He'd blow up the entire city of l took to keep her alive...

The explosion was satisfying. He hit the floor, taking her with him, as flying glass peppered the bar. The sound was horrendous, alcohol and Sterno fumes igniting and glass whickering through the air. He covered her body with his and caught a stray breath of a clean, pure scent. She was soft and slim, and he remembered what it was like to bury his face in the softness of her throat and hear her sigh as he—

No time to think about that, they had to move.

He rolled up to his feet in a swift crouch. His forehead burned, blood dripping into his eyes. He yanked her up, fingers slipping in warm wetness. Was she hit? He hoped not. The thought of her wounded did something funny to his chest.

"Back door, angel," he said, and they went. She gasped with each footstep, dragging herself along. He hit the door open with the palm of his left hand, his right holding a gun again, and pushed her through after checking behind it. And there, above the stacked cases of liquor and other odds and ends, was the Exit sign.

Acrid smoke billowed through the door. It was burning merrily in the bar now, tables, chairs and plush carpet fueled by spilled liquor. A wave of heat groaned through the entire bar.

"I think I'm going to throw up," Rowan said in a high, thin, breathless voice. She slumped against him, still clutching at her leg. Was she hit? God, he hoped not.

His chest was on fire, his nerves twisting with the need for Zed. *Get her out of here. Get her out and away from them. Get her out* now.

"Wait until we're out in the alley," Delgado heard himself reply. "Goddammit, woman, I told you to run."

"Wasn't leaving without you." Stubborn. Always so stubborn. "Where have you been?"

"In hell, angel." He kicked the fire door open, waited a beat, and spun out, covering the likely angles. Nobody there—the alley was clear. The Sig team guarding it was probably pulled in to help deal with the mess inside. He'd known it was clear. His own psychic talent worked overtime to tell him so, spurred by Zed withdrawal and adrenaline, but it was nice to have confirmation. "In hell. It's nice to be back."

Dedication: *To my grandfather, Jim Schuler, who has always served with honor.*

Acknowledgments: The first acknowledgment goes to my husband James, who patiently bears with a writer's uncertain temper, and who gently reminds me that even writers need to take a break once in a while. (He is, after all, my best friend.) Also deserving thanks are my children, Maddy and Nicholas, for their gentle daily lessons in how to be a better person.

Thanks are also principally due to Linda Kichline, publisher, editor, and friend, who puts up with me with cheerfulness and ease. Without Linda, I would still be scribbling notes in my basement and moaning over rejection slips; she was the first to believe in me and is, to me, a living embodiment of strength and finesse. Also deserving a bow is my agent Miriam, my staunchest advocate and ever-faithful friend.

Thanks also to my family: my mother and father, who have not batted an eyelid at the strange course my research sometimes takes; my sisters Tricia and Alison, who prove that blood ties can also mean friendship; and my grandfather James Schuler, who has served his country and community in peace and war with diligence and patience.

Last but certainly not least, a huge thank you to my Readers. You are, I daresay, the most wonderful bunch of people on the planet, not only for your support and good humor but also for the letters and emails I receive full of encouragement, suggestions, and support. Let me again thank you the way we both like best: by telling you a story.

Other Books by Lilith Saintcrow

Dark Watcher
Storm Watcher
The Society

Coming Soon
Fire Watcher
Cloud Watcher

Hunter, Healer

***

Lilith Saintcrow

Hunter, Healer
Published by ImaJinn Books

ISBN: 1-933417-80-3

10 9 8 7 6 5 4 3 2 1

Cover design by Patricia Lazarus

ImaJinn Books
P.O. Box 545, Canon City, CO 81212
Toll Free: 1-877-625-3592
http://www.imajinnbooks.com

One

Amor animi arbitrio sumitur, non ponitur.
—Syrus

Kick. Another kick. Knee. Solid contact. Move in. Move in, get going, do it faster, faster, precise, put your weight behind it, sweetheart! Do it. Punch. Ouch, don't flex your wrist, throw an elbow, keep going, stitch in side. Move. Move. MOVE!

Rowan Price, Society operative and psion, stood shaking and sweating, her head hanging. Her hair fell on both sides of her face, curtaining her off from the outside world. The punching bag swayed, its chain creaking. Her hands burned. The CD player set on the chair by the door gave out a throbbing bass beat. She threw another punch, unwinding all the way from the hip, then moved in. Her fists almost seemed to blur. Good solid strikes thudding into the heavy bag, hands numb, arms on fire, shoulders jolting with pain.

He'd be proud.

"Ro?" Cath called over the music.

Rowan dropped her head even further, hunched her shoulders, and drove another punch into the bag. Another. Another. Low and dirty, the way Justin had taught her.

Don't. Don't think about it.

Another flurry of punches. Elbows smacking the bag as if it had personally offended her.

"Jump-off in thirty," Cath finally called. "Henderson needs you in fifteen."

Rowan turned away from the bag and met Cath's eyes. Her cheeks were wet, her shoulders dotted with beads of sweat. The sports bra was damn near soaked through, and the waistband of her shorts chafed a thin line into her back and belly.

"Ro?" Catherine, her hair cut short in an inky black pixie instead of a punked-out blue Mohawk, reached down and turned the CD player off. The silence was instant and shocking. Cath was plump-cheeked and pretty, or would have been if not for the sheer amount of metal on her face. Nose rings, earrings marching up the curve of each ear, pierced lip, and pierced eyebrow. Rowan didn't want to *know* about any of the other piercings. And of course, she wore a shoulder holster, the butt of a Glock snug under her left arm. Cath also usually wore a boot knife and a stiletto up her sleeve. For a Society operative, that was damn close to lightly armed.

Especially considering current events.

Rowan's ribs heaved with deep controlled breaths. A thin trickle of sweat slid chill and tickling down her back. She swiped a few damp tendrils of hair back from her forehead. "I'll be there. Thanks, Cath." It was an effort to be polite, to keep her voice toneless.

"You're being a real bitch lately," Cath informed her tightly, crossing her arms as if in self-defense. Sometimes she really did appear very young, despite her shell of prickly confidence.

Pot calling the kettle black, anyone? Rowan sighed, blew the tension out between pursed lips. "Sorry." *I don't sound sorry at all.* "Really, Cath. I am."

The short, muscled girl shrugged, the chain at her belt jingling. Her violet eyes turned cool. "You're worrying about him again, aren't you?"

Well, you get the grand prize for stating the obvious. But guilt pricked at her. Cath didn't deserve her ire. "Shouldn't I? It's been three months." Rowan stripped her gloves off, tossed them down on the CD player. "He's trapped somewhere, Cath. Sigma's got him."

"He'll come back for you." The girl sounded certain. "I mean, he said he would, didn't he?"

Don't remind me, Rowan thought, and set her jaw. "I'm sorry," she repeated. "I'd better get cleaned up if Henderson wants me. Thanks for telling me."

"There, that's the Ro I know." Cath grinned. The change was startling, a flash of how she would look without all the metal. "I'll meet you for jump-off. Cool?"

I'm not cool at all, Cath. I'm about two steps away from very, very uncool. "Chilly cool."

The girl bounced out of the small room. Rowan looked down at the futon folded in the corner. No books and no plants, because they had to move every few weeks. Nothing but her kitbag and some clothes, and the never-ending tension. And Sigma always yapping at their heels.

Rowan sighed, shutting her eyes. Her hands hurt inside the padded gloves, her shoulders twinged, her legs and lungs burned both from the side kicks she'd been practicing and her morning bout on the treadmill. The place where Justin should be inside her head was empty and aching, and her mind kept circling it like a tongue poking at a toothache. A phantom limb, phantom pain. If he was able to come back, he would have by now.

She tossed the gloves over on the futon and worked the ponytail holder free of her wet, clinging hair. *I'd better get cleaned up, Henderson wants me. Probably to try and talk me out of it.* She headed for the bathroom, rubbing under her sweat-soaked hair and grimacing. She should have dyed it. The ash-blond mane was too distinctive by far. Even Cath had gotten rid of her trademark Mohawk, but Rowan couldn't bring herself to dye her hair.

That would be like admitting Justin was really gone. Like admitting she was on her own. *As if I'm some idiot of a fainting maiden who keeps waiting for her man to come back. He cometh not, she said wearily, as she looked from her tower window.*

Her mood was getting worse and worse; she was even irritating herself. She kept breathing, deep down into her stomach, trying for calm.

The shower warmed up quickly, and she ducked under the water and started scrubbing. She only had a few minutes before the General wanted her. No time to luxuriate in the hot water.

Ten minutes later, she pulled the white cotton tank top down and zipped up her jeans, tossing her wet hair back over her shoulder. She'd braid it in the comm room. She attached her shoulder holster, checked her Glock, and shrugged on her hip-length leather coat. The knife went in her boot, and she scooped up her kitbag, the canvas messenger bag that held an operative's toys and tricks, settling it so the strap ran diagonally across her body. She turned the CD player off and paused, looking around the bare white room.

If Justin was here, he'd stop by the door and smile at me, ask if I was ready. She shivered, gooseflesh rising on her skin. *Maybe Cath's right. Or maybe he's dead. Maybe they killed him and I'm going to waste my life on a wild goose chase.*

But it just didn't feel right. She would *know* if he was dead. Wouldn't she? Sigma hadn't killed him. They needed to use him against the Society. He was alive, and if he was alive he would come back to her. He'd *promised.*

And of course I believe him, don't I?

Rowan swore, threw one last punch at the heavy bag, and left as it creaked back and forth on its hook sunk into a stud in the ceiling. This house was nice, and they'd been able to stay here for a little while. But soon enough Sigma would close in with uncanny accuracy, and they'd be on the run again. It was as if the Sigma psions had suddenly gotten better...

...or as if someone was helping them.

She didn't want to think about that, either.

* * *

Henderson pushed his wire-rimmed glasses up, his sharp nose wrinkling slightly. "Morning, Rowan." he said. "You ready?" The patch of white hair at his temple had grown in the last three months, but his steel-colored eyes were still bright and interested, and he moved with the same fluid precision as always. She understood why they called him "the General." His air of command and cool confidence was almost archetypical in its depth.

"Ready as I'll ever be," she replied, glancing down at the table and collating the maps with a swift glance. He was going over the layouts of the building again, each exit, the city in a few blocks in either direction, and routes out of the metropolis. She knew he probably had everything memorized, but Henderson's innate precision wouldn't take "already memorized" for an answer. Not when it had to be perfect, and an operative's life was on the line.

Her life, today. She might have cause to thank him for being anal-retentive before sundown.

Her fingers flicked as she finished braiding her hair back, tied the thick rope off with an elastic band. "What's the chatter?"

"They've scheduled the move-in for 1600 when he gets home from work. They're planning on a primary penetration unit and a net." Henderson tapped a printout with one blunt, callused finger. Before Headquarters had been destroyed he'd been the chief of covert operations for the Society. Now that the handful of psions fighting Sigma had been scattered, he was the closest to a leader they had. Rowan had never really found out just *who* was the actual leader of the Society, but she suspected Henderson's name would have been on the list of candidates. "With you to get in and get close, we should get him around 1100 *at* work. Is he ready?"

She nodded. "It was the file that convinced him. And the

reporter that died of a 'heart attack.'" Her lip curled. *I told Lewis it would happen. Then again, I wouldn't have believed it either when I was a civilian.* Her throat closed. Another life ended by the monsters who had killed her father.

And was Rowan responsible because she'd initiated contact with Lewis?

She tried not to think about that, either. "Sigma's pushed him right into our hands." *Just like they pushed me.*

"They have a habit of doing that. It'll be nice to have another precog. Eleanor will like training him."

Rowan cleared her throat a little uncertainly. "General?"

He knew what she was going to ask. The comm room was deserted—Yoshi's laptop sat on a desk and Cath's Dr. Who scarf was draped across an ergonomic chair. Henderson started rolling up the maps. "I can't send you to Vegas, Rowan. I need you too much. You're my second."

Now that Justin's gone? Hot anger flooded her. *I'm not qualified for this, General. You know that.* "I'm not a replacement."

"No," he agreed. "You're not. But you've stepped into the breach admirably. You're cool under fire, you're competent and talented, and you got us all out of the disaster at Headquarters."

I didn't "get us out." I nearly got us trapped and stuffed. "All except Justin," she reminded him.

Henderson moved with exacting slowness, his hands steady. "Just be patient, Rowan. He'll come back."

"It's been three months." She swallowed, her voice husky. *I never used to get angry. The very idea of getting this angry used to be foreign to me. What happened?*

She knew what had happened. Sigma. They had stolen everything from her. Her father, her best friend—and Justin.

"He'll come back." Henderson's voice was the epitome of calm faith. "I can't send you to Vegas."

You aren't listening. Just like Dad, set on your own opinion. "We need the money," she pointed out, pitching her voice low and reasonable. "We've only got another eight weeks of operating funds, less if we're unlucky. Until we get the new Headquarters fully up and running and drain the old resource net, we're going to burn our budget down to the bone. I'm going to Vegas, Henderson. Send Cath with me, if you're so worried. Or Yoshi. Either of them will be able to help."

"You just don't give up, do you?" Henderson arched a dark eyebrow. "I don't want to lose you, Rowan."

But you're okay with losing Justin? That was unfair, she told herself. Unfair. But she still thought it. "You won't," she assured him. "But we need the money, and Cath and I are the best bet. You know that."

A slight scuffing sound from the hallway alerted her. Yoshi appeared. "It's showtime," he said, flashing her a quick grin and scooping up his laptop. The slim Japanese man wore a blue cable-knit sweater and jeans despite the scorching summer heat outside. Maybe his sandaled feet made up for it. Then again, he'd be in an air-conditioned van unless something went terribly, dreadfully wrong. "Everyone's waiting for Cinderella."

Rowan's eyes met Henderson's. She hadn't known him too well before, but now she could read the faint iron smile he wore. She'd won the argument with cold logic, it seemed.

"All right," Henderson barked. "Let's get moving. And, Yoshi, do a workup for a Vegas run for Rowan while we're waiting, all right?"

"Love to." Yoshi's dark eyes sparkled. He'd already done the workup a week ago, at Rowan's quiet request. "Gonna play the horses, Ro?"

"You bet. Right after Cath makes us rich at roulette," she answered, and felt her pulse rise slightly. Adrenaline began to tang copper in her mouth, she lowered her respiration and pulse with a few moments of attention. She couldn't afford to get nervous now. "Thank you, General."

"Don't thank me," he growled, sliding the maps into his battered olive-green map bag. "It's dangerous, and Del would have my hide."

"He's not here to protest," Rowan said flatly, and followed Yoshi out of the room.

Two

Green eyes, wide and dark, she stood with Andrews's hand around her upper arm. Motionless, she was too sedated to recognize the danger, trusting Delgado completely.

He wasn't ready for that.

Pale hair, lying damp and dark against her forehead. More rain kissing her skin and sliding into Del's eyes. Stay still, *he thought.* Just stay still. *Moving, every muscle strained, every nerve screaming.* Stay still until I can get to you.

Andrews sneering, certain he had both of them—but Delgado whirled, throwing the knife. His other hand came up, the weight of the gun strangely familiar. The bullet took out the other Sig as the knife buried itself in Andrews's shoulder with a meaty thunk. Rowan made a thin noise and swayed again.

He caught her arm. "Are you all right? Rowan? Goddammit, Rowan, talk to me."

Agent Breaker woke up, his arm flung across his face and the dream fading into unreality. Again. The metal shelf was hard beneath him, and he strained as he did every morning to *remember*.

It didn't work. Whatever he'd done to himself seemed permanent. Even the Colonel's star psions couldn't reverse it, and the Colonel seemed a little upset. This Price girl, whoever she was, managed to hop one step ahead of every Sigma trick. They seemed to blame Del for that too.

If he'd trained her, he'd done it well.

The door to the concrete cube they called a room slid aside and Del curled up to sit on the bed, a hand closing around a knife hilt. It was damp and chilly down here, but he didn't care. The bed was a single metal shelf, the cube had a drain in one corner, and two blankets and a bare light bulb were recently accorded luxuries. The single metal bar for exercise—pull-ups, inverts, and the like—sliced across the cell, low enough that he had to duck to avoid it. This room wasn't made for comfort.

Not like a room he remembered with scarves scattered over the bedstead, books stacked on shelves, and a clean warm perfume in the air. Sunlight fell through the window and French door of that room in the most secret corner of his mind. Del had the idea that if he waited long enough, was still and silent enough, he might catch a glimpse of whoever owned that room—maybe the woman they were so eager to find. It never happened, but that room had held him during the worst of the beatings and the deepest of the drug-induced questioning sessions.

That room had saved his sanity.

Andrews leaned against the doorjamb, without Jilssen for once. "Hey." His deceptively-sleepy blue eyes, under short wheat-gold hair, moved over the concrete cube, as if Del was holding contraband in some corner.

He was, but he wasn't about to let the Colonel's second-in-command know it. "Hey," he returned, the knife lifting a little, playing through the sequence that would end with it whipping through the air and burying itself in the lean man's throat. It would be immensely satisfying to see Andrews's eyes bug out and hear him choking on steel, maybe with his fingers scrabbling at the hilt while Del moved in on him. Del could strip him of weapons and grab his magkey, but there were armed guards at either end of every corridor, as well as the security net. And the trackers.

Don't forget the trackers. Wait for your time, Agent Breaker. Just wait.

Where was Jilssen? The traitorous doctor who had allowed Sigma to take Society Headquarters had been coming around less and less—maybe because of the way Del stared at him, aching to tear the man's throat out. It didn't matter—Jilssen was a small problem in the scheme of things. Sooner or later Del would have his opportunity, of that he was sure. Patience brought a man everything he needed, especially when there was nothing left but endurance and the dream of revenge.

Andrews shrugged under the supple, oiled leather of his rig. Del had copied the Sigma rig pattern for the Society. He could remember that clearly. He'd altered them to make them easier and lighter, a few material adjustments. He could even remember buckling a rig on someone, testing it. She'd been a little shorter than the usual woman and her nearness had made his hands shake imperceptibly.

Who? He shook the memory away. His hair was cut short now, none of the longhair crap the Society let its members indulge in. Del had never gone in for that, but his hair *had* been longer when he'd come in. He remembered that, remembered the click and buzz of the electric razor against his scalp. So he'd been growing it out, he guessed. Something to do with the hole in his memory.

His arm itched, the creeping fire of Zed wearing off. They'd drugged him hard, always asking the same question.

Where is Rowan Price? Whoever she was, they wanted her badly.

That was enough to make Del hope they didn't find her.

"We've got jump-off in forty. Get your ass up, you're coming topside with me. We've got a snatch and grab to do."

"Fine." Delgado coiled himself to his feet and noticed Andrews tense, his muscled shoulders rolling under a black T-shirt. "Who we grabbing?"

Andrews stepped back. He might look lazy, but he was ready. Del wondered if his shoulder was hurting from the old knife wound.

The blond man's lip curled as he looked over the inside of the concrete cube. Del didn't rate even a mattress pad yet; he might never. They were confusing his inability to remember with stubbornness. Del didn't blame them. If he'd had a choice, it *would* have been stubbornness.

"Some psion the freaks have been courting. We've got a shot to bring in a whole busload of them. Including the golden girl who's been running me around the goddamn country."

Del let one corner of his mouth tilt up into a smile. He seemed to remember a time when a smile had started to feel natural. But he was back in Sigma now. Every expression, the most minute of facial tics, was a weapon or a betrayal now. You never knew who was watching, who would report what, or when the fist would come down hard.

I never really thought I'd escape, he realized, as he did every day. *I was just waiting for them to scoop me back up. Deep down, I knew it. Knew this would happen.*

"She's been putting you through your paces, huh?" *The more I hear about this woman, the more I like her, you son of a bitch.*

"Oh, yeah. It's almost like hunting you, you sarcastic fucker. Come on, we've got to kit you out." Andrews didn't sound happy.

Of course not. For three months this Price had been eluding him, slipping through his fingers like water. Sigma couldn't exterminate the last few vestiges of the Society no matter how hard they tried—and Delgado's knowledge of the ragtag assortment of psions and their usual procedures hadn't helped as much as Colonel Anton had hoped. No, despite picking his brain for every scrap of information that could be gotten out while a cocktail of Zed and sodium pentothal was forcibly pumped into Del's veins, the Colonel was no closer to eradicating the persistent thorn in Sigma's side.

And the Society had even started, incredibly, to fight back. A whole Sigma snatch team had disappeared off the map a month after Del's recapture. Civilian psions Sigma had targeted for acquisition suddenly vanished, reappearing fitted out like Society members, recruiting new psions and damaging Sigma with a persistent guerilla war. Slowly, incredibly, and successfully, the Society had managed to stay together and fight the massive tentacles of a well-funded black-ops government agency.

Del kept his face a mask and silently cheered. He gave all the information he could—he had no choice, not if he wanted to end up anything other than a brainwiped Zed-shattered hulk. The beatings hadn't helped. Andrews was sadistic, and his trained bullyboys not much better. Del didn't want to give them any more reason to bark at him. He'd just barely gotten over the last goddamn thrashing they'd given him.

So Anton was letting Delgado out to play, was he?

I can use this. Maybe escape.

But if he escaped, how would he break the Zed habit? He wasn't sure he could do it again. Once was enough for *that* particular hell, thank you very much. The drug was meant to give you withdrawal so bad you'd do anything for another hit. Without a full detox unit to help him through the worst of the physiological effects he might find himself in an even worse place than he already was now. Strange as *that* sounded.

And if he escaped, where would he go? How the hell could *he* find the Society?

More importantly, would they trust him once he found them? Probably not.

He slid off the bed, his rig coming with him. He buckled it on, rolling his shoulders to make sure it fit right. Slid the knife back into its sheath. Giving him a few weapons didn't matter. One man, no matter how gifted or well-trained, couldn't extricate himself from a full-size Sig installation. It would be insanity even to try. "Well, we'd better go, right?"

"We'd better. You think you can bring this girl in, Del?"

I'd rather firebomb this whole goddamn place and dance on your burning grave, you sadistic son of a bitch.

"If I trained her like you say, I should be able to." *But if I do find her, I'm not bringing her in. I'm going to help her get so far away you'll never find her.*

"You better be careful," Andrews said. The bastard was smirking, his blue eyes alive as if he was contemplating someone's pain. Probably Del's. "If she keeps this up the Colonel might decide she's better dead, even if she is a golden girl. Jilssen has a hard time convincing him to bring her in alive anyway."

Del shrugged. "If I cared, I wouldn't be here." *I escaped you once before.* But he was past lying to himself, and the thought was merely reflexive. Empty bravado wouldn't help him.

What would help him was finding the genius who could outthink Sigma, hold the shattered Society together, and direct an organization like this back from the brink of disaster. A genius like that might have an idea or two Del could use.

A genius like that might be able to help Del figure out what he'd done to his own head—and what he couldn't remember.

Andrews laughed, sidling back out the door. "Yeah, sure you don't care. Come on, Breaker. For this assignment, your ass is mine."

"Color me excited," Del mumbled, and followed him out the door into the blinding white-tiled corridor beyond. They were underground in the high security warrens, armed guards with personal dampers everywhere, and trackers in special cells on every level. Someone down the hall screamed—probably undergoing their first reeducation session. Zed and a beating, just the right way to wake up in the morning.

Sigma. Back home in the bad old cradle. They were going to send him out on an assignment for the first time since his recapture. And any assignment, however well-planned it was, might offer Del a chance to do something other than keep being a Sigma lapdog. Excitement rose, but training clamped down on his hindbrain, regulating his pulse back to a steady, even thudding. Even a heartbeat could give him away.

Escape was just a vanishing possibility, though. It was far more likely that Anton and Andrews were going to use Del like a ferret in a hole to smoke out any Society operatives possible. They had all the weight of the government behind them, and they had learned a few things since Del's last escape. Whoever this Price girl was, she was still playing in a rigged game. Del's unwilling acquiescence to Sigma might be the thing that tipped the balance against her.

Whoever you are, Price, keep running, he thought. *I hope I did train you, I really do. 'Cause that's the only thing that's going to save you if they somehow make me hunt you down.*

Three

Rowan's head began to hurt as soon as they got within ten miles of the office building, navigating the van with no trouble through midmorning traffic. Skyscrapers rose up, the downtown of this city beating around her like a heart. She waited while Henderson drove, closing her eyes and stilling herself, reaching for that place of quiet calm that seemed to grow deeper each time she used it. It was the calm that allowed her to do some of her more showy tricks, like quick-healing a cut or a scrape. The training Miss Kate and Henderson—not to mention Justin—had given her had triggered a deepening of her talents, and it was like a muscle. The more you trained it and the more you used it, the better you got and the bigger the talent got. She'd reach her limit soon, probably; there was a ceiling to every psion's gifts. After that ceiling, you courted backlash, the body protesting once the mind was pushed past its limits.

Rowan hadn't found her ceiling yet. And the massive effort she'd used during the attack on Headquarters—shunting aside the collective force of massed Sigma psions and also striking at the pilot of a helicopter that had been firing at Henderson's Brigade—seemed to have torn something inside her. A thin protective barrier that had kept her from going all wacky with the woo-woo.

You could incite riots, Justin had told her. *You could start revolutions.* He'd been utterly serious. She didn't think she was quite *that* powerful, but there were certain things she could do that seemed far above the norm. *Norm.* As if that word applied to any of this.

Rowan had never been normal, really. Finding lost articles, hearing people's most intimate thoughts shouted into her head, calming her ward of mental patients, sensing the moods of those around her—no, normal was not the word.

The massed attack, several Sig psions in a circle around a target site or funneling their talent through a single point, was an evolution in their tactics according to Henderson. Just like Rowan was an evolution in psionics, according to him.

And so, she had learned to trust her instincts. Especially when they were so painfully, exquisitely loud.

Is this just pre-job nerves, or is there a good reason for me being so edgy?

The deep calm inside her returned an answer Rowan didn't much like.

"Sigma's here," she heard herself say in that queer, floaty voice that seemed all she could use when she did this trick. "I think they're planning on getting him."

"Good," Cath said from the back seat. "I want a little payback."

"Bloodthirsty's not the way to go," Henderson said severely, as he did every time.

Boomer, sitting next to Cath, made a rude snorting noise. Yoshi laughed. Rowan felt their jagged nerves and reached to soothe them, stroking away the rough edges of pre-operation jitters.

"Yeah, right." Boomer's sideburns would be wagging side-to-side in disbelief. "When was the last time you let a Sig get away alive?"

"Focus, people," Rowan said softly, returning to herself. "We aren't Sigma."

Silence filled the car, a silence that almost turned into words.

But Delgado was. Even Cath wouldn't say it to her, but she was suddenly sure they had said it to each other.

Sometimes being a psion was a bitch. Rowan kept breathing.

It had been cold the night Justin had come over for dinner and ended up carrying her to his car because Sigma burst in and shot her father and best friend. And afterward he'd always been there. They'd taken to calling him *Rowan's shadow*, because wherever she was you could find Justin Delgado—leaning against a wall and watching, drifting behind her, or buried in the shadows in the most defensible corner, his eyes on her.

But now he was gone, and Rowan didn't even know herself anymore. The mental hospital's nursing station she'd worked at seemed a million miles away, as well as her house with its green kitchen and her yellow bedroom and Dad's painting of Mom in the front hall. The person she had been was equally gone.

The funny thing was she still *felt* like herself. Except for one thing—the empty, nagging, raw place inside her head. Where Justin should be.

That, and the aching grief of her father's death, turned into a cold, clear anger that frightened her while it gave her the strength to go on. Anger should not feel this *good.*

The black van braked to a smooth stop, and Rowan's hands moved efficiently, checking her gear. She looked back over her shoulder at Yoshi, who sat in the middle seat with his laptop balanced on his knees. He smiled at her. "You ready?"

She nodded and reached back with her left hand.

Yoshi's fingers touched hers—but another meeting took place, a mental handholding. Rowan wasn't quite used to the ease with which she seeped into the borders of Yoshi's mind, but she let the connection sink below her conscious control. *You can hear me.* It wasn't a question.

Loud and clear. Yoshi's mental voice tasted, as always, of circuits and wires and the jittery dance of electricity, black coffee and a strange bittersweet incense smoke that made Rowan think of offerings in clean, pure pagoda-roofed temples. His calm steadied her. "Good luck, Ro."

"Thanks. If all goes well I won't need it." But her head prickled with pain, and her stomach felt sour.

Sigma.

She always felt sick around them.

"Ro?" Henderson, now, sitting in the driver's seat, looking out the windshield at the street he'd chosen to park on. "Be careful. Don't take any chances."

She felt her lips stretch in what she supposed was a grin. "Don't worry, old man." She reached for the doorhandle. "I'm a professional."

It was just the sort of thing Justin might have said.

* * *

The building was tall and glittering, a spike of iron and glass throwing back the morning sun. Heat simmered up from the pavement. Rowan's lower back was soaked with sweat by the time she reached the glass door and swung in, her eyes moving in an arc over the lobby and taking everything in, just as Justin had taught her.

Exits—two. Elevators, a bank of six. Escalators, four. Fire escape stairs, there and there, mezzanine level above. Christ, what a security nightmare. The escalators flanked a wide central staircase made of faux white marble. The plants were all fake, and the people were all in end-of-week business chic. Lewis worked as an accountant for a huge company and the dress code was only relaxed on Fridays.

People—lots of them. An espresso stand tucked into one

corner of the lobby. A tide of business-suited and khaki-and-short-sleeves deadhead people. The elevators dinged frequently, releasing more of them at regular intervals.

"Deadhead," the term for those without psychic powers. Slightly disparaging, but she'd fallen into the habit of using it. It was apt; they noticed nothing. Then again, they were living normal lives without having to worry about guns, knives, targets, critical zones, and casualty percentages. Lucky them.

Sunlight speared through the glass, robbed of its power by air conditioning but still somehow reassuring. There were two bored security guards near the elevators, one with his hand resting on a holstered gun. They were both too pudgy to be of any real use. *Even an idiot with a gun can be dangerous*, Justin's voice reminded her, floating up from memory.

So many things to do—juggle the confusing wash of sensation from the ordinary people, sharp pinpricks of guilt or fear in the sea of boredom and frustration. Scan for any whisper, any *breath* of anything out of the normal. She had barely sensed a Sig coming the first time, now it was like an aching tooth or a fresh bruise each time they got close.

She was hunting for a particular mind, a mind she'd brushed before. She drifted with the crowd, peeling off to walk toward the doors that most likely led to the fire stairs.

I'm in. The channel to Yoshi was wide and smooth with the ease of long communication. They sometimes meditated together too, sitting face-to-face in the comm room, strengthening the bond so Rowan didn't have to use a comm-link to talk to him. Of all of them, Yoshi was the one who...well, not comprehended, but *understood* what she was feeling. *Where the hell is our precog, Yosh?*

Yoshi's answer: *Twenty-fifth floor.* Clipped, he was typing, the feel of the keys against his fingers. Acrid undertone of worry—something was going on.

Get him down here. Rowan's mental voice was equally brusque. Her stomach flipped. Sigma was close. Very close.

Too close. Her stomach flipped again. *They're onto us, Yoshi. Get moving.*

Leave no man behind. Furious concentration. *Rowan, they're closing in. I've got him on his cell. He's coming down the fire stairs.*

No. Elevator. Have him take the elevator. A plan began to form, loose and haphazard as all Rowan's plans tended to be. She frequently ran on intuition instead of logic, something that often caused Henderson a bit of worry. Then again, trained intuition was as good as magic sometimes.

Sweat trickled down her back again, even though the air-conditioning was icy.

Yoshi didn't argue, even though it was against a primary rule—never take an elevator if you can help it. It was just too easy to get caught.

Elevator it is. On my mark, one...two...oh, goddammit, Rowan, get the hell out of there. Tightly-controlled panic, tasting like smoke, colored his mental voice. *Get the hell out of there. They have a net going, they're all over. They're serious this time.*

What, like they ever play games? I'm not leaving without our precog. Steel in her mental voice, the bleak taste of determination. Her eyes moved over the crowd again, marking, evaluating as she leaned against the wall. *Where is he, Yoshi?*

Ro, Henderson says to get out. That's an order. Yoshi didn't sound happy. As a matter of fact, the wash of purple-red panic coming from him was distracting. She was too sensitive, and his fear scraped raw against her brain. Rowan's heart began to pound, she took a deep breath. It was almost second nature to blur the perceptions of the people around her. They wouldn't see the woman with the long ash-blond braid and the gun under her coat. Electromagnetic resonance meant that camera footage would be blurred and useless too.

Another trick Justin had taught her.

She'd managed a whole thirty seconds without thinking of him. It was a new world record.

Rowan eased the gun free of its holster. There was a time she would have been too afraid to hold a heavy, lethal piece of metal capable of killing someone. That time, that woman, had died on the floor of her father's kitchen as she heard the chilling little gurgle of Dad's last breath. She'd died there, hadn't known it—and been reborn months later, sitting on the bed in Justin's room when the fierce determination to make Sigma *pay* had surfaced, giving her a reason for living.

Yoshi? You're in the building's intranet?

Henderson says—

I don't give a good goddamn what Henderson says. Trigger the fire alarms. Now.

Mercifully, he didn't argue anymore. Instead, there was a

sense of frantic action from him as Rowan eased forward, cutting across the line of people heading for the escalators—businessmen, secretaries, flickers of almost-psions. Her palms felt slippery even though she knew they weren't. A trickle of sweat eased down the shallow channel of her spine, tickling like a sharp knife tip brushing her skin.

A down-coming elevator dinged, and Rowan felt a familiar bright, clean mind inside. Lewis Emberson stepped out, his beaky face pale and dewed with perspiration, just as the fire alarms began to bray.

Rowan moved forward smoothly and took Lew's arm. He was thin, with black-rimmed retro glasses and an indifferent haircut. He wore a pair of khakis and a blue T-shirt. Today was casual day at work, and Rowan had counseled him to wear something he could move in. A pair of high-end, obviously new Nikes decorated his feet. He was a precognitive, and if Sigma got their hands on him he'd be full of Zed and working for the black sector of the government in no time.

Not while I'm around, Rowan thought fiercely.

His watery brown eyes blinked behind his glasses. "Rowan," he said under the sudden chaos of alarms and people starting to move for the exits. "Something's wrong."

Gee, you think so? "I know," she soothed, as his eyes found the gun in her hand. "You're with me, Lew. It's gonna be okay. Come on."

I wonder if Justin ever felt this frightened while he was moving me around.

They joined the mass of deadheads crowding for the exits. *Give me a mark on where they are, Yosh,* she said, her stomach suddenly full of bile. They must be moving in. Brass spikes of pain jabbed at her temples, driving into her brain. She took a deep breath, bringing her heartbeat down a little. She didn't need to start exhausting herself with terror.

Moving in. But the deadheads... Sudden sharp jolt, like a fist slamming into her solar plexus. She almost doubled over, the shock was so intense—Yoshi's fear becoming hers through the mental link between them for a dizzying moment before she could block it out. *Goddammit, Rowan, they've locked on you. They've got a visual! Move!*

A visual meant they were in the building. And then, to cap off the entire damn situation, gunfire popped and zinged. Rowan lunged forward, dragging Lew with her as glass shattered.

The Sigs were aiming high to spook the crowd instead of kill. If Lew hadn't been right next to her the Sigs might have been able to scoop him up separately in the confusion. *Where are they? Give me some help here, dammit!*

A flood of information in reply. It was too late, because she felt the glow of other psions and saw the long flapping tan trench coats. So they'd changed their fashion sense—the other Sigs she'd seen had worn black. *Maybe it's Sig summer wear,* she thought privately, squashing the lunatic urge to laugh. *The hot new fashion in government weirdoes.*

They were coming down the escalators and stairs, shoving through the crowd, firing from the mezzanine to drive the mass of frightened humanity out through the doors and spill enough terror into the air to slow her down. Rowan could either stay and be caught, or get out on the street and run straight out into the Sig search net.

Lew made a high whining sound. She didn't blame him—getting shot at had that affect on a person.

"Come on!" she yelled, shoving aside a blonde with a briefcase and clacking high heels. Lew mercifully obeyed, running with her. They bowled through the crowd at an angle, heading for the other exit. She was going to have to get creative really soon.

Rowan *reached*, blurring the other psions' perceptions of her as well. The number of hands she had free to juggle mental eggs was rapidly decreasing. Her heart pounded. She didn't have any energy left over to regulate her pulse. Her body knew she was being shot at, and her mind couldn't convince her body that it wasn't an emergency that *deserved* a racing pulse.

The other stream of people heading for the secondary exit—out onto the street on the other side of the block—swallowed them. Rowan deliberately didn't return fire, though she ached to pick off a few of the Sigs. Her primary objective was to get Lew out, not work a little hurt on them. More gunfire, more glass shattering, they were going to start aiming for real soon. They must be desperate to risk this kind of open attack. Generally Sigs didn't like public shootouts in which the cops could get involved. They could cover up just about anything, but that took time and resources, and the less government agencies involved the more chance everyone could keep their mouth shut.

Ro, Ro, come on. The net's almost at the building. You

don't have a lot of lag. Move out of there, can you? Yoshi's voice held the deep purple shade of tightly controlled excitement, shot through with brittle crystal lattices of professionalism.

Rowan pushed Lew in front of her and did the single riskiest thing she could—she pointed her gun straight up and fired twice. With screams and gasps, the crowd exploded away from her, people diving for cover or panicking. The swirling flood of emotional energy acted as "static," blurring her even further to the other psions' perceptions and giving her a short-term boost in energy. One she'd pay for later, but nothing was perfect. She tapped in and triggered the mood of the crowd, directing the frightened people with deft mental pressure. Some of them found themselves blindly pelting for the stairs, keeping the Sigs back with a crush of bodies, others spilled out irresistibly onto the street, providing her and Lew with cover.

And for my next trick, she thought with grim amusement, *I'm going to disappear. Watch this.*

The sudden crush pushed Lew and Rowan out through the door, the heat like oil bursting against her skin. She shoved Lew in one direction—up the block, where Henderson would be waiting until it got too hot to stay around here with a van full of comm equipment and psions, no matter if they were shielded.

"Run!" she yelled, and Lew took off, not waiting to argue.

Thank God. At least he has some sense.

Then Rowan dropped a few layers of mental defenses, sending out a very public wave of fear and pain. To the Sigs, it would feel like she'd gotten shot and made her first mistake.

Crystal cold clarity fell over her, the adrenaline freeze Justin had told her about. Everything seemed etched into memory, every fleck of glittering mica in the pavement and the sound of the sirens approaching, the screams and horrified yells of the people behind her, whooping fire alarms and braying sirens. Her own breathing, harsh and desperate as she flashed along the sidewalk.

I'm drawing them off, she said, and broke the link with Yoshi. She would need all her strength for eluding the net that now turned on itself, pivoting as the Sigma-trained psions moved their flank to encircle her. Now Henderson had a clear field to extricate himself from the critical zone and swing around to pick her up—once she got through the goddamn net, that was.

Pounding feet on the pavement, her boots flying. She had

their locations now—the net was thick and tight, three deep. Rowan strained her memory for the layout of the city block Lew's office building was on. There was an alley—but that was a dead end.

It was punch through the net or nothing.

Rowan dashed out into the middle of the street, narrowly avoiding being hit by a silver BMW. Horns began to blare. She was deliberately making a lot of goddamn psychic noise.

And then...*contact,* another mind sliding against hers, through every lock and defense. Brushing past all the walls Rowan had painstakingly built to keep herself sane, keep everyone else *out.* There was no denying this touch. She catalogued it out of habit, though her entire body *knew* it, a wave of new strength flooding her bones. She grabbed for him the way a drowning woman would grab for floating debris.

Who the hell are you? The voice was clear, familiar. Male, with a touch of bitterness over a deep well of reined anger. Rowan gasped and kept running up the yellow line, relief giving her feet fresh speed. The bafflement in the voice was a little worrying, but she didn't have time to think about that right now.

It's me! She sent a wordless flood of gratitude as she saw two Sigs on the sidewalk. Cars were honking, and the two women in tan trench coats—one with close-cropped stubble, and the other with longer, jet-black hair framing a dead-eyed face—stared at her. Then the dead-eyed one jostled the shaved one, whose eyes swung down Rowan's body.

Rowan felt the psychic attack like thunderstorm prickles along her upper arms and shunted it aside. She didn't even break stride—but the new voice inside her head suddenly *reached*, full of furious, frustrated pain. He flooded her like the sea inside a channel, using her as the equivalent of a booster station to increase his range and actually force his own psionic talent *through* her.

She had only intended to knock the Sigma psion's attack away from her, spending its energy uselessly. Instead, the girl with the shaved head stiffened, her head thrown back. Blood burst from her nose and she howled, a sound that cut through crowd noise, screams, sirens, and the horns of traffic now snarling from the mess down the block at Lew's building.

What are you doing? Rowan's mental voice hit a pitch of anguish that drove steel-tipped spikes through her brain. *Justin, no!*

If you're going to get out of there, was his imperturbable reply, *you'd better move. Who the hell are you, and why are you in my head?*

She didn't have time to answer, having run out of mental hands to juggle with. The collective psionic pressure increased, trying to snag her, slow her down. Every step was a physical battle no less than a mental one. Gasping, her side on fire, Rowan ran. Everything now depended on speed.

She used to love running. Still did, even though she had to run on a treadmill instead of a track.

It's me, she thought, desperately reaching for understanding, for the reassurance he had never denied her before. *Don't you remember me?*

I don't know what the hell you're talking about. Get off the goddamn street. Justin's voice was as cold as a gun barrel pressed against her temple. She smelled cordite, bullets zinged past her. *Cut left at the next intersection. Do it!*

She saw the intersection up ahead. Almost lost the battle of keeping the collective pressure of Sigma away. Pain exploded in her chest, in her side. How many other psions was she fighting? Ten? Fifteen? Where did they house them?

It doesn't matter. Move. He sounded utterly calm, but there was an undercurrent of something else—what was it?

The voice was familiar, but he sounded like a complete stranger. As if he didn't know her. A complex stew of bafflement, rage, and incomprehension tinted his mental voice, added to a deep wash of disbelief.

Rowan bolted through cars brought to a standstill by the chaos behind her. She zigged left at the intersection, gasping for breath, car exhaust and heat burning her eyes. The smell of fried food from the teriyaki joint with its doors propped open hit the back of her throat, she bowled into a man in a business suit and sent him flying. More zinging sounds—snipers.

Great. Her breath tore in her throat, a sudden stitch grabbing her side.

They were trying to shoot her now, probably just to slow her down. The sound of shattering glass tinkled sweetly, a bright note in the song of exhaustion her body had become. The stitch bloomed in her side, gripping along her ribs almost all the way up to her armpit.

It didn't matter.

Justin! Where are you? She reached for him frantically. He was here. She'd heard him, and she *knew* he was here. Heat simmered up from the pavement, and she was sweating, but goose bumps thrilled across her skin as if she was cold.

Bam!

A hammer smashed against her right shoulder, drilling fiery pain. Rowan stumbled and saw blood bloom on the pavement. She kept going, but she tripped over her own feet and almost fell headlong. Heavy gelid warmth flowed down her right arm, slipping against the inside of her coat sleeve, the lining now slicked with blood that dripped off her fingertips. The sense of heaviness fighting every step eased. She had made it through the concentric rings of psychic pressure.

Like a gift, the black van appeared, its side door open. Boomer leaned out, his face contorted with effort as his limited telepathic ability reached toward her, a fine, thin thread of help Rowan grabbed at, and she fell gratefully into his arms. He yanked her inside and Henderson jammed the accelerator down as Cath dragged the door shut.

But Rowan didn't care. She closed her eyes, the leftover pressure of the Sigma psions snapping as soon as she was in the van's shielded interior. The vehicle swayed as Henderson took a corner, rocketing toward the freeway on-ramp and zigging at the last second to plunge the van into the shadow of a tree-lined lane. The Sig net was left behind, and there was no pursuit. The cops were too busy trying to sort out the mess at Lew's office building. "Lew?" she whispered in a cracked voice.

Nine-tenths of her didn't care, was hunting frantically for the *contact*. It had been familiar, as familiar to her as her own breath. It was *him*, and she'd felt the dizzying electrical crackling over her skin that told her he was close. Very close.

"She's bleeding pretty badly," Boomer said. "Winged her, went right through the meat in the upper arm. Damn lucky there's no bone."

"We got him, Ro," Cath said.

More pain grated against Rowan's shoulder as someone's hand clamped over the bloody wound. There was the rip of a pack of sterile gauze and the hiss of an antiseptic pack. "Just relax. Lew's safe."

"Justin," Rowan whispered, and passed out.

Four

Delgado leaned against the alley's wall, his head pounding no less than his heart. *What the hell did I just do?*

If he wasn't so sure he was sane, he might have wondered if the Zed had finally cracked him. Andrews was in the van, leaning out the open side door while collating and doing damage control, conferring with two handlers while warily eyeing Agent Breaker. Delgado wasn't needed, so he simply stood with his back against the brick, his only avenue of escape blocked by the van, his arms folded, apparently composed. Inside, his heart labored and his breathing threatened to short out completely.

What the hell had happened? One moment they'd been tightening the net, ready to bring in Price and the precog—Lewis, whoever the hell he was—and snare the other Society members too.

The next moment it had all gone to hell in a handbasket. The woman thought quickly on her feet. She had worked the crowd like a pro. She'd also managed to tangle up the collective will of several Society psions set in a circle around the site, all concentrating on bringing her down. It was incredible. He wouldn't have believed it if he hadn't seen it himself.

But the most incredible thing of all had been the wave of fear and pain rocketing out from Price, as if she'd been shot. Delgado's stomach had flipped, and every psion in sensing range had flinched. Hard on the heels of that psychic cry, Del had realized she was deliberately broadcasting to throw them off, and the knowledge had frozen him in place. That should have been *impossible*, both for her to do it and for him to know her intent. Andrews had shoved him out of the van, and he'd made it to the ground and moved smoothly and habitually into the prescribed guard position, unwilling to let Andrews suspect he was having any deep philosophical thoughts.

Bitter copper flooded his mouth, the taste of adrenaline. The heat out here was incredible, simmering even in the alley's shadow. A hot stink of garbage rose, everyone ignored it. The comms inside the van crackled—cleanup taking place, the Sigs coordinating with each other.

If the van hadn't been there, Delgado might have tried to get the hell out and disappear.

"Get me a trace," Andrews said. "Something, anything. Now."

Delgado filled his lungs and tried to force his heart to stop pounding. She had *linked* with him, her mind sliding through his apparently with ease and familiarity.

And she knew his name, the name he'd left behind as dead. *Nobody* called him that, it was Del, Delgado, or "Breaker," not *Justin*. But she'd said it as if it was old habit, as if she'd resurrected that name for him. Hearing it was like waking up in his own grave with a mouth full of dirt and his skin wet with mud.

Had he known Rowan Price? Was that what he'd *pushed* himself to forget? How well had he known her? Had they been friends? Teacher and student?

Justin, no! Her horrified mental scream rang inside his head again.

Lovers? No, probably not that. He was too damaged.

It's me. Don't you remember? A lovely contralto husk of a voice that made his body tighten with recognition, a wash of complex feeling boiling through him—desperation, relief, and a deep aching he couldn't name. If she hadn't been so hurried he might have gone a little further, instead of simply reaching through her to strike at the Sig with the close-cropped hair and guiding Price free of the net. The instinct to protect her had been deep, immediate, and full of a terrible fury.

But the most incredible, absolutely unbelievable part? It hadn't hurt.

Agent Breaker, whose talent could crack a mind like an eggshell given the proper motivation, had one severe drawback. His Talent killed or drove people mad. He literally couldn't make mental contact without pain for his subject and himself.

But linking with her hadn't hurt. Suddenly, he was intensely hungry to do it again—feel the brush of that clean, deep mind against his, feel the strange sense of calm sinking into his skin with a crackling electric glaze.

"Delgado," Andrews barked.

Do I kill him now or later? It was tempting. For a moment Delgado considered unleashing his talent on Andrews. It would be satisfying, if agonizing, to break the Colonel's lapdog. And then he could elude the Sigs and follow the woman who had turned all their careful plans and procedures into a complete clusterfuck.

Easy as pie, right?

Only one consideration stopped him. He had to get as much information as he could from Sigma before he made his break for freedom. It was the way he'd done it before.

A mind I can make contact with, without pain. And she knew something about him, something he had *pushed* himself to forget. The hypo-marks in his arms burned, reminding him that very soon he'd need another dose of Zed. If he wanted to break the addiction again, could he? It had been hell the first time.

But now he had an objective to pursue, not just a simple escape to plan. And if there was anything Sigma had trained him for, it was the single-minded pursuit of a target.

"Delgado!" Andrews repeated. Del stiffened reflexively.

"What?" *She got away from you. Good luck catching her now. I must have trained her; she's too good for anything else.*

Anderson's blue eyes blazed. For a moment Del wondered if he was going to unleash his own talent on Del. That wouldn't be comfortable for either of them.

Maybe Andrews remembered that, because he only snarled, "You fucking well trained her, what's she going to do now?"

Yap, yap, little dog. That's the wrong question. The right question is, what is Henderson going to do now? He'll wait for a little less than twenty-four hours and then break camp and move everyone out, after Sigma thinks he's already blown town. If you want to catch them, you'd better start setting up grids now.

"They'll be heading out of town," he lied smoothly. "As fast as fucking possible, they'll head for the city limits. They'll be gone in two hours max. Not enough time to get a full-scale grid going."

For you, Miss Price, he thought. *I'm not going to let them catch you until I've had a little chat with you myself.*

The woman probably couldn't hear him. There was no answering echo inside his head. The need to feel her again was almost as bad as the need for Zed. If he put the two addictions together, which one would win out?

I don't want to be caught in the middle of that. He was still trying to track down the third emotion she'd drowned him with. Desperation, relief, and what else? What had she been feeling? It bothered him that he couldn't find a word to describe such a clear beautiful feeling. It was too pure, and he had nothing to compare it to.

Andrews's blue eyes narrowed. "Why?" he challenged.

"Because it's what I'd do." *I wouldn't. I'd button everyone down and stay tight unless you were running grids.* "And I supposedly trained her."

"Did you train her?" Andrews hopped out of the van-turned-impromptu-command-center, landing as lightly as a cat. If Del was going to attack him, the time was now. He let the moment pass.

"She's too good for anything else," he replied. His voice was steady, and his pulse had returned to its regular rhythm.

"Where's she going next? How can we track her?"

Get a fucking grid going now, you idiot. "Set up check teams on every major avenue out of town for the next couple of hours. Then you're going to have to shift to chatscan." Delgado shrugged. "If you sent me out with a full team and support, you might be able to catch her."

Andrews laughed mirthlessly, his hand on the butt of a gun. *If he draws I'm going to take him,* Delgado thought, and felt the clear calm of adrenaline freeze lower over him. *And if I take him, I have to take everyone in the van, too, and then figure out some way to get the hell out of here.*

"You think I'm going to send you out with a full team? I'd never hear the end of it. All right, we'll set up check teams and do chatscans as well. She won't get away this time. One of the snipers got her in the shoulder. The rats'll have a wounded golden girl to get out of the city, and that'll slow them down."

Not likely. Everything he'd seen from her pointed to a resourceful enemy who wouldn't *let* a wound slow her down. And if Henderson was able to command a severely-compromised group away from the wreck and ruin of the Society's Headquarters, he was capable of getting a team with one wounded member to safety. All things should be so easy.

But the thought of her hurt, the idea of a bullet in the body that housed that clean, deep mind…He had to exert control, keep himself still and collected.

"—the Tracker," Andrews said.

Del replayed his mental footage. *They're going to send us the Tracker.*

What the hell?

"You mean that blind guy?" Delgado's skin went cold. *Please tell me I didn't just hear that.* "With the Japanese bodyguard?" *The one that never loses his target—or he didn't, until they set him to hunting me. I'm the only one that got away from him, and I had to nearly get killed to do it. If it wasn't for Henderson I* would *have been dead.*

"Yeah." Andrews grinned like a death's head. "I'm waiting for confirmation from the Colonel, but I think we'll get him out here by tomorrow with that Jap watchdog. Your favorite buddy Jilssen, too. And then we'll hunt her down like a dog."

The grin widened when Delgado didn't respond. "Cheer up, Del. When we catch her, I might even let you have a taste."

Five

Rowan came back to herself in stages. Her shoulder hurt as if a drill was burrowing into the flesh—her healing talent working overtime. The only drawback to healing a lot more quickly was that all the pain got compressed into a shorter time.

I'm doing well for only the second time I've gotten shot, she thought hazily, swimming up through the fuzzy gray blanket of shock. Her head hurt, a pounding relentless ache curiously removed from the rest of her.

"Justin?" Her own voice, soft and slurred.

"She's coming around." Yoshi, sounding tired. "Rowan, just relax. We're safe."

"No," she objected immediately, her voice slurred and breathless. "He was there. We have to go back." *Listen to me, I sound like I'm drugged.* "He was *there*."

"She's saying it again." Sound of movement, clicking of keys. "I don't like this. They're suspiciously quiet out there."

Henderson sighed. "I know. Just keep digging, find the channel they're using, and break it. I've got one of those feelings." The quiet warmth of the General's attention spread over her skin, his dry, steel-hard fingers taking her pulse. "Rowan, quit trying to get up. Just relax. We've got a couple hours."

She took a deep breath, drawing in the familiar smells of a clean house—fabric softener, computer fans going full-blast, Cath's strawberry incense, the smell of gun oil and healthy human animals. And the crackling smell of fear—their fear.

I'm their talisman, she thought. *A protection. And I just got shot again.*

Two and a half months ago, Sigma had found them again as they scrambled to salvage what they could from the ruin of Headquarters. It had been Yoshi's quick thinking and Zeke's berserker rage that had saved them. Rowan had been ingloriously shot in the first few moments of the attack and spent the rest of the mad scramble bleeding and feverishly trying to be of some use.

She opened her eyes, feeling the electric buzz of dampers against her skin. *I never get used to that.* She was on the cot in the comm room, with Henderson squatting right next to her.

"Hey," he said quietly. "Welcome back. Lew's safely on his way to Eleanor in Calgary, and we're all in one piece. If we still had a Headquarters and infrastructure I'd court-martial you."

"Nice to see you too," she managed. He knew the first thing she'd be worried about was Lewis. "Water?"

He helped her sit up. Her shoulder was tightly bandaged, and a wave of fierce hot pain made her bite her lip. Then the old man handed her a bottle of Evian, thoughtfully twisting the top open for her. She took it in her left hand and took a few deep swallows. Her stomach boiled, flipped, and decided to keep the liquid down. She cast a practiced eye over the room—Cath's Dr. Who scarf was gone, and so were the chairs. They were preparing to blow this town now that they had Lewis and Sigma had shown their hand.

"That was foolish, Rowan." Henderson looked grave. His mouth turned down at the corners, and his gray eyes were pale and cold in a way she had rarely seen before. "They could have caught you."

"They didn't," she pointed out. "Henderson, Justin was there. He helped me escape."

"You saw him?"

"Not precisely." Her cheeks felt hot. Was she *blushing?* "He made contact, linked with me. He..."

He killed the woman with the cropped hair, she realized. *A Sigma psion. The other woman must have been her handler*. And Justin had reached through Rowan, using his talent to crack a mind like an egg.

"He reached through me to kill one of the Sigs and told me how to get out of the net. He was *there*."

Henderson sighed, reaching up to rub at his steel-colored eyes behind his spectacles. He looked tired. "Are you sure?"

Rowan's shoulders sagged. A fresh jolt of pain tore through the right side of her body, making her vision swim and her eyes fill with reflexive tears. "Of course I'm sure." *You trusted my instincts before, General. Why not now?*

"If he's here, he'll show up when he can. You disobeyed a direct order." Henderson didn't look mollified in the slightest. His eyes were sharp and his mouth was a thin line. "Don't do that again."

"I had to get Lew out," she answered. "And draw them off."

Still not mollified. Not even close. "You're not superhuman. You're only human, with some very special talents. You're acting suicidal, and that's bad for the team. Clear?"

"Crystal." Rowan had to suppress a sigh. More irritation rose, fighting with the incredible eye-watering pain for control of her stomach. *I did what I had to do, General. You wouldn't have hesitated either, in my place.* "What's the plan?"

"We're going to lay low until they've passed us by. Boomer's already gone to take Lewis up to Calgary. You and Cath will head to Vegas, and Yoshi, Zeke and I will peel off and start causing trouble northwest. I've got a mind to make a run on a Sig installation." The old man's eyes glittered behind his glasses.

"With only two support staff? Now who's suicidal?" Rowan's jaw set. Her legs ached. Had she pulled something? She hoped not. "Don't do it, Henderson. Go back with Brew and Boomer."

"If you're going to Vegas, I want Sigma chasing their own tails. We're not going to *take out* an installation, just make a run and cause some confusion." His jaw was set, and Rowan felt a faint whisper of alarm. It wasn't like him to be feckless. "And if Del's in town, he'd approve. I shouldn't be sending you to Vegas at all. He's going to be upset."

Do you, or do you not, understand that we need some cash if we're going to get Headquarters running smoothly? And do you, or do you not, understand that I felt *Justin, I* know *he's here?*

She gathered the last scraps of her patience and tried to keep her voice even. "He's here, Daniel. Please...don't do this."

"Um...guys?" Yoshi broke in. He didn't sound happy, and Rowan's nape started to prickle. She moved to swing her legs off the cot, and her shoulder ran with acid fire. She almost wished she didn't heal so quickly. The compressed pain tore into the wound and made it difficult to think clearly.

"What?" Rowan's eyes locked with Henderson's. "What's going on?"

"I don't like this," Yoshi repeated. "I've found their channel and cracked it. Their chatter says they're setting up scans and checks, and there's something about a tracker."

"Any names?" Henderson's shoulders hunched as if warding off a blow.

"Just one. Carson. Mean anything to you?" Yoshi blinked, his fingers still tapping the keys. He'd fitted a comm-link in one ear and was monitoring Sigma's use of a comm channel. "He's due to arrive about twelve hours from now."

"Oh, *Christ.*" Henderson closed his eyes briefly. Rowan's stomach turned over, settled uneasily. "We've got to get everyone out of here. Now."

"Who's Carson?" Rowan tried to stand up. Her knees shook, and the cot threatened to tip until Henderson put out a hand and steadied it. Then he looked up at her from his easy crouch.

"Pray to God you never meet him, Miss Price. Yoshi, get everyone in here. Now."

"You got it, boss." Yoshi tapped at his keyboard and then spoke into a small handheld comm-unit. "Everyone, the General wants to see you. We're blowing this taco stand."

Six

Sigma had their central command in a partially-constructed building downtown, which was their first mistake. Their second, Delgado noted as he was brought into the command center, was that they weren't changing chatter channels every few minutes. *Yoshi*, he thought. *Dammit, boy, be listening. Get a lock on them. Please.*

He could remember the thin, quiet Japanese man and the General's steely eyes. He could remember Cath's punk haircut and Zeke's blunt fingers. He could even imagine Brew's wide white smile and perfect, burnished ebony skin.

But he couldn't remember *her*, no matter how hard he tried. The wall he'd *pushed* himself to erect still stood firm. Frustration tasted bitter and familiar, hopelessness acrid like tar.

One of Andrews's two bullyboys pushed Del forward. "Go on." The man was grinning. He'd been one of the ones who had administered the initial beatings to soften Del up. Thickset and broken-nosed, he looked a little like Zeke, but he had none of Ezekial's careful movements or self-deprecating humor. For a moment Del considered striking out with fist and mind, killing the man with a quick upward strike to the nose and simultaneously ripping his mind free of its moorings. The thought sent a warm, gratifying feeling through him, almost like the oozing fire of Zed.

But his veins began to creep with the slow, painful needling of his addiction, and he walked slowly across the unfinished flooring, stepping over thick cables running to the computers. This would be an employee lunchroom when completed. One end of the room had a half-finished wall through which late afternoon light bounced. When done, this place would have no light at all except fluorescents. Delgado gave an internal sigh. You couldn't expect people to eat under buzzing tubes every day. It would drive even deadheads mad.

Two horseshoe-shaped banks of monitors, hard drives, and keyboards hosted the nerve center of Sigma's operations here. Andrews's team was in one horseshoe, murmuring back and forth. Papers were signed and the machinery of the chain of command went on. The other horseshoe held shaven-headed commtechs with handlers and psychometric or precognitive talent, monitoring and searching for any disturbing trace in cyberspace or the city's grid, any sign of the vanished Society members.

Andrews leaned over a commtech, watching as the shaven-headed kid spider-tapped at two separate keyboards at once, his jaw slack and the monitors above bathing his face in a spectral green glow. A thin thread of drool wandered down the kid's chin. His handler, a tall chestnut-haired woman, stood with her arms crossed, scowling at Andrews.

"Get a lock on them," Andrews snarled. "Do it now. If they haven't gone past the check scans they *have* to be in the city."

Not necessarily, Del thought. *You're an idiot, Andrews. This isn't like you.* He must be frantic to catch them. This Price girl was making him look bad.

Del should play it safe, keep his head down and try to get as much information as he could. But he knew, miserably, that he'd made up his mind to escape ahead of schedule. Now it was only a question of *how*.

The third mistake was almost imperceptible—Andrews didn't immediately notice Del approaching. That meant two things: that Del was no longer considered a threat, and that Andrews was severely distracted.

The skinny, shaven kid began to make a small moaning noise, though his fingers didn't stop blurring over the keyboards.

"That's enough," the handler said. "He won't be useful if you keep pushing him. Lay *off*, Andrews."

Andrews's upper lip pulled back. "He's finished when I *say* he's finished. You'd better watch it, or I'll have Breaker convince him."

The handler seemed supremely unconcerned. She reached down, her fingers circling the boy's wrist. "Come on, Jarrod." Her tone was kind, and the boy stopped moaning and froze. "Let's go get you something to eat."

"I didn't—" Andrews began, but two of the monitors began to flash red. "Aha! Fine, take him. A couple of check scans have given the flag."

Delgado watched as the boy made it to his feet and shambled away, grinning vacantly while his jaw worked, drool coating his chin. Everything burned out but his psychic talent, harnessed to his handler's voice. *I could have ended up like that. I still might.* The thought he'd cherished ever since they'd recaptured him—*I will do whatever I have to do to escape you*—returned, circled his mind once, and vanished. Now he had to work.

His skin chilled slightly, the pain from his Zed addiction kicking up a notch.

"You're jonesing." Andrews tossed him a small black medical pouch, and Delgado caught it reflexively. "Here. Have a ball, and make it last. Go back to your room. We won't need you until we've brought her in."

Del nodded. *Are you insane? You're giving me my own stock of Zed?* "You've got her?"

"As good as. They've split into two—" Andrews glanced up as another monitor began to flash red. "Three—" Another. "What the hell?"

The rabbits have divided, or they've found a way to trip all the checkpoints at once. Good thinking. He weighed the bag, backing up while he looked at the monitors. More of them began to glow red. *There'd be no reason for them to trip a bunch of checks unless they're getting out. If they're getting out, I could lose them. It'll take me too much time to track them down again.*

There would never be a better chance.

"What the *hell*—" Andrews was just a fraction of a second too slow. Delgado was gone before he finished the sentence, slipping out of the command center and into the hallway beyond. With any luck, the sadistic bastard would have his hands too full to notice Del's absence and would assume he was holed up in his airless little room hyping himself on Zed.

Delgado unzipped the bag a little as he walked down the hall. Three hypos. Enough for six days, twelve if he stretched them to the point of pain. He had a few weapons—two knives and two guns—and his talent for cracking minds. And his wits. It would have to be enough to escape a full-scale appropriations team and track down the foes that slipped so smoothly through Sigma's nets.

The first order of business was getting out of this building. He would have to take the stairs.

He heard chaos erupt behind him, Andrews barking orders. It wasn't like him or the colonel to let Del out of their sight without an armed guard, but Del had his veins full of Zed and had shown none of his former defiance since his recapture. And Andrews had lost sight of the mission. He was now emotionally invested in Rowan Price.

She seems to bring that out in a lot of people, Del thought, already running over the building layout in his head. There were some unfinished stairs on the east side, but it was chancy at best.

Del turned east, slipping the bag with the hypos into a small loop attached to his rig that would keep them safe.

"Rest easy, sweetheart," he muttered, hardly aware he was speaking. "Agent Breaker's coming to get you."

Seven

The phone buzzed and Cath flipped it open. "Yeah?" Long pause. "Great. Great news. 'Kay, we'll see you at home, baby. Tell Zeke I said *smoochas*." Her fair, young face broke into a grin as she hung up. The pixie cut suited her more than the Mohawk had.

She shifted the blue Subaru into reverse and pulled out of the rest stop parking space. "Everyone got out okay," she said. "How you doing?"

"Hurts," Rowan said in a colorless voice. And it did—four hours after she'd been shot the agony was enough to draw a gray curtain over her vision. She was sweating, her cotton T-shirt sticking to her armpits and the small of her back. "Better soon."

"I hope so. You look like hell." Cath bit her lower lip, slid the car into "drive," and began to roll forward through the rest stop. The air-conditioning came on full-blast. Rowan managed to open her eyes.

The gray-green blurs pressing against the edges of her vision were trees hung with Spanish moss. The small brick rest stop, housing two bathrooms and a map proclaiming Georgia to be a *Peach of a State!,* receded as Cath accelerated onto the long driveway that would connect them to the freeway. It had taken most of Rowan's waning strength to simply stay conscious and *boost* Yoshi as Henderson—with his trusty pendulum—found the Sigma check teams, and Yoshi used his talent for electronics to long-distance trigger their equipment. Both the General and the slim Japanese man were in bad shape as well, having stretched their talents to the limit. Zeke would get them out, and Boomer and Brew were well on their way with Lewis and several pieces of gear, heading for the Canadian border. Rowan, for now, was Cath's responsibility—at least until the mind-numbing pain stopped and Rowan could think again.

She squeezed her eyes shut, tears trickling down her cheeks. "Justin," she whispered. He was back there, in the city they'd just escaped. Why did she feel like she was abandoning him again?

"It's okay, Rowan. If he's back there in the city, he's probably got his hands full. He'll find you." Cath popped her chewing-gum, her violet eyes focused on the road.

"It's been three months." *I sound like an idiot.* Her mouth was dry. The pain in her shoulder gave one more excruciating twinge and, thankfully, began to recede.

"And you just got proof he was still alive, right?" Cath smashed down on the accelerator and the car leapt forward, merging with heavy afternoon traffic. "What do you want for dinner? We'll stop for something—oh, like Mexican. Mexican sound good?"

"Fine." Rowan forced her eyes open. "How are we for supplies?"

"Got plenty of everything, including ammo. There's the real Rowan. Nice to have you back." Cath popped her gum again. "Think of this like a vacation. We'll be Thelma and Louise."

"Christ, I suppose I'm Louise." It was a pale joke, but Cath giggled anyway.

"You better believe it, sweetheart. Now, if you're not still moaning, dig out that map and start naggervating me." Cath began to hum as she felt around in her purse—a khaki army-surplus map bag that doubled as her kitbag—for a pack of cigarettes. "And push the lighter in, will you?"

"Give me a few minutes, Cath. I got *shot*, for God's sake." The pain receded quickly, leaving Rowan sweat-soaked and chill in the blast of cold air from the air-conditioning. Four hours of hell, and her shoulder felt tender and dislocated. It would be better tomorrow, and in two or three days the scar would begin to shrink. Her old childhood scars—a small one on her right knee and the long one on the underside of her left arm from a bicycle mishap—had started to shrink too; a consequence of her breaking whatever psionic barrier she'd smashed the night Headquarters was breached.

"Yeah, but you're a quick healer. Look at you. Bet it's all closed up by now. That's some voodoo you got, baby."

Rowan closed her hand tentatively over her wounded shoulder. It felt hot even through the corduroy jacket Yoshi had made her take. He'd packed her clothes and kitbag, too. The canvas messenger bag rested between her hip and the center console. She was armed and dangerous, as the old police shows would have said.

Funny, she thought through the swell of pain. *I wouldn't have known what to do with a gun a year and a half ago.*

Now I feel naked if I don't have one. And I understand so much more about Justin now.

Like what it might have cost him to drag a sedated Rowan across the country, eluding Sigma traps and nets to get her to safety. Like what it might have done to him to watch her sink further and further into grieving apathy.

Like how he must have felt when she'd insisted on becoming an operative. She'd thought he was being brutal, but he'd simply had to be twice as tough as the Sigs would be, to prepare her to face an enemy with no conscience and few scruples. It must have tortured him to act so coldly toward her in the practice room.

Rowan sighed, her hand tightening on her shoulder. A jolt of fading pain lanced across her chest. She was exhausted. "I've got to get some sleep," she said heavily. "Wake me up for dinner."

"Sure thing." Cath's lighter clicked, she inhaled and then cracked a window to ventilate the smoke. The heavy smell of swamp and heat began to blow into the car's interior, and Rowan fell asleep thinking about juicy green vines and the life rioting wildly out of still stagnant water and sodden ground.

Eight

He picked west because something too deep to be instinct stirred vaguely in him at the thought. Besides, it made no sense for her to go north, that would bring her closer to some of Sigma's thickest-scanned areas. South would pin her against the Gulf with no escape routes after a major brush with Sigma, and east would do the same with the Atlantic.

So west it was.

It had been absurdly anticlimactic to escape. All he had to do was *push* one heavily-armed guard at the bottom of the murderously unfinished stairwell. Apparently even Andrews thought only a suicidally insane person would brave the rickety, no balustrade, leap-over-gaps Delgado had done.

Maybe they were right. In any case, one bored guard smoking a cigarette was no match for Del. He wanted to take the man's wallet and gear, not to mention weapons, but for maximum confusion he needed to simply vanish without a trace.

Negotiating the security net on the ground floor and the three-block radius outside the building was another matter. It took him two precious hours to traverse those three blocks. To keep himself invisible from the psionics and their handlers, he had to use every shadow-skill he possessed—he had to avoid killing one of them and leaving a hole, too. The wet heat and slowly increasing need for a hit of Zed made it even more difficult to concentrate. He even crouched behind a Dumpster for a full twenty minutes, less than six feet away from a precog and her handler, only escaping when the handler needed to take the thin bald girl in to a 7-11 bathroom because she had started to moan softly and sway with her knees pressed together.

I could have ended up like that.

And maybe this faceless Rowan Price could have ended up like that. The thought of that clean, deep mind broken, and maybe a brutal handler to add to the fun, made sheer red protective fury rise in him.

What the hell am I doing?

His first need was money. Thankfully, it was now in the prime hours of dusk, and he found himself in a bad part of town. He summarily relieved three crack dealers of their cash and left them with blinding headaches. He could have also taken a very nice Glock 9mm, but he wasn't sure if it was a clean gun. Del broke it down and left the parts in two separate Dumpsters. A cab ride later, he found a small teriyaki shack unlikely to have surveillance cameras and put away three bowls of rice and chicken. He wanted to buy some ibuprofen because he felt as if something monstrous was being torn from the center of his brain, but he didn't have time. Hunger would slow him down, but he could live with pain for a while longer before needing to deal with it.

He made it out of the city with thirty-eight hundred dollars and a ride hitched in a DariMilk semi that was actually, according to the garrulous mutton-chopped man driving it, carrying grape mash for winemaking.

"Yeah, ain't no money to be had in carrying fuckin' milk," the driver said as Del settled back in the seat and watched the asphalt slip away under the wheels.

"Guess not," Del replied with a thin attempt at humor.

The driver was feeling chatty, and his rig reeked of cigarette smoke and old sweat. The initial *push* to make him friendly hadn't been hard. Larry the Truck Driver was a lonely man, glad for someone to talk to. Del made the appropriate noises, one part of him monitoring the chatter from the CB radio and the patterns of traffic in front of and behind the semi.

He'd done the easy part. Now he had to find Rowan Price.

Nine

"This has got to be the bleakest part of the country," Rowan complained the next day, leaning against the back of the car as Cath deftly smacked the gas pump nozzle into the car like a teat into a piglet's mouth. "I mean, *look* at this."

Rolling hills lay flat and pleated, covered with whatever grew on Oklahoma sod. The landscape stretched from horizon to horizon with nothing to break its monotony but the highway's dips. Deep blue sky was scored with the blazing eye of the sun, mercilessly beating down on humid black dirt and matted grass. The faraway shape of a water tower lifted like a distant pregnant elephant, another welcome break in the flatness. Insects hummed in the fitful hot breeze and sweat lay like oil against Rowan's forearms, between her breasts, against the curve of her lower back and behind her bare knees. She was glad she could wear shorts, even if she had to wear a T-shirt because of the glaring chunk taken out of her right deltoid. It was an angry bright red and didn't look like a normal wound should. Because it was healing too quickly, it looked weeks instead of days old and paradoxically fresh.

Cath glanced around. "Nothing but sod, huh? But the hills break it up a little. Not like Wyoming. You ain't seen a whole lot of nothing until you see Wyoming." She scratched at her cheek, the tails of her Dr. Who scarf stirring in the low, warm breeze. At least it wasn't the cloying heat of the city; this heat was fractionally less muggy.

But the insects are worse. Rowan slapped at a bite on her forearm. The sky was a deep venomous blue, no trace of a cloud except in the south, where a thick band of black smudge promised a thunderstorm later in the day. *I never thought I'd miss Saint City rain. Rain four days out of every five, rain until you grow mold between your toes. God.* "How are you feeling, Cath? Want me to drive for a while?"

"We should make Amarillo late-late tonight, and we'll stop for some real food and a real bed. We've made good time. Wish we didn't have to go through New Mexico, even for a minute. How's your arm?"

The sign proclaiming *Gas-Food-Ice* squealed as the restless wind mouthed it. "My arm's okay." Rowan massaged her left shoulder, feeling only a slight twinge—probably psychological. "We *have* made good time. I wish we could know how the others are doing."

"They're probably fine. Worry about us first." Cath popped her Juicy Fruit gum again and the gas pump clicked off. "I'm going to go get my change and some Doritos. You want anything?"

"A cold Coke, if they have it. That bathroom dried my mouth out." Rowan grimaced, and Cath laughed as she strode away toward the ramshackle mini-mart attached to the gas station. It had an actual *Dirty Harry* movie poster tacked to the window, Clint's sneer turning as yellow as the rest of him through the dingy glass. Rowan stood and waited, leaning against the car and blinking as the dust-laden wind rose again. The asthmatic ice machine on the store's front porch wheezed and made a cluttering thump.

It was actually nice to be out in the country, with precious few people emitting confusing bursts of thought and emotion. Instead, there was the clean sweep of wind—full of chemical stink, probably from oil fields since the wind was from the south, but good enough. Rowan caught a flash of focused thought just as a hawk dove out of the deeply blue sky and caught some poor small bundle of fur. The hawk's satisfaction was a thread of gold spilled through the song of tough stubbled grass, weeds, and the ribbon of the highway.

Rowan closed her eyes, letting the wind blow through her, hoping the space and sky would ease the creeping guilt chewing at her chest. And the nagging hole in her head, where Justin should be.

"I got us some Pop Tarts too," Cath said at her elbow. Rowan nodded, her eyes on the sky now. There was no sense of peace to be found in the deep blue haze. "And a couple of Tiger Tails. Come on, we're on a field trip, we might as well live a little dangerous."

"If preservative-laced sugar isn't dangerous, I don't know what is," Rowan muttered good-naturedly, and Cath stuck her tongue out.

"Says the woman who can eat a whole pound of bacon at one sitting."

"Only if it's crispy enough." Rowan stretched. The wind was beginning to fall off, and she saw a distant flash among the black clouds gathering on the horizon. *I wonder if they get big storms all the time,* she thought, and shivered. "You need me to drive?"

"Hell no. I need you to hand me my Tiger Tail when we

cross the state line. Let's go."

* * *

They did indeed make Amarillo late, so late Cath had to shake Rowan awake, her violet eyes bloodshot. "Come on," she said, yawning. "I've got us a room, and there's a greasy-spoon diner."

"Mrgh," Rowan managed, opening bleary eyes. "Christ, I'm sorry."

"No problem. I'll shoot you later. Help me carry the gear."

Half an hour later, with the room clean and countermeasures in place, they crossed the weed-choked parking lot to the slightly better-lit, flat, cracked asphalt lot unrolling around what a buzzing neon sign proclaimed as Babe's Blue Hole Café. Cath lit another cigarette and coughed, deep and racking. "Want one?"

"I'm trying to cut down," Rowan returned, deadpan, rubbing at her left shoulder. Her hair felt greasy, her face felt leathery and dry, and her shoulder ached. Her entire *body* ached after two whole days in the car, catching only broken sleep as Cath drove, Cath napping as Rowan piloted the car over the gray ribbon of highway after highway. "I'm dying for a club sandwich. And an apple."

"I think they can only help you with the sandwich. This part of the country ain't known for health food." Cath stepped over onto the pavement. "You're worrying again."

Rowan nodded. "I'm sorry, Cath. I know I should be focusing on—"

"The thing I can't understand," Cath said, bowling right over the top of Rowan's sentence, "is why you picked *him*. I mean, he's *Delgado*, for chrissake. He used to be Sigma, and he's *scary*. Was it just because he rescued you?"

"You don't know him," Rowan said flatly. "They did terrible things to him, Catherine. And he..."

How could she explain that he was the only person who had truly seen her? Sigma saw her as a resource to be obtained, and the Society saw her as a powerful psionic to be kept out of Sigma's hands. Her father had seen her as his little princess, and even Hilary had only known Rowan as her slightly weird and geeky best friend. The only person who had *seen* Rowan as thoroughly as Justin Delgado had been her mother, long dead of a stroke.

"He's different," she finally said, as they walked up the sidewalk toward the front entrance of the restaurant. Mellow electric light shone out through the windows, and she saw a few nighttime customers and braced herself for the familiar wave of chaos that was normal minds.

"You can say that again," Cath snorted. She exhaled a long stream of cigarette smoke. "He's scary different. You know what weirded me out the most? How he would just appear out of nowhere. One second, nobody there. Next, *boom*, Del's there saying hi. Freakiest fucking thing in the world. He even freaks Zeke out, and nothing scares Zeke."

I know just how scared of him you all were. Rowan took a firm grip on the remains of her failing patience. *Nobody ever thought that maybe he was traumatized by what those bastards did to him. Drugs and electroshock. And beatings, although he never really talked about those. What was it he said? "They wanted what I could do, and I was...resistant."*

The way he would stand so completely still, as if he'd forgotten to breathe, staring at Rowan with that oddly intent look on his face. How shy he was—and that was something the rest of the Society wouldn't have believed. They thought he was superhuman and coldly, efficiently robotic. Just a killing machine, a training machine. None of them saw the man who had slept in a recliner for months while Rowan took over his bed and eventually his entire room. She still cringed at the thought of how she had blithely assumed the room empty because it had no betraying personal marks or possessions other than a few clothes and Justin's weapons.

"He's not scary," she said quietly, holding the door open for Cath, who hadn't even bothered to ditch her cigarette. "They tried to break him. I'm not sure they didn't do it, in some ways. Emily asked me this too, you know. *Why him?* Well, he needs someone. Maybe I'm just a sucker for people who need me."

"Well, we need you too." As usual, Cath didn't sugar the pill. "You keep insisting on chasing him down everywhere we go and you're going to get someone killed—maybe one of us and maybe you. Let it *go*... Yes, table for two. Smoking. Thanks, sweetheart."

Rowan sighed, exhausted. Even keeping the faint blur that would disguise the fact that she was armed was a heavy weight against her mind. The leaden bottle-blond waitress shuffled them to a back booth and settled them with overheated coffee, plastic menus, and glasses of tap water. The smell of fried foods drenched Rowan's skin, and she was suddenly very tired of running and hiding.

Even at Headquarters it had felt like hiding.

I don't just want to stay alive, she thought. "I want to destroy them." Her low murmur caught her by surprise.

"Destroy who? Sigma?" Cath took a slurp from her water glass, and then inhaled another lungful of smoke. Her pack of Dunhills was placed ceremonially on the table, a battered Hello Kitty lighter on top of the rich red glitter. "Me too. But they're too big."

"They are big," Rowan agreed. "But I'm serious. I want them to go to jail. I want them to be *accountable*."

"Good luck. They *own* the courts." Cath blinked through a veil of cigarette smoke. She looked far older than her nineteen years. "Don't go all Caped Crusader. You'll burn out."

They both fell silent as the shuffling, tired-eyed waitress returned. "Hey I'm Blair. What canna getcha?"

A little bit of hope, Rowan thought, *and a plan to take down a secret government agency. You got one in your back pocket?*

"Club sandwich, please, on sourdough if you have it. And french fries." *I might as well. I probably won't live long enough to get clogged arteries.*

"Chicken fried steak and baked potato, with the clam chowder," Cath said cheerfully, collecting Ro's menu and handing it to the waitress. "Can I have a side of Ranch dressing too? You're a doll. Thanks a million."

She lit another cigarette with the burning stub of her first as the waitress trundled away. "I mean it," she continued. "You're going to burn out. And if that happens we're dead in the water. I don't know *what* we'll do if we lose you. I thought we were goners after Headquarters bit it. But you managed to keep Henderson from going nuts and organized us, and we're actually *fighting back.* Stop thinking you have to go save Del. He's tough enough. He can save himself." She blew twin jets of smoke out her nose, the sheaf of earrings on each ear and her nose ring glittering.

She'd actually be quite pretty without all the metal, Rowan thought again. "I've done my duty," she said quietly. "If it was up to me we never would have left him behind."

Cath made a short disgusted sound. "You know your problem, Price? You're too goddamn serious. Now get out the map. I want to look at our next day of fun and games."

Ten

He lay sprawled on the cheap bed, the thin blanket rasping against his bare left arm; his right was flung over his eyes. The hypo sat on the bedside table, but he hadn't used it yet.

Not while he had this to do.

Outside, Lubbock pulsed with light under an endless star-scarred Texas sky. Del had managed to get this far by hitching rides with truckers, but he needed a car of his own. That meant he would need all his talents, which meant he had to use one of the precious hypos of Zed so he could think clearly for a few hours.

But first, there was something he had to do.

The smooth, blank wall inside his head taunted him. The wall had remained firm under the sodium pentothal mixed with Zed and the beatings. They hadn't dared to use electroshock. That might have destroyed vital pieces of information. And the telepaths had been unable to read him without excruciating pain and possible death, Del's own talent extinguishing the mind that sought to probe it.

Every mind—except hers.

He felt along the wall again. Smooth and sheer, he had locked something in the deepest recesses of his mind. Something precious.

The image of that half-remembered room, with scarves tossed over the bed, plants growing lush in every corner, and sunlight spilling along shelves of books, returned. The room looked familiar and unfamiliar at the same time, his only refuge while they tortured his body. The room held a faint, beautiful perfume he'd never smelled before. He kept his eyes closed and imagined himself there, standing on the mellow-glowing wood floor, the edge of his hand warmed with sun pouring through the French doors, and the smells of paper and bindings and wet earth—*she just watered the plants,* he thought—rising to his nostrils. The thought was gone as soon as it appeared.

Nothing else in the room but the faint, almost imperceptible odor of a woman's skin, clean and fresh.

He was in three places at once—his body, lying on a cheap hotel bed in Lubbock, another part of him in that room full of sunlight and clean peace, and a third part crouched in front of the blank, smooth wall and scraping at it with fingers turned to bloody claws.

Let me in. Let me IN!

The answer, when it came, struck as hard as a fist to the gut.

You pushed *yourself to forget. Now* push *yourself to remember. Then you'll know where she's going, and who she is.*

It was risky. He might end up a crippled, mind-shattered hulk if the *push* ricocheted. And if Sigma caught him again, he doubted he could force another *push* through his memory in time. They wouldn't just beat him up and fill him full of Zed. They wouldn't stop until he was dead. He'd outwitted them twice now, and was too dangerous for any profit his talent could bring them.

So this time was for keeps.

Del lay in the dark with his arm over his eyes and gathered himself, feeling the need for Zed burning in the subtle traceries of his veins. If he took the hypo now, he wouldn't have the concentration necessary for the *push*, and he'd foul something up. No, this would be painful anyway, best to just get it over with.

He reexamined the wall, searching the smoothness for any weak spot. Looking at it like someone else's mind, shielded and shut tight, but still vulnerable. Very few minds were completely impenetrable—only Zeke's. That was why they called Zeke "the Tank," because he was curiously inoculated against psychic attack. Even Del couldn't crack him.

Delgado thought of the woman's voice, her husky contralto. *Justin! No!* The flood of feeling from her, underlaid with something too pure to be described, a feeling like—

He *pushed*, gathering all his talent in one single, undeniable thrust. Battered the wall with the sound of her voice, pain striking and curving into his brain's map, black explosions against his eyelids as his back arched and his arms twisted uselessly, his heels drumming the mattress.

And the wall...broke.

But Delgado was finally, mercifully, unconscious.

* * *

He came to hours later, dried blood crusting his nose. His head throbbed, every nerve twisting with excruciating pain. He fumbled for the hypo, pressed it against the inside of his elbow and heard more than felt the airpac discharge. Numbness, blessed relief, crawled chill up his arm, spilled past his shoulder. Crawled through his chest and reached his legs, headed for his brain to short him out.

Oh, God, was his first thought. *Oh, my God. No.*

Echoes inside his head. Echoes of a woman with long ash-blond hair, her green eyes dark with pain, and her mouth clamped in a thin line. Memories flooding him, of running halfway across the country to escape Sigma, of training her to be an operative, of her voice crackling through a comm-link as the rest of the world turned to gray fuzz because he'd been shot in a raid on a Sigma installation. She had literally pulled him back from death.

Her voice, the exact color of her eyes, the taste of her skin where the fragile pulse beat just above her collarbone. *Rowan.*

He remembered now, remembered why he had *pushed* himself to forget. He'd sacrificed himself to get her out and away from the ruin of Headquarters, wiped his own head so he couldn't be used against her, because she was the only thing he cared about. The only thing in the world that mattered to him.

And Sigma was now frantically trying to find her while Delgado, his mind almost shattered by agony, Zed, and his own talent, lay on a hotel bed and began to laugh out loud, a keening unhealthy laughter.

He was going to find her first.

Eleven

Vegas rose, shimmering spikes of light bristling into the desert night under small, flinty stars. Outside the window, the city thrummed with an electric bath of greed and light, but it was, for all its desperation, a relaxed town—probably due to the amount of alcohol being consumed, fuzzing all the deadheads out.

This far away, the city looked like a carpet of colored bonbons. Radioactive bonbons. Cancerous little sweets.

Rowan set her bag gingerly down on the burgundy bedspread. "My entire body hurts," she said mournfully. "My ass most of all."

"Stretch out." Cath was unsympathetic. She flung herself down on the bed on her back, her short black hair puffing out like thistledown. "I'm gonna check the room."

Rowan nodded, her fists against her lower back. She bent back like the old painting of the Lady of Shallott, shaking her hair out and stretching. There were probably cameras everywhere. She'd kept the baseball cap on the entire time to cover her hair. She probably looked like the world's worst case of hat-head by now.

Cath closed her eyes. Breathless silence filled the room as a faint psychic crackling, like faraway crickets, swept from one corner to the next. Rowan, her mental defenses still absurdly sensitive, shivered and crossed to the windows, looking out on the carpet of light in the distance.

It's beautiful, she thought. *Hilary would have loved this.*

Thinking of Hilary, with her sleek cap of dark hair and her charcoal suits, still hurt. It was probably a blessing she couldn't remember seeing her childhood friend dead. That was one memory Justin had refused to share with her, even though she'd asked. *Don't, Rowan.* He had stroked her back, his fingers gentle, kissed her temple and hugged her tighter. *You don't want to see that. You don't need to see that.*

The old pain rose, and the old rage with it. She stared out at the lights, then reached up and spread her hand against the chill glass. Mist outlined her fingers, living warmth meeting cold hardness.

Justin was alive. She had hoped, prayed, thought...but not *known*. Now she knew. And if he was alive, was he following her? Had he already made contact with Henderson?

The strangeness nagged at her. *Who the hell are you?*

As if he didn't know, or didn't remember. Had Sigma done something to him, made him forget? It was ridiculous, but...perhaps. If she could *touch* him without hurting them both, someone else might be able to. If that someone was a Sigma operative, they might well try to strip him of every memory he had of her, both to try to catch her and to break any emotional attachment he might have to her. It was standard in Sigma to break up relationships that didn't serve the purposes of the handlers and higher-ups, psions moved around like human chess pieces, manipulated like puppets.

Spears of night-burning light pierced the desert sky. Cath sighed from the bed. "Room's clear," she said, in the heavy slurred voice of exhaustion. "Get some shut-eye. Tomorrow's a busy day."

Yeah, we have to score a few hundred thousand and get out of the city without anyone noticing. Her eyes burned with fatigue. At least her shoulder wasn't hurting. No, the only thing hurting was her chest. Or to be more specific, her heart. It was a fresh pain, a pain she thought she'd left behind months ago when she had finally accepted Justin wasn't coming back. That Sigma had stolen him too.

"Go to sleep," she told Cath. "I'll turn in, in a few."

But the girl was already asleep. Her even breathing filled the room. Rowan didn't mind. She had learned not to like sleeping alone. It was nice to have the sense of another psion near. If she pretended hard enough, she might be able to believe it was Justin for a few moments.

Rowan sighed, eased out of her jacket and unbuckled the shoulder holster. Tomorrow she'd wear a full rig. It would cost her in energy to keep it hidden from the crowd of deadheads and security cameras, but it would be worth it if trouble occurred. And the way her nape and upper arms were prickling, trouble was a definite possibility.

This trip should fund them through the next critical period as well as finishing the remodeling of the new Headquarters. By the time that was accomplished, the rest of Henderson's preparations should be in place to tap into the reserves the Society had left. It was slow going, because they had to make sure that Sigma hadn't trapped or frozen the financials from the records they'd acquired at the wreck of the old

Headquarters. The safeguards had probably protected most of it, but Henderson wanted to be sure before he drew on the funds and brought a whole house of cards down on them.

Rowan rubbed at the back of her neck, sighing. She should be sleeping. If anything untoward happened tomorrow, she was going to need every scrap of energy she possessed.

She couldn't help it. She gathered herself and sent a thread-thin call through the city, subtle as a single gold thread buried under wool carpet. There was only one other mind that could find that call, one other mind that would possibly answer her. *Are you there?*

Nothing. Her hook slid through dark waters, not a nibble. No bite.

Please, if you're there, if you've followed me, please talk to me. I miss you.

She waited, the call blurring as her concentration faded. Nothing. If he was there, he wasn't answering. Why? If he had been there while she was running for her life, where was he now?

She sent out one more wistful call. *Please. I miss you.*

Nothing.

She sighed, laid the shoulder holster on the bed, and slipped the gun free. It was loaded, a baby Glock with a full clip and one in the chamber, functioning perfectly. She set it on the nightstand and stripped down to her T-shirt and panties, breathing a sigh of relief when she unsnapped and struggled out of her bra under the shirt. Given Cath's habit of stripping down, she shouldn't worry about being modest, but old habits died hard, if at all.

The sheets were clean, smelling of bleach and industrial fabric softener. Rowan lay still, feeling the strain of exhaustion weigh on her, muscles unwilling to let go of wakefulness. There was a certain point of nervous endurance past which it was almost impossible to fall asleep. She closed her eyes and began to breathe long, deep breaths, just like meditation. Just like sitting with her back against Justin's, feeling his brain shift into the smoothness of alpha waves and doing her best to follow. Finding that magic space, sinking into a timeless eternity. It was like meditating with Yoshi, only with the absolute safety of Justin's attention closed around her. Even while he slept he never lost track of her, his mind never quite slipping free of the borders of hers.

Rowan exhaled, peace loosening her muscles. She drifted closer to sleep, closer, closer.

Just before she went over the edge, she seemed to feel a brush against her cheek. Gentle fingers, callused from practice, skating over her cheekbone.

Just rest, angel. Comfort wrapping around her, a familiar touch. She would have tried to wake up, but she was tipped into the black well of unconsciousness before she could protest.

* * *

Rowan looked at the laptop's blue screen. "We're going to hit the Venetian first. I feel a little bad about this."

Cath shrugged, leaning back on the bed. She checked the automatic's slide and racked a clip in, the sound loud in the room's hush. "Why? They have more than enough."

You don't get it, do you? Cath was not overly given to deep analysis. Maybe it was her age. *Was I ever this oblivious?* "It's not our money. We're basically stealing."

Cath chambered a round and slid the gun into the holster under her left armpit. Next went a pair of stilettos up her sleeves. Her fair, round face was serious, set in its childish lines, her soft mouth drawn tight. She'd taken out her nose piercings, her tongue stud, her eyebrow ring, and most of her earrings as well. "You're right. We are. But people come here to throw their money away. We need some of it to fight Sigma. What the hell's wrong with you?" Her hair, damp and slick from the shower, lay seal-sleek against her head.

"I just feel bad, that's all." Rowan finished the last string and looked at the results. Code flashed; she barely saw it anymore. The message was clear. "Looks like Yoshi's worked his magic, as usual. They're all fine." *And Henderson's getting ready for a run on a Sigma installation. Wonderful. If I didn't know him better, I'd say the man was suicidal.*

"Good. Now worry about us." Cath sounded uncharacteristically nervous. When Rowan glanced over, she saw pale cheeks and tasted a shimmer of acid yellow fear.

Rowan wondered if this was what having children was like. She was just as nervous as Cath but hiding it better. If *she* went off the rails Catherine would go nuts. "I *am* worrying about us, porcupine girl. Relax. This is going to go like clockwork. All you have to do is tickle the little roulette ball and let me worry about the rest. We'll hit a couple of casinos and make up the rest at the track this afternoon and tomorrow."

"I hate horse races." Cath's mouth pulled tighter. Muscle moved under the goth-pale skin of her arms as she rolled her shoulders back. Her holster would chafe if she insisted on wearing just a tank top and the light overjacket. Then again, this was a desert town. It was going to be a scorcher. "You sure you're okay, Ro? I got a bad feeling about all this."

"Just nervousness. Everything's going to go fine." Rowan closed the laptop and looked around the room. If all went well, she would never have to see this room again. They would find another hotel for tonight and be well out of town tomorrow night, after they finished at the track. Moving around was the best way to avoid unwanted attention.

The curtains were pulled tight, but the desert morning outside was already beginning to send spears of light through the cracks. There was a narrow strip of light under the door, too. *Just the thing for scorpions to scuttle through*, she thought, and shivered a little. She set the sleek black deck aside and unplugged the telephone cord, wrapping it deftly and stowing it in the larger kitbag. Then she busied herself getting her own gear on. She was going to sweat today; there was no way around it.

The clicking sound of clips checked and slid in, rounds chambered, and the soft sliding sound of each knife's action tested were all familiar, comforting. She was getting better at throwing knives due to Brew's patient tutelage. Still, she would have felt better if Justin had been here. He was an acknowledged master of making a blade do things it shouldn't theoretically be able to do. *A slight side-effect of Sigma training,* he'd once remarked wryly to her, working a knife out of a block of wood. *When you want quiet, quick, and dirty, it's knife work. Sometimes the poor bastards even forget they have guns.*

Finally, she shrugged into the cream-colored linen suit jacket Yoshi had given her. *Very Miami Vice. All I need is stubble and loafers with no socks. I am* so *not ready for this.* "As ready as I can be," she muttered, and looked up to find Cath watching.

The younger woman's eyes were wide. "I remember when you came in. You didn't even know what end of a gun to hold. I used to think Del was crazy, trying to teach you the way around a sparring match."

Me too. It had taken Rowan months to snap out of her

daze of apathetic fear.

"I learned," Rowan replied, crossing the cheap brown carpet and peering out into the bright floodlight of a Vegas morning. "Just like you did, just like he did." The parking lot already shimmered with heat above the pavement, the freshness of morning boiled away by a merciless sun. "Shit, we're going to sweat today. We should have gotten up earlier."

"We'd be conspicuous. There'll be a good crowd there by now to hide us." Cath levered herself off the bed. "You look nice. Wish you'd let me dye your hair."

"Everyone today is going to swear I'm a brunette, and the tapes will be scrambled anyway once we leave." The corner of Rowan's mouth tilted up. She could feel the lopsided smile. "So much simpler than going to a salon."

"Clairol for Psions." Cath grinned, the tension breaking and peeling away. "Only for you, I'd pick a nice deep purple. Or mahogany, seeing as how you're such a straight-arrow."

Rowan heaved a mental sigh of relief. If Cath got nervous in a casino, they would have a harder time doing this.

"My reputation precedeth me." One final check of the parking lot. Ranks of cars gleamed under the assault of sun and dust, their dashboards almost visibly popping with heat. The glare of light refracting off windshield glass left a green-gold veil over Rowan's eyes as she blinked and looked back into the suddenly-dim cave of the room. "Looks clear. And I don't feel like I'm going to throw up, so we're probably clean."

"We look clean, cute, and harmless. Curse of my life. Got your game face on?"

"Absolutely. Wish us luck." *With the pre-job jitters we're getting, it will be a miracle if we pull this off. And my neck is prickling again. I think we're going to have some trouble. Please, God, let there be no trouble, what do you say?*

Cath gave her a thumb's up and a wide smile, seeming to shake nervousness aside like a dog shakes off water. "Luck. Let's hope we don't need it."

Twelve

Delgado found the pay phone, fed in quarters and dialed. No answer. Tried another number. It was only a vanishing possibility, but one he had to explore.

The truck stop lay under a coat of thick dust and evening blur. The Taurus he'd paid cash for in Flagstaff—a necessary indulgence—hunched tired and green under a street lamp. Its paint job was suffering, but the engine was good, and the little tingle in Del's hands told him it would go until its heart gave out.

Kind of like him. He'd always liked mechanical things. They were far less messy and judgmental than people.

And then, miracle of miracles, the phone was picked up. No sound, not even breathing.

"Delgado," he said. "Code in alpha-zulu-henry-bravo, 31142."

"Jesus *Christ!*"

He recognized the voice. Wanted to smile, dispelled the urge. "Hey, Yosh. How are you?"

A click, while Yoshi scanned for traces. Del could almost see the slim man's fingers tapping over a computer keyboard, his face bathed in monitor glow. "I thought you'd call in. Rowan swore you were alive."

His heart gave one shattering leap and started pounding hard enough to burst. He leaned against the side of the phone booth, blinking the omnipresent dust out of his eyes. "Did she? Good girl. Takes more than Sigma to keep me down." His arm burned, reminding him he would need more Zed soon. The back of his throat was slick and dry. "Thought you'd like to know they're bringing in Carson to hunt my girl. I'm tracking right now, going to do all I can to throw him off."

"Ah." Another click. "The line's clean."

Good boy. Yoshi wasn't committing to anything. He had no way of knowing if Del was talking with a gun to his head, or looped out on Zed and going to report every bit of information to Sigma handlers.

But the mistrust still hurt a little, even though it was what Del would have done himself. "Of course it's clean. I've slipped the leash again. If they catch me they'll kill me for sure, not just hook me on Zed and give me some love taps."

"SOP says for you to come in from the cold, operative."

Delgado swallowed. He needed food and rest. He would only get dinner. He was too far behind Rowan for resting. "This isn't standard. I'm looking for Rowan. Care to give me a hint?" *You can't. Tell me you can't.*

"You know I can't."

"Come on, Yoshi. I'm calling in on a clean line and obviously myself. Just give me a goddamn clue. A name, a sign, anything. Please tell me she's not on a fucking run." His voice cracked.

There was another click. Then another familiar voice, crackling with impatience. "Del, where the hell are you?"

"Fifty miles out of Vegas, General." It was closer to fifteen, but old habit made him mislead. "Tell me you didn't send my girl in there."

"You're supposed to come in the approved way. If you do, you can see Rowan, Del. That's the only offer you're going to get." Harsh, but with an undertone of something else—Henderson was trying to tell him something. Or at least Del hoped he was.

Come on, old man, I'm tired and blunt, give me a little something here, anything? "You think I'd do anything to endanger her?"

"I'm going by protocols you yourself laid down, operative. Come in. That whole sector's crawling with Sigs."

Aha. Very tricky, old man. And very nicely put. "There're three blind mice on her trail, General. I'm not coming in unless it's with her." *You sent her on a fucking run. Dammit.* Fresh on the heels of that thought came a wave of almost-panic. The situation must be incredibly bad. *Tell me you gave her Brew as backup. Tell me you've sent her in with a full team. Goddammit, General, talk to me!*

He knew the old man couldn't. Couldn't take the chance, couldn't trust Del's voice on the phone. He wouldn't have trusted Henderson if the situations were reversed, especially not with Rowan's safety on the line. "Let us bring you in, Del. Nice and easy. We can bring you in and you can see Rowan's pretty face again. She's been missing you."

That bit of information made his heart pound even harder. Even if it wasn't true, he still wanted to believe it. "Likewise," he managed. "Just so you know, I'm tracking her. I'll come in when she does. Warn her to be on her toes." *Carson's after her. Carson and that goddamn Japanese psycho. And*

Andrews as well, but now Andrews has a big hard-on for me, too.

"You're wasting your time, Del. Come in."

"See you soon." He laid the phone back in the cradle and listened as the box clicked with his change. Night was cold out here, under the hard jewels of the desert stars. Las Vegas was a volcano of light in the near distance, especially the sword of the Luxor's spotlight.

Delgado rested his head against the chill glass of the phone box, keeping the door open with one foot. The smell of sagebrush and diesel, plus heat simmering away from cooling pavement, rose to touch his cheeks. He was running on nerves and instinct, rubbed raw by the aftereffects of the *push* and the Zed addiction. He only had one hypo left. He needed food, some kind of ballast. He suspected he'd pulled a mental muscle or two by using the *push* on himself.

Didn't matter. What mattered was finding Rowan and watching over her until she could bring him back into the Society.

He found himself hyperventilating. Bad, the first stage of withdrawal. He wasn't going to last much longer.

Not without her. Making himself forget had served one other purpose: Sigma was unaware of Rowan's ability to nullify Zed addictions. Maybe Jilssen hadn't known either. Del had certainly done his best to keep it quiet. If they'd known, he would never have escaped them.

And something about his escape bothered him too. It had been too uncharacteristically easy.

Don't start getting paranoid now. Focus on what matters.

What mattered right now was getting something to eat, and then driving into Vegas proper to take a look around. He'd need to figure out which casino they were most likely to hit, see if his luck and his instinct held.

Or maybe he was just chasing his own tail?

No. He *knew*, a clear, deep, undeniable knowledge that settled in his gut and twisted, hard. She was probably asleep in a hotel room right now, with whatever backup Henderson had managed to send with her. *Please, not Cath. The goddamn punk girl will get them both killed.* He stepped out of the phone booth.

First things first. Some stick-to-your-ribs road grease, and then he'd be on his way. Thank God truck stops were mostly cheap. He would have to replenish his cash posthaste. Impossible to hide without money.

Just stay safe, angel, he thought, trying not to remember her face. It was impossible. Now that he did remember, there was precious little else he could think about. *Just stay safe until I can get to you. I'm on my way.*

* * *

It was nice to be back in the city again. He worked best in an urban setting. There wasn't much room to hide in small towns or out in the vast stretches of wasteland that were America's heart. Mom and Pop and apple pie, and Sigma working behind the scenes to scoop up every psion that wasn't nailed down. Wipe 'em with Zed and put them to work for the American dream. Nobody was even sure what war they were fighting now, since the Russians had started cannibalizing themselves.

It made his mouth sour just to think about it.

Morning dawned bright and clear, but he didn't think she'd be out that early. There was no crowd cover. It was afternoon when he drove the Strip, obeying every traffic law. Two things became immediately apparent: he was feeling better and better about this every time he saw the Luxor, and Sigma was in town.

Please don't tell me Rowan's hitting the place that looks like a giant pyramid. The security in there is too good. Stick with the smaller ones, what do you say? Except the smaller ones will get sticky over the type of payoff we're talking about. Or are you doing the horses, angel? With your precog it won't be hard to pick a winner or two.

No, that felt wrong. It was the casinos, and in particular, it was the one that looked like Ramses had thrown a despotic fit in the desert again. Great.

He almost didn't spot the three black vans tucked into alleys at even intervals down the Strip, almost didn't catch the crackle of psychic electricity coming from some of the strolling tourists. Most of them were free ops like Andrews. They wouldn't bring in the brainwiped until they had a lock on her and wanted the heavy guns.

He left the car in an underground parking lot and decided to penetrate on foot. It was problematic. If the Sigs were around, they might need a fast getaway. He couldn't afford to have them recognize him first-off by driving right into their critical zone.

It was too warm, and he was in T-shirt, jeans, rig, and boots, not to mention the loose leather jacket. He would simmer in his own sweat before long.

He wandered with the flow of the crowds on the hot pavement, tourists coming to see the big pile of neon and broken dreams. *You don't belong in this town, angel.*

She belonged in some Ivy League, ivy-covered northeast village, one where the houses were old and there were bookstores on every corner. He remembered her coming home with bags of books and stacking them in his room, rescuing plants and nursing them back to health. Remembered her house, quiet and trim and neat before Sigma destroyed it with bullets and tear gas. Remembered watching her while she slept, a book dropped onto her chest and her face quiet and serene in the wash of winter sunlight coming through his window.

That had been the best winter of his life, squiring her around Headquarters, watching her learn to use her talent. Thank God he had *pushed* himself to forget. If they had caught her…He almost shuddered just thinking about it, controlled the movement. He didn't want any passersby to register him.

The pyramid towered above him, and he caught the flow of people pressing in through the front door. Cavernous lobby done in tawny colors, touches of royal blue, palm trees in pots, and the smell of air-conditioning. Welcome coolness flooded him, made him more aware of how the Zed tracks on his arm were itching. He would start to twitch before long, withdrawal torturing his nervous system, begging him to jack out.

Slot machines whizzed and burped electronically. The mood of the place—savage and desperate, with a thin veneer of fun—washed over his raw psyche. He needed that last hypo of Zed, but he couldn't afford to use it now. He needed to get a zero on a pale head of hair, a slim, small, graceful woman with wide green eyes. What if Henderson had made her dye her hair for camouflage? It would be the smart move, but Del's heart hurt to think of that long pale mane altered. Hurt to think of it cut short, although he would still be able to run his fingers through the silky mass of it and—

Wrong thing to think. He'd end up distracting himself. He drifted to the buffet and saw nothing but hungry tourists and gamblers. The vast open space above him—each floor with its own balcony looking down into the well of the pyramid—pressed down, cavernous and cool with air-conditioning. He smelled cigarette smoke, sweat, heat, perfume, carpeting, and reheated coffee.

He worked his way into the pit, ignoring the décor. It meant nothing except for possible cover and escape routes. He brushed past a heavyset woman with her arm around her teenage daughter. The daughter, wearing a tight pink *Freezewire* T-shirt, rolled her eyes. "It's *Vegas*, Mom. Live a little, will you?"

Goddammit. He ducked into the bar, ordered a double Scotch to calm his nerves and tipped the bartender. He bolted the alcohol. It would dull him a little, but that was to the good since his nerves were starting to burn from Zed and crackle with…

What was that? Felt like a lightning storm coming, little bits of electricity dazzling over his skin. Electric honey, a sensation he remembered.

It felt like Rowan.

Goddamn. He ordered another Scotch, downed it as fast as he could and left the bar, plunging into the crowd and working his way to the pit. They had chosen a good time to come out. Everyone was looking for a giveaway at the buffet and a few minutes of gambling. She was here; he'd bet his life on it.

He *was* betting his life on it. Because not only was he almost out of Zed, but he had the sneaking feeling Sigma would close in on this place too, unless she was very, very careful.

Thirteen

Rowan stood next to Cath's chair, her arms crossed, playing the disapproving best friend. "You're going to waste it," she said, loud enough for the man fiddling in the back to hear. They'd been taken to this plush, soulless private office on the fifth floor to cash out the chips—and probably so Security could get a good eyeful of them. It wasn't every day two women walked in off the street and won two hundred thousand dollars at the roulette table after winning in another casino, too. They had cleaned up just under a hundred thou at the Venetian and made it out safely.

But hey, this was Vegas. The house always won, and if the women weren't on blacklists or doing anything illegal they would be encouraged to blow their gambling gains on more gambling or the high-roller nonsense. If not, the casino would make it back within minutes with other poor suckers. Someone had to win, even if the house always got you in the end.

It was, Rowan reflected, the perfect scam.

The identities Yoshi had crafted were holding up, and due to Rowan's deft mental pressure they were about to take a duffel bag of cash instead of a cashier's check up to a "courtesy" suite. If all went well, in half an hour Cath and Rowan could be out of here, with enough of a stake to clean up nicely at the races tomorrow, and head home with a cool quad of hundred thousands to keep the Society going until Henderson could get more legitimate funding up and running

So close. So why did Rowan's head suddenly start to hurt, like little crystal needles driving into her temples? Was it the strain of keeping the shield of illusion tight and seamless so none of the people looking at her noticed she was wearing a gun?

No, that's pretty easy. Nobody expects to see a mousy brunette with a sidearm in a casino. It goes against expectations. Their eyes want *to be fooled, even this man's. I shouldn't be feeling like this.*

But she was.

"I am *not* going to waste it." Cath played the whiny winner so perfectly Rowan was hard put not to laugh. She also did a dead-on nasal Eastern seaboard twang, something Rowan had no idea she could do. "I just don't see why I should cash out if

I'm on a winning streak."

"Trust me," Rowan said dryly. "Haven't I been right about everything else?"

"Shut up." Cath shot her a murderous look, blue-violet eyes flashing, and the urge to giggle rose again.

The man came out with the bag. "We'll count it in front of you," he said pleasantly. He was one of the casino's security officers, a nice heavyset man with a sharp Armani suit and a diamond stud winking in his left ear. He'd smoked a full bowl of pot this morning. Rowan could *smell* it on him, though it wasn't a smell any deadhead would notice. It was more like a psychic color, the mellowness of the depressant closing him off to her random brushes against his mind. She actually had to work to press him into doing what she wanted. It was an unexpected relief, even if it meant more effort. Her head was really starting to pound.

"Anyway," Rowan remembered her part with a small mental struggle, "I doubt you'll do anything smart with it, like put it into investments. Sure, you can count it. Though I'm sure it's all there." She restrained the urge to bat her eyelashes at him, and the man preened. He must have been used to women flirting with him. His job handled a lot of things gold-diggers would be interested in.

He actually blushed a little, setting the bag on his desk. "Well, it's policy. There will be a lot of people wanting to shake your hand, Miss Ernhardt. Luck makes you a lot of friends out here in Vegas. Where did you say you were from?"

It was the second time he'd asked that. Trying to trip them up? Suspicious? Or just making conversation and forgetting what he'd already asked?

Cath rose to the occasion, her eyes twinkling with what anyone else would have called flirtatiousness but Rowan recognized as sarcastic glee. "Rhode Island. But they don't have anything like this out there. My husband's going to *freak*." She looked too young to have a husband, but that wasn't anybody's business.

Not here in Vegas.

Rowan was about to give her next line, a comment about the husband, when a familiar *touch* blazed through her mind like a star, its contact sliding against every nerve in her body. Training took over and clamped down on her reaction. She didn't stumble or sway. Yet Cath glanced at her nervously, her eyes suspiciously wide and her lips parting. If the man behind the desk had been even the slightest bit sensitive, he would have caught her unease.

Lucky for us we get a casino employee with a head made of brick and dulled with marijuana. It was a snide thought, there and gone in a flash, a thought Rowan wouldn't have recognized before as her own. She'd grown sarcastic, it seemed. Then again, being chased down and hunted like an animal would make even Pollyanna a cynic.

Rowan juggled the touch, trying to remember what she was supposed to say. "Sandy's a nice man," she heard herself say frostily, the words coming out of nowhere. *That's right. I'm supposed to be her sister-in-law.* "He'll be very happy. Might even want to build a rec room onto the house."

Justin? She sent out the "call," hoping, praying. It was him. She would know that touch anywhere.

There was a flood of urgency in return, tinted red with concentration. Something was dreadfully wrong, and he was close. So close she restrained the urge to look back over her shoulder.

Cath slanted her another nervous glance, and Rowan moved. Not physically—her body did not so much as flicker an eyelash. But she suddenly strained, stretching in two directions—toward the man with the bag full of cash, and toward the aching call tugging at her mind.

The heavyset man with the diamond earring stopped dead as Rowan's mental push unbalanced him. She tied off the strands deftly. The man suddenly stood behind his desk, eyes half-lidded, a virtual zombie until Rowan released him or the *push* faded. "He'll remember counting it for us," she said hoarsely. "We've got to move, Cath. Something's wrong." *Justin? Talk to me, dammit! Justin?*

I'm here, angel. A flood of reassurance. He sounded like himself again, instantly recognizable, and this time she did stagger. The relief of feeling him in her head again was too intense. She grabbed the back of Cath's chair, steadying herself. He was here. He was *here*. She'd been right.

Cath bounced out of the plush cushioned chair and to her feet in one elastic motion. "I'm shorting the cameras," she said, the Rhode Island accent gone as soon as it had arrived. "Goddammit, what is it now?"

What's happening? She sent a wordless flood of relief

and hoped she wasn't distracting him. *Justin? Talk to me?*

There are four full Sig teams down here on the bottom floor. They're working through the pit. Get out. Get out *of here as fast as you can.* She felt his concentration, and a sudden burning swept through her, making her flinch.

She'd felt that before. *Oh, God. Please, no*. This thought she kept to herself. To Cath, she said, "Four Sig teams, down on the ground floor. Cath, Justin's here."

"I don't want to hear that shit," Cath hissed. "Keep your mind on business and get us the hell out of here!"

Two guards outside. The men were waiting to escort the big winners to their courtesy suite. Rowan would have to deal with them. Cath would have her hands full stretching her moderate telekinetic ability to keep them from electronic eyes.

Justin had closed himself off from her, fiercely and definitely. She caught a sense of movement—he was moving, doing something, but what? A plan. He had some sort of plan, one he wasn't letting her see.

Then, to add insult to injury, a wild braying split the air. Cath flinched, and Rowan let out a sharp yelp of surprise and grabbed her arm. "Fire alarm!" she yelled over the noise. "Come on!" *Thank you, bless you, thank you—*

He didn't reply. He probably had his hands full.

No time for subtlety, Rowan *pushed* as she hit the door. The two beefy men, dressed in ostentatious casino security uniforms, dropped in the hall, and Rowan's head began to pound in earnest. She hated knocking people out. It felt…well, *rude*. The old Rowan wouldn't have done something so drastic without a good bit of guilt and dithering. She stepped over one of them, having to stretch. He was so tubby he'd probably look rectangular from the back. She felt a wild hideous laugh welling up inside her at the thought of this lardass protecting *anyone*.

Then again, if someone went after his potato salad I bet there'd be a battle to end all battles, she thought, just missing the other man's hand with a skipping movement that almost tipped her into the wall. Not very graceful, but it got the job done.

Cath was right behind her. The hall was long, lit with fluorescent lights, and seemingly endless. But at the end, under a flashing Exit sign, was a door that probably gave onto the stairwell. *We're on the fifth floor,* she "told" Justin, *heading for the fire escapes. Where are you? What can we do to help you?*

Just get the hell out of here, angel. The words were hard and clipped, and there was another drumroll of pain against his nerves. *They haven't ID'd me yet, but if I hook up with you down here—oh, shit. Get out, Rowan. Get out as fast as you can and* run. *Don't wait for me.*

Rowan set her jaw, her hand finding Cath's arm. "Get out of here," she yelled. "Split up, I'll draw them off!"

"No way!" Cath yelled back over the assault of the fire alarm. It was eerie, the way no other door in this hallway opened, even under the sonic wail. Little lights in the walls were flashing, and Rowan glanced nervously up at the ceiling. If the sprinklers went off this could turn into a right royal mess. "We're supposed to stay together!"

Losing patience, Rowan shoved the girl. Cath stumbled, her other arm weighed down with the duffel bag of cash. "*Go!*" Then, to show she was serious, her right hand reached for her gun.

Cath ran. Her short black hair bobbed as she bolted for the stairwell. Rowan didn't waste time, just turned on her heel and lunged for the second hall branching off from this one. *Hang on, Justin. I'm coming.*

No! Sheer refusal. *Get out. Get your backup out. Go now!*

How had they found her? Well, where else could the Society replenish their coffers in short order? Go where the money is, that was a standard law. Maybe they'd just been waiting around for someone to make a run, or maybe her codestringing with Yoshi this morning had tripped an alarm.

I'm coming, she told him, stubbornly. *I haven't gone through the past three months to lose you now.*

Another stairwell, as she'd predicted. *Know your exits.* She could still hear Justin's voice in the long, dim, faraway region of time that had been her training. *Knowing your exits will get you out of any number of tight spots.*

Now he sounded angry. *Get the hell out, woman! There's nothing you can do here.*

"Like hell there isn't," she muttered, and hit the door at full speed, spilling out into a concrete stairwell. In here there was no carpeting or smooth pale paint or little Egyptian knickknacks, only the stairs and confused people. The mood of the entire casino tipped and spun, scraping against Rowan's sensitive brain. She didn't care how she looked now, barely keeping her feet under her as she bolted down the stairs.

It took less time than she'd thought to reach the bottom. The alarms hadn't been on long enough for the crowd to really start massing at the doors. She broke out onto the first floor and found herself at the end of another long hall, restrooms on one side and the glow and tingle of slot machines at the other end. *Justin!* She "reached" for him frantically, almost reeling under the wave of burning agony that slammed through him. What was it? Had he been injured? It felt *familiar*, somehow, if she could just think—

No time for thinking, because two women in tan trench coats moved across the end of the hall and paused, seeing her. Rowan's head gave another agonized flare of pain and her stomach flamed with hurt, the veggie omelet she'd eaten that morning rising in rebellion.

Revolting food, she thought, wondering why she always had the urge to laugh at the most inappropriate of times. *Revolutionary hash browns, anyone? Resistance pancakes?*

One of the women reached under her coat. Rowan sped for them, her eyes locking with the shorter woman's eyes, hazel and wide and full of the sparkle that told her this was a psion. The nausea twisted inside her belly again. She had a split second to reach for her own gun, clear leather and decide if she was going to take a life here in this gawdawfully decorated place.

The first woman dropped, her legs folding under her. The second paused, her hand closing around her gun—then she buckled too, her eyes rolling up, and her military-short blond hair ruffling as she hit the ground with a thump audible even through the fire alarms. And there, behind them, slipping something back into his pocket, was Justin.

He looked like hell. He was gaunt, his cheekbones standing out, and his hazel eyes were just as dead and flat as ever. Tall man, much taller than her, stubborn dark hair cut military-short like her father's. *Why did he trim his hair?* He'd just been growing it out the last time she'd seen him. He had a nice face, even cheekbones and a firm mouth drawn tight and haggard with pain now. Same clothes as usual—dark hip-length leather coat, jeans, and a pair of engineer boots. Easy to move in, if a bit too overdressed for the Vegas heat.

But there was the shadow of a bruise on his face, dark

circles under his eyes, and the way he moved would have told her he was in pain even if she couldn't feel it against her own nerves.

Rowan flung herself down the hall. When she was less than four feet from him, the crackling jolt of his nearness ran along her skin.

She ran to him. He didn't move aside, just opened his arms slightly. When she hit, his arms closed and he whirled, using the momentum to help her down to the ground as she heard a popping, shattering noise.

Gunfire. The slot machine nearest them exploded in a shower of glass and shredded plastic, change zinging out from its ruined bottom and sparks flying. The noise was incredible. Rowan gasped and swallowed a shriek.

"Justin! *Justin!*" She was yelling his name, over and over again.

They hit hard, her cheekbone bouncing against his shoulder, and fireworks spilled across Rowan's vision. She let out a short cry of pain, and Justin rolled, untangling himself from her. He had a gun, too, somehow coming up into a low crouch and returning fire.

"I *told* you to get the hell out!" he yelled over the sudden screams and shattering glass. It sounded as if he'd hit something. Her head rang, both with pain and his nearness, and her stomach twisted against itself again. "*Move*, woman!"

Nice to see you too. But he was all business, clear and cold, with the peculiar fierce concentration he used while under fire. A machine. Sigma had trained him to be a machine, and he'd trained so many Society operatives to move coolly and think clearly under fire that his reputation had turned him into something of a legend. Her own gun slid into her hand as she scrambled along the row of slot machines. Justin followed her. *Here. He's here.* Childlike, the way her chest suddenly eased. *Everything's going to be all right. He's here. He's alive. He's all right. He's here.*

His hand closed around her upper arm, hard, and she stopped dead. He pushed her aside and scanned the end of the row of slot machines. They were in a back corner. It would be almost impossible to shoot their way out through the large open place where the roulette and blackjack tables were. The short, cheap carpet ground under her boots as she half-turned, looking over her shoulder to make sure their six was still clear. She smelled cordite and felt air-conditioning chill the sweat on her skin. Fear rose sour in her throat, her heart pounding. No one was braving this aisle of slot machines yet.

"Who did you come with?" he barked. "Who's your backup?"

She swallowed, her throat suddenly dry. "Cath. She's getting out. I told her I'd draw fire."

He swore, his fingers moving automatically as he slid another clip into the 9mm. The movement was habitual. He didn't even look at his hands, pointing to a fire door with his chin. "Go that way, out the fire escape. I'll clean up in here and find you."

She set her jaw and shook her head. "I'm coming with you."

"Goddammit, do what I *tell* you!" Frustration made the words sharp, and he glanced over her shoulder, scanning the blackjack tables again. "I've found you once. I can do it again. Get out."

Her eyes flicked past him. She lunged forward, intending to run for the aisle and the blackjack tables. If she went, he'd have to follow, and there would be no more of this *get out of here and leave me behind* nonsense.

He grabbed her, yanked her back and pushed her toward the door with its blinking green *Exit* sign overhead. She felt a sudden sharp flare of bloodlust and threw herself instinctively down, her feet tangling. He also fell, just as more bullets whizzed overhead. *Well, wasn't that lucky. Instinct saves the day again.*

Rowan's knee hit hard and he dragged her back behind the shelter at the end of the aisle. He had his left arm around her, and his right hand with the gun pointed carefully away. His heartbeat thudded against her ear, and she felt absurdly comforted.

Options were rapidly closing down on them, and she could feel his mind clicking through alternatives, working percentages, calculating how to get her out of here alive.

Justin, please, goddammit, I'm not leaving you! Desperation, flavored acrid yellow.

"Come on," he said in her ear. His arm tightened around her, electricity tingling on her skin from his nearness. "Keep up, move with me, and for God's sake do what I tell you."

She nodded. Her own gun, useless for the moment, was

clasped in her hand. The adrenaline freeze began, details standing out sharp and clear—he hadn't shaved that morning. She could see the roughness of charcoal stubble on his cheeks, a crack in the shoulder of his leather coat, and a fading bruise spreading over his left eye. Someone had hit him awhile ago. Sigma? Why?

Then, wonder of wonders, he pressed a rough kiss onto her damp temple. Stray strands of her hair had come loose, and his lips pressed one against her sweating forehead. Rowan's speeding heart seemed to crack in half. More gunfire chattered and popped. *Why are they shooting?* She didn't mean for him to hear the thought, but he did.

"Drive us out, make us break cover." He got his legs under him and pulled her up into a crouch. "We're going to have to move fast, angel. You ready?"

She nodded, biting her lower lip. She gained a shaky equilibrium, staying as low as she could.

"They're going to shoot to kill. They can't afford to let me get away." His flat, dark eyes searched her face. "You understand?"

He's saying that if they're shooting at him, they may hit me. He thinks I care about that?

"I understand," she managed. "Let's get the hell out of here."

Fourteen

If Delgado didn't remember training her, he would have now doubted that he had. It was a stupid move, letting herself be caught in the trap with him. He'd given her a clear shot at escape. Why hadn't she taken it?

She was even more beautiful than he'd remembered. How had he forgotten her clear, pale skin, her aristocratic nose, graceful cheekbones, flawless mouth that was even now pulled down with worry, and her pearly teeth sinking into her lower lip? Dark circles under her eyes only served to underscore how green they were, again. She looked like she hadn't been sleeping well. Her hair was still the same pale, fine ash blond pulled back and braided. He couldn't wait to get it free of the braid and wrap his fingers in its dense silkiness. Not only that, but she *smelled* beautiful—shampoo and soap and the clean scent of female under a thin veneer of sweat from healthy effort. Her forehead was damp, a few random strands of hair sticking to the skin.

She smelled like *home*. There was no way he should have let her get involved with this.

Delgado closed his eyes for a moment, thinking. It wouldn't do to get all hurried and blow their chances of escape with something stupid. How was he going to get both of them out of this?

He knew, of course. There was only one way. One thing they wouldn't expect.

"All right." He gained his feet, and she rose with him. "Come on. Stay close."

She nodded. A slender woman, she only came up to his collarbone. She wore a man's linen suit jacket over a T-shirt, jeans, and her rig. He wanted to keep his hand around her arm, feel that crackling glaze of electricity that was her talent brushing over him, but he needed both guns out. He shot a glance out into the pit and down a long corridor of slot machines. He could hear screams, staccato bursts of gunfire—casino security, maybe, battling it out with Sigma. That was enough to bring a hard delighted smile to his face, the grin of a fox hearing the hunter tangle with his own dogs. He simply ignored the noise from the fire alarm he'd pulled, one more thing that didn't matter.

He moved down the long corridor, his back roughing with gooseflesh. Sweat collected along his lower back and under his arms—his body's response to combat. With the heat around here, a sweating man was no big deal. No need to waste energy trying to control an autonomic function.

When they reached the end of the corridor, a single sweeping glance told him everything he needed to know. Three Sigs were down in heaps of tan trench coat, and the rest were moving into the far end of the pit. They had a group of casino security guards pinned behind a makeshift barricade. It was utter chaos, especially with the fire alarms and a tide of screaming tourists to deal with as well.

He'd spared himself half a moment to *push* one of the security guards to open fire on the Sigs, saving a whole lot of time and trouble even if it was putting a civilian in the line of fire. He'd feel bad about that later. Much later, when he had Rowan out of here and safe.

He led her across the corner of the pit, moving from cover to cover. There was even an overturned blackjack table. *How the hell did that happen?* Bullets chattered. The security guards wouldn't hold out much longer. The Sigs were better armed and better trained. Delgado smelled spilled blood, hot lead, cordite, and the leather-peppermint-pepper smell of deadly exertion.

"Goddammit," he whispered, pulling her down behind the table. "Keep your head down."

She nodded. She was deathly pale, but two spots of hectic color burned on her cheekbones and her eyes gleamed.

He wanted to kiss her again. The feeling almost made his hands shake. But that wasn't what made him curse. The Sig team was sweeping in from the entrance, cutting across the grand taupe-colored lobby, their boot heels clicking on the faux stone floor. They were cutting off one route—the easiest route—of escape, and they would zero in on Del and the woman—*his* woman—in less than ten heartbeats.

Delgado moved. He squeezed off two shots and sent them scrambling for cover, then he bolted for the bar. Rowan matched him stride for stride, and he heard her breathing as if it was his own. *Keep up, angel. For God's sake keep up...there. Move, move, move.*

They burst through the swinging glass doors and into the dimly-lit hell of the bar. Cigarette smoke hung in the air, fouling every surface, and the door shattered as a hail of bullets caught it. She let out a short breathless cry and stumbled. He had one hand free and reached over, dragging her along. Ridiculous, dangerous—he should have kept both guns out.

Glass popped and sparked, the reek of spilled liquor mixing with the fuggy lake of cigarette smoke. Nobody in here, thank God. And there, behind the bar, the door that led to a back hall and probably a fire door.

No time, no *time.* Instead of staying down and cautious, the Sigs were coming straight for the shattered lounge door. Del caught sight of a baby grand piano sitting on the stage, spotlit against a blue velvet curtain. *All we need is an Elvis impersonator singing over the fire alarm. Viva Las Vegas.* He shoved her up and over the bar and followed, his boots grinding in broken glass. He squeezed off a couple more rounds to keep them back from the door and ducked down. "You okay?" He wasn't gasping, but he was close.

"Fine." Rowan was paper-pale, visibly trembling, her mouth compressed. Her pupils were so wide her eyes looked almost black in the dim light, and she clutched at her leg.

Hope she's not hit. He had to crouch further as gunfire chattered, broken glass tinkling from overhead. A fine spray of rum drifted down. At the curve of the bar, there were Sterno cans with low blue flames under the chafing dishes for keeping the hors d'oeuvres warm. He pushed Rowan down, grabbed the nearest two and tossed them, burning, over the bar. He almost got shot for his pains as more glass shattered and more booze oozed down.

Need something more. He found what he wanted—a half-full bottle of Stoli, racked below the bar. He holstered his right-hand gun and pulled down the bottle.

"Give 'em a couple of rounds," he said, digging in his pocket for spare cloth. He found a thin, torn strip of rag, useful for wiping fingerprints or any number of things, and unscrewed the cap.

Rowan complied, taking a quick glance over the bar and popping two shots off with a short, sharp cry that sounded painful. She rubbed her wrist as she fell back to the floor again, grimacing.

Of course, her hands are so small she has a hard time with the recoil. Poor girl.

"In ten minutes this will all seem like a bad dream," he told her, twisting the end of the rag and forcing it into the bottle's long, thin neck. *Have to keep it loose enough or the gas won't ignite. Do it right, Delgado.*

He pulled a stiletto from his sleeve and jammed the rag further in. Then he found a dish of matches. A cigarette lighter would have been better. *A fine time to wish I smoked. Say something, keep her focused.* "We'll find ourselves a nice quiet place and get acquainted again, what do you say?"

"Sounds good to me." Her voice shook with gasping pain. Not a whisper of whatever she was feeling escaped, though. She was holding up under the pressure like a pro.

He jammed the stiletto back into its sheath, grabbed a bottle of rum, and broke its neck with a swift sharp smack against the counter. After dousing the dry part of the rag liberally, he hefted the rum bottle up and over the counter.

Shots, again. "Goddammit," he said, shaking the vodka bottle to get it nice and angry. "Throw a couple more bottles over the counter, sweetheart, while I get this lit."

"You're so much fun to hang out with," she shot back, and grabbed a bottle of Kahlua, lofting it over the counter and following it with another bottle of Stoli. The reek of spilled liquor filled the air. There was enough fuming booze out there to make his eyes water. She managed to get a good eight bottles thrown with one hand, her other hand clamped onto her leg as if she had a cramp in the quad muscle, as well as two more Sternos she worked free of the racks with quick deft yanks. While he struggled with the matches, they were getting closer, closer, closer. There was one in the door now, and Del could hear the crackle of another psion's thoughts, a well of bloodlust.

The rag caught. He waited until the flame had a good purchase and switched the impromptu cocktail to his left hand. "Cover your eyes," he said, not wanting her to catch any flying glass. *Let's hope this works. If I believed in God I might be praying now.*

She did as he said, obviously willing to trust him, and hunched down behind the bar as more glass shattered. Del tossed the cocktail as he rose to his knees, his right hand bringing up his own gun. More glass shattered and the whole world narrowed. He shot twice at the Sigs looming in the shattered door and dropped.

The explosion was satisfying, to say the least. He hit the floor, taking her with him, as flying glass peppered the bar. The sound was horrendous, alcohol and Sterno fumes igniting and glass whickering through the air. He covered her body with his and caught a stray breath of a clean, pure scent. Her hair touched his face, a slippery satin rasp against his stubble, and her hip pressed into his belt buckle. She was soft and slim, and he remembered what it was like to bury his face in the softness of her throat and hear her sigh as he—

No time to think about that, they had to move. *Not bad for thinking on my feet, but don't congratulate yourself yet, operative. Get her out of here.*

He rolled up to his feet in a swift crouch. His forehead burned, blood dripping into his eyes. He yanked her up, fingers slipping in warm wetness. Was she hit? He hoped not. The thought of her wounded did something funny to his chest.

"Back door, angel," he said, and they went, duck-walking just in case anyone out there still had a gun and the presence of mind to use it. She gasped with each footstep, dragging herself along. The fire alarm was for real now, and he could hear sirens. He hit the door open with the palm of his left hand, his right holding a gun again, and pushed her through after checking behind it. And there, above the stacked cases of liquor and other odds and ends, was the Exit sign. It was a fire door. The delivery door was off to the left. But since the alarms were already going, it wouldn't matter, would it?

Acrid smoke billowed through the door. It was burning merrily in the bar now, tables, chairs and plush carpet fueled by spilled liquor. A wave of heat groaned through the entire bar.

"I think I'm going to throw up," Rowan said in a high, thin, breathless voice. She slumped against him, still clutching at her leg. Was she hit? God, he hoped not.

His chest was on fire, his nerves twisting with the need for Zed. *Get her out of her. Get her out and away from them. Get her out* now.

"Wait until we're out in the alley," Delgado heard himself reply. "Goddammit, woman, I told you to run."

"Wasn't leaving without you." Stubborn. Always so stubborn. "Where have you been?"

"In hell, angel." He kicked the fire door open, waited a beat, and spun out, covering the likely angles. Nobody there—the alley was clear. The Sig team guarding it was probably pulled in to help deal with the mess inside. He'd known it was clear. His own psychic talent worked overtime to tell him so, spurred by Zed withdrawal and adrenaline, but it was nice to have confirmation. "In hell. It's nice to be back."

Now, let's get a car and get you out of here.

* * *

Heat shimmered up from the pavement. Rowan clamped her hand over the wound on her left thigh. It was still bleeding. Merciless sunlight beat down. Delgado had wiped the drying blood off his face, and his hair was dark enough that, at a casual glance, the blood crusted in it wouldn't show. He wasn't upset over his own wound, caused by a shard of flying glass he was happy missed his eyes. It was her serious, bloody injury he was worried about.

His stomach turned over. *Later,* he promised himself. *Feel bad later. Right now, get her somewhere safe.*

Christ, I'm saving up a hell of a lot to think about later. Then he reminded himself not to think about that.

Until later.

"It's up here on the left," she whispered in the same colorless, tiny voice. Her eyes were closed, and she had stopped stealing little glances at him. Her hair stuck to her forehead with sweat. "Poor Cath. I hope she's okay."

I don't give a damn. He didn't give a good goddamn what happened to *anyone* as long as Rowan was all right. The whole fucking world could go to hell in a handbasket for all he cared. He had nothing further to lose now; nothing except her.

I'm just as dangerous to the Society as I am to Sigma right now, he thought, and saw the sign for the Hotel Doze-Inn. "There it is," he said. "Room 25?"

"That's it." She'd already handed over the room key. A rendezvous with Cath, and getting all three of them out of here, was just what the doctor ordered. And once he had a few moments he was going to tell Rowan just how good it felt to be near her again. "I'm bleeding all over the seat," she said. "I'm sorry."

You're sorry? Jesus Christ, you could have died back there. You got fucking shot! What the hell are you apologizing for? He clamped down on himself. Hysteria was not what he needed now. What he needed was a good stiff drink and a chance to bandage her up. "No worries, angel. Unless we need get you to a doctor."

"No. *No.*" She sounded panicked, and he cursed himself.

"It'll be fine," she said. "Look, it's stopped bleeding. Now I just have to wait for it to heal while it hurts."

He pulled into the parking lot, checking the rearview mirror yet again. Still no sign of pursuit. "We look clean."

"Is the car…" She gulped down air, and he caught a flash of pain. Oddly enough, that touched a spark of fury deep in his gut, a fury that managed to rise in a sheet of red flame. Hurt her. They had *hurt* her. "Oh, God. Is the car here?"

"Blue Subaru, Georgia plates, just the thing for evading Sigs? Yes, it's right there. You've got the keys?"

"I shouldn't… I shouldn't…" Her head lolled back against the seat. The delicate traceries of sweat on her face made her look even more pale and delicious. He had to restrain the urge to lean across the seat and kiss her cheek.

Goddammit, Rowan. I almost lost you. I almost fucking lost you in that bloody mess. Why didn't you run?

"No need to worry, angel." He saw a familiar figure leaning against the side of the Subaru, shading her eyes with one hand. Cath had ditched the blue Mohawk for a short black gamine haircut that suited her much better. She'd even taken most of the metal off her face for the Vegas run, and her Catholic-schoolgirl prettiness shone out. She was going to be dangerous in a couple of years. Zeke would have his hands full keeping her out of trouble.

Not my problem. It was a relief to find something that *wasn't* his problem. "There's Cath right there. You just rest. She and I will take care of everything else."

True to form, when he pulled up Cath didn't waste words. She peered in through Rowan's rolled down window—the hot air that came in was like standing in front of an open oven—and examined him for a long moment. "About damn time," she said crisply. "Holy hell, Ro, what happened to you?"

"I got shot again," Rowan whispered, and unceremoniously passed out, her head spilling back and her mouth opening slightly. He tried not to think about that, tried not to feel the flare of frustrated heat that went through him.

Cath cracked her chewing-gum. "All right, Del. How we gonna do this?"

You're taking this rather well, considering I've been away for months and might be a Sig mole. Sloppy, Cath. You should be holding a gun on me and looking for signs of pursuit.

He held up the room key. “Is the room clear?”

“You bet it is. Knew you’d show up.” She wore a cute pair of heart-shaped sunglasses, very *Lolita*. He was surprised she wasn’t smoking. Cath without a cigarette hanging out of her mouth was strange indeed.

Del suppressed a flare of irritation. “Then get the keys turned in and let’s blow this Popsicle stand. You got a medkit?”

The telekinetic shrugged. “She won’t need it. Already closing up.”

“Get me the goddamn medkit, kid. And then go and turn the room keys in. We’ve got to get out of here *now*.”

Fifteen

The pain was incredible, spearing through her left leg and twisting with white-hot pincers. Rowan bit her lower lip, feeling flesh yield between her teeth. Her leg hurt so badly she didn't notice the trickle of blood sliding down her chin until Justin wiped it away, his fingers gentle under the rough paper of the McDonald's napkin. They had stopped for lunch, and Rowan had managed a few sips of Sprite before her stomach closed and she couldn't drink any more. She sucked on a chunk of ice Justin slid between her lips, and shook her head when he tried to give her more.

The desert scrolled by in taupe bumps and sagebrush blurs outside her window. She was in the back seat with Justin. Cath was driving and smoking like a fiend. As the city fell into the distance she felt a great relief, when she could think through the waves of agony rolling up her leg. She'd taken a bad hit—one she was almost sure could have been fatal, if not for her freakish ability to heal. She'd even managed to try to walk through the rocky shoals of tearing pain. She barely remembered Justin dragging her to a car, saying something in a low, fierce voice.

When the breaker of agony retreated again, she opened her eyes just a crack to find Justin staring at her. His eyes had come alive, instead of the flat darkness she remembered, their depths curtained by a screen of indifference. Now they were terribly present. He stared at her face as if he wanted to peel it off and take it home with him.

What a gruesome thought, Rowan.

But the intensity with which he was looking at her was nothing short of frightening. His entire body seemed focused on her, while Cath drove with the windows down and Johnny Cash playing, bright scarves of music and cigarette smoke furling out into the jet stream.

"Hey" he said quietly. "Still hurting? It's stopped bleeding again, and it's closing up."

She didn't look down. His hand was clamped over hers. This was not at all how she had expected a possible reunion to go. "Justin," she whispered. "I knew you were alive."

"I didn't," he replied, with such a straight face she wasn't sure if he was joking. His eyelashes were so dark, she had forgotten that. Had forgotten the way his face made her breath catch, the way her skin felt alive with electricity when he touched her. He was sweating, too. She could almost feel his pain as well as her own. “You’ve been a busy girl, haven’t you? You’ve had their tails tied in knots looking for you. All over the damn country.”

A ghost of a smile touched her lips. The next big jolt of pain was coming. She could feel it gathering like rain on the horizon. “Had a good teacher,” she whispered. “Always keep moving. Do it by the book. Never leave a man behind.”

“You better believe it, angel.” He was smiling now, but it was a pained smile. “Rowan.”

The pain swelled, crested over her. She bit her lip, not wanting to cry out. It would frighten Cath, and if Rowan let her guard down even for a moment she might broadcast and give Sigma something to latch onto.

“Scream if you need to,” he whispered in her ear. He’d taken his seat belt off to lean closer to her. She wanted to chide him for it, but couldn’t find the breath. “I’m here, angel. I’m not going anywhere.”

Oh, but you’ve said that before, she thought before the pain roiled again and she succumbed, going down into the depths without so much as a murmur. But this time, he was with her, his mind wound in hers. Rowan could feel his own pain and unwilling need.

Zed. They had addicted him to Zed again.

Which meant he might still be a Sig after all. They might have broken him. It didn’t seem likely, but…

Rowan fled into unconsciousness.

* * *

Warmth, close and unfamiliar. A feeling of comfort.

Rowan opened her eyes, slowly. The hotel room blurred around her. She saw the edge of pale curtains keeping the sun out, and a mirror fastened above the dresser where a dark television crouched. There was a small table near the window with two chairs, looking more suited to a hospital waiting room than a hotel room, pushed halfway under it.

The curiously naked feeling of dampers roared over her skin. How had Cath gotten her into the hotel room?

Gingerly, she moved her left leg, and she let out a sigh of relief when it was only tender, not screaming with pain.

Then came the clichéd question.

Where the hell am I?

She rolled over gingerly and looked up at the ceiling, her back sinking into the mattress. There didn't seem to be anyone in the room, but the shower was running behind the bathroom door. She heard Cath's tuneless humming, familiar from spending so much time with the girl in different houses. It sounded now like Cath was trying to sing *Cat Scratch Fever* and failing miserably but with great relish.

Rowan blinked. Memory roared in. Justin.

Where is—

The door rattled.

She pushed herself over on her side, reaching for the nightstand and the gun that lay there in its habitual place. Had he put it there?

Where was he?

Her fingers closed on empty air. She lunged and caught the gun as the door opened, letting in a blast of hot air and the smell of car exhaust and high plains wind. Justin stepped inside, shaking his head, and closed and locked the door. Cath had apparently found him a new shirt, but he wore the same hip-length jacket and jeans. As usual, he looked maddeningly precise. The haircut helped the image. So did the set, grim expression on his face. Somehow he never looked rumpled, even with the fading bruise over his left eye.

Rowan lowered the 9mm just as he turned around, his shoulders dropping. He regarded her over the space of empty air between them. The new T-shirt was blue, and it made his eyes seem even darker. Cath's singing continued in the bathroom, underscored by the splashing of hot water.

"You can put that away," he said finally, his eyebrow lifting just a little. He was pale, fever-spots standing out on his cheeks. He looked like hell, with dark circles under his eyes and his jacket hanging oddly on his frame. He'd lost weight but still looked deadly, muscle flickering as he crossed his arms over his chest. And his eyes were new, burning and fully alive, hazel coals in his pinched, gaunt face. "I was checking the parking lot. Nothing stirring. I think we might be okay."

Rowan blinked. She laid the gun back down on the nightstand and then pushed back the covers. Her jeans had been cut away and the bandage was glued to her thigh with dried blood. She peeled it carefully off. Her leg twinged roughly as she looked at the bloody hole and wide stain on the denim.

"God," she said. The heavy material was stained all the way to her ankle. She'd bled a *lot*. She felt pale just thinking about it, didn't want to imagine the scar the wound would leave behind.

Doesn't matter. The scar will close up and fade like all the rest. It was a chilling thought.

"Why didn't you tell me you'd been hit?" He yanked one of the chairs out from under the spindly table and dropped into it gracefully. Then he seemed to go absolutely still, his eyes sweeping the hotel room and then coming to rest on her.

She found her voice. "You had enough to worry about."

This wasn't like any reunion she'd envisioned either. She'd imagined…what? Falling into his arms and everything going back to the way it was before—her father still alive and Hilary still working for the newspaper and calling or dropping by almost every day to visit? Or had she imagined waking up at Headquarters and finding out that it had all been a dream, her normal life *and* Justin's capture?

Instead, this gaunt man stared at her, seemingly content just to sit and watch. He reminded her of an alley cat, all nerves and dark eyes, every muscle taut and ready. The sudden mental image—Justin as a cat, prowling in a dark corner, disdainful of a plate of food, and reminding you he could leave at any moment, that he was just visiting—would have made her smile if it wasn't so sad.

"I'm sorry." He even *looked* sorry, his mouth pulling down and his eyes turning even darker. The shower shut off, she heard Cath switch to *I Will Survive* and felt her mouth want to twitch again.

"Why? You didn't shoot me." She took a deep breath. "I've missed you."

Three inadequate words, completely unable to convey the longing and frustrated guilt she felt. Rowan hunched her shoulders and dropped her eyes to her knees, one pale and streaked with dried blood, the other still covered with her sweat-soaked jeans. She reeked of sweat, coppery blood, and spilled alcohol.

"I *pushed* myself," he answered, almost inconsequentially. "To forget. Forget everything about you. I had to—Sigma had me. Then when I got loose, I *pushed* myself to remember. You're in trouble, angel. They're sending Carson to hunt you."

A cold finger slid down her spine. Who was this Carson

character? The General hadn't said much, just that he was bad news and for Rowan to be very careful.

"Henderson told me." *I need a shower. And I need to get dressed. Why is he looking at me like that? Why won't he touch me, talk to me? Really talk to me? He sounds like he's giving a report back at Headquarters. Nice and impersonal.* "Justin?"

He shook his head, as if shaking away a sudden bath of icy water. "Never figured out why you called me that," he muttered, his eyebrows pulling together. He actually *scowled*, an expression light-years away from the calm, precise man she remembered.

What had they done to him? "It's your name," she whispered. *It's what I've always called you.* "Don't you…don't you remember?"

"Just Delgado. Or Agent Breaker." He shrugged. "Makes no difference. Look, how soon can you be ready to move? I've got to get you out of here."

Rowan's entire body turned to ice. Her heart gave one wounded, incredible leap and fell back into her chest with a plop, like a stone tossed into a pond. She'd been so sure he would come back—maybe wounded, maybe bloody but relatively unbowed. And she had also assumed that he would want to pick up where they'd left off. But that presented another problem, didn't it?

I hate you! she'd screamed at him in the training room, after he'd pushed her too far. *I wish I'd never seen you!*

She hadn't meant it. It had only been frustration and agonized grief speaking. But what if he'd thought she *had* meant it?

Of course, if it wasn't for me the Society would still have *Headquarters. Sigma was after me, and they killed everyone they could find at Headquarters to get me because Justin brought me in. He's had time to think this over and remember what a jerk I was to him.* Guilt flashed through her, bloomed into a hideous certainty. *And I didn't go after him. I left him to suffer there.*

"I can be ready in twenty, as soon as Cath gets out of the bathroom," she answered tonelessly, sliding her legs off the bed and rocking to her feet. She swayed, her knees weak. *Blood loss will do that, even if you are the Super-Healing Freak,* she thought bitterly. She scooped the gun off the nightstand, checked it habitually, and winced as she tested her left leg. The cut leg of her jeans flopped. She tasted bile, feeling the crusted denim against her skin.

"Henderson's going to be happy to see you," she tossed over her shoulder as she hobbled toward the low wide dresser. She recognized her duffel bag sitting next to Cath's and let out a sigh of relief. Fresh clothes sounded heavenly right about now.

"Rowan." Justin's voice was harsh. "They hooked me on Zed again."

She nodded, her lips compressing, as she limped to the dresser and unzipped her bag. *Oh, thank you, God. Clean clothes.* "I know. Don't worry, I've got detox down to a fine art. We'll have you fixed up in no time." The fake cheerfulness in her voice hurt. It was the same tone she'd heard other nurses use at the mental hospital. She had always hated that, hated the teeth-gritting falsity of trying to jolly the patients along for their own good.

"Rowan." He sounded as if he was about to say more, but the bathroom door opened and Cath banged out in a puff of steam.

"Christ," she said cheerfully, "you'd think a place in the desert would have more hot water."

Great. A cold shower. Thanks, Cath. Rowan sighed and made her escape to the bathroom's sanctuary, thankful that at least the younger woman had left her a few towels.

She tried not to wonder why tears welled up and traced down her cheeks as soon as she closed the door.

Sixteen

Delgado hunched in the back seat next to the kitbags. Cath drove, lighting yet another cigarette. Rowan sat in the passenger seat and frowned at the map.

He was almost literally boiling with frustration. They shouldn't have put him there next to the guns and the gear, but evidently they trusted him. They trusted him too much, as a matter of fact. For all they knew he could still be Sigma, especially since he was still hooked on Zed.

He'd lied, of course. He hadn't been checking the parking lot. He'd been looking for a place to hunker down and slam the last hypo, but hadn't been able to. The thought of her eyes, dark green and lit from underneath with clarity, had stopped him.

No, that wasn't true, either. What had stopped him was no private place to shoot up. He ran the risk of having the cops called if he jacked in and zoned out for an hour in a motel parking lot. Self-loathing crawled along his skin, burrowing in. No wonder she didn't want to look at him. He could barely stand to look at himself.

Now his hands were shaking, and the unsteady lightning-bursts of pain were getting closer and closer together, his nervous system crying out for a jack and his overstrained will digging its heels in, refusing. He slumped in the back seat, letting the wind play over his face. It smelled of water and thick, rank growing things, hills rising green and blotting out the empty sweep of sky he'd become used to in the desert and traveling through Wyoming.

We'll have you fixed up in no time. A door had slammed behind those beautiful eyes. He'd done something wrong. She had obviously been glad to see him at the casino, but now the distance was palpable, her lovely face closed, cool, and professional. Cath didn't help, either. Her normally abrasive manners had gotten even worse, if that was possible.

Had he done something wrong? He didn't think so, but his memory was a little spotty. He'd forgotten how gorgeous Rowan was, how a few silken strands of her pale hair could fall into her face and make a man think of brushing them back, which would lead naturally to touching the curve of her cheekbone, a curve that begged to be kissed just like her flawless pretty mouth or the vulnerable inner hollow of her elbow, not scarred with hypo-marks like his.

He had forgotten just how it felt to look at her bowed head, see her nape because she'd pulled her hair up in a loose knot, and feel his entire body tighten.

He'd been trying to explain why he hadn't been back earlier. Why he had stayed so long instead of fighting tooth and nail to escape and get back to her even if it killed him. He had fouled up somewhere. He hadn't known what to expect—tears, maybe. She'd cried in his arms plenty of times before, her grief at the loss of her father and best friend still raw and sharp.

He'd been trying to remember why she called him by his first name, and her face had closed with an almost audible snap, her eyes going dark and distant. And since then, she had treated him with a polite cheerfulness that made him want fifteen minutes with a heavy bag so he could let loose a little of the rage he was feeling.

Just a little.

They were heading back northeast to rendezvous with the rest of Henderson's Brigade. Cath's description of the situation—punctuated with such colorful terms as *absolute fucking disaster, Del*—left him wondering if the Society was worse off than he'd thought. In light of what she was telling him, it was a miracle they had managed to elude a government apparatus with damn near unlimited funding and highly trained support staff.

But then again, they had Rowan.

If she had felt like a thunderstorm before, her talent prickling along every exposed edge of his skin—and quite a few that weren't—she now felt like a smooth deep river of force, deceptively placid on the surface with a riptide underneath. She seemed even more powerful now—and more self-contained than he had ever seen her, her former guilt and insecurity washed away. He'd trained her well, and functioning under fire with the Society for the past few months had evidently taught her a few things. And he'd missed it, dumb useless bastard that he was, cooped up by Sigma and forgetting—however temporarily—that she existed.

They'd left Cheyenne early that morning and were now in the lower end of the Black Hills. The scenery was grand, but Cath snorted when Rowan remarked wistfully that she'd always wanted to see Mount Rushmore. Delgado pushed down the urge to strangle the girl, who had slid most of her metal jewelry back on—nose ring, tongue stud, the earrings marching up each ear, the hoop in her eyebrow—and correspondingly started acting the disdainful teenager instead of the seasoned Society operative. Warm summer wind poured in through the open windows, and the windshield was peppered with murdered insects.

I've never liked South Dakota. Delgado went back to studying the curve of Rowan's neck, the slope of her shoulder, everything he could see about her. Looking at her made the persistent burning need for Zed fade a little bit.

Thinking about touching her made a different kind of pain worse. The kind of pain he hadn't realized he was feeling for months, a gnawing emptiness inside the middle of his chest. He wanted to reach over, cup his hand over her nape, and whisper something in her ear—anything to erase that solemn frown as she stared unseeing at the map. Were those tears in her eyes? Big, fat, shining tears?

Oh, Christ. He leaned forward, unable to help himself. "Rowan? You okay?"

She actually flinched, as if he'd tried to touch her. "Fine." Then she turned to look out her window, so he could see nothing but the back of her head. He'd chosen the driver's side seat in the back so he could look at her profile, and now he found himself denied even that. "It's just dusty, that's all."

"Is your leg hurting?" Cath, now sounding concerned. For all her brash impoliteness, she seemed to sometimes care how Rowan was feeling.

"No, it's fine. Almost healed up. The worst is over." Was there a telltale hitch in her voice? Did she sound a little choked? "Are we stopping in Pierre?"

"Maybe just outside, for a snack. You hungry?" Cath sounded hopeful. Of course, she'd been stuffing herself with junk food the entire trip, if Del guessed right. *Nutrition* did not seem to be a word in her vocabulary. It was a wonder how she stayed rail-thin with all the calories and preservatives she swallowed.

"A little. Jus—ah, Delgado? Are you hungry?" Rowan had to half-shout to be heard over the rush of wind.

Delgado. The name hit him like a sucker punch to the gut. *She called me Delgado.*

Not Justin. *Delgado*. The name the rest of them used.

She's changed her mind. Doesn't want anything to do with me. What am I anyway, but a junked-out Sigma? She's probably already dating someone else, if she has time. God knows there were enough men at Headquarters that would have jumped at the chance.

His heart burned, cracking in his chest. It felt like a goddamn cardiac arrest. The road slipped smoothly under the Subaru's tires, pavement singing and engine purring. Sunlight fell thick and liquid across the dash, tingled in Rowan's hair, picked out the crisp whiteness of her button-down shirt, worn open over a tank top. They were supposed to be tourists, just another car with Georgia plates, a man traveling with two pretty women, maybe a wife and a niece.

Stop it. Goddammit, stop it. If there was one thing he couldn't afford right now, it was fantasy. She didn't want anything to do with him.

"Not hungry," he said. It was only half true—the withdrawal was killing any hunger pangs he might be feeling, and he wouldn't want food anyway. The only thing he needed was to be near her. "Better stop anyway, to take a look at that wound."

"I'm *fine*," Rowan protested.

"It'll slow us down," he answered harshly, almost hating himself. "Another fifty miles or so, Cath. We'll stop for a late lunch, early dinner."

"You got it." Cath apparently had no problem with taking direction from him. *Old habits die hard,* he thought, and didn't miss the flash of irritation, like a bright dart of sunshine, that jetted out of Rowan.

Too bad, angel. The stubborn endurance that had carried him through the last few months of hell rose up now, bright and hot. Sigma hadn't broken him. They'd just hooked him on Zed and beaten him up a little. He could take that. He'd broken a Zed habit once and could do it again—especially if this pale-haired angel let him stay near her. He didn't ask for much, just to watch over her while the Society rebuilt itself.

Del, you're a fucking fool. She's beautiful. Just look at her. And you can't get rid of a Zed habit by yourself again. It nearly killed you last time.

Remembering that time almost made him shudder—beating his head against a wall until the skin broke and bled, hours spent at the heavy bag just pounding away the furious frustrating weakness and torturing pain, prowling the halls of Headquarters because he couldn't sleep with his skin feeling like red-hot ants were swarming over it—but *she* could cure him. He remembered the first time she'd done it, cured a woman they had rescued from a Sig installation already moaning and eye-rolling when they brought her in. It had taken Rowan awhile, but she'd somehow treated a Zed addiction without a system flush plus detox and the implied risk of cardiac arrest for the victim.

The thought of how close it had been intensified the cold sweat standing out on his skin. If Jilssen had found out, if Del hadn't *pushed* himself to forget, Sigma might have gone to even greater lengths to acquire her. She was a high-priority target anyway, but if they found out what she could do, it was likely to become capture-or-kill, no price too high and no mandate too broad to bring her in or neutralize her.

If that happened, she would need him. They would need an operative who knew every dirty trick Sigma could pull because he'd been one of them.

Del touched the small bag nestled against his hip. Inside, the last hypo was cupped in its antishock foam, clipped in and just waiting to detonate inside his head, wipe out the burning he felt in all his nerve channels. It was only going to get worse. Withdrawal was no picnic.

I've got to ditch this, he realized, with a sinking sensation. He settled himself to wait for the next stop, his heart hammering and his sweat smelling sour even to himself. The voice of self-preservation shrilled inside his head, but he paid no attention.

One way or another, he was going to keep Rowan Price alive and free. If she didn't like him, that might actually be better. The kind of man she'd feel proud of wouldn't do half of what Del was prepared to do if Sigma didn't leave her alone.

* * *

The rendezvous with Henderson's Brigade was in, of all places, Fargo.

The landscape was entirely flat—flat enough that Del thought privately it was a wonder anyone who lived here didn't die of sheer boredom. But by the time they reached the small suburban house, he didn't have time to think about the landscape, or the fact that Rowan had brightened perceptibly the closer they got. He was too busy fighting off the need for Zed and cursing himself for tossing the last hypo in a rest stop garbage can twenty miles out of Pierre. Not to mention wishing he could wrap his hands around Cath's skinny neck and *squeeze*. The girl's abrasiveness didn't matter so much as the way she treated Rowan, like a not-too-bright den mother.

It was dark, and soft early-summer air came in through Rowan's slightly rolled down window. The heat was muggy and oppressive, and he saw lightning flashes in the distance. An early-summer plains storm. The neighborhood was the best kind for rendezvous and clean houses—middle to upper middle class with fenced yards and neighbors who were too busy climbing the food chain to be curious about new folks. Cath idled in the driveway in front of the three-car garage for a moment, waiting, and the garage door began to lift, slices of warm electric light knifing out through the cracks.

Rowan drummed her fingers on her right knee. She was only limping slightly now, refusing to eat very much, and looking more thin and tired with each passing hour. Her hair, pulled up in a messy chignon and secured with a ponytail elastic, glowed in the sudden light. The familiar dead-air feeling of dampers closed over Del like water over a drowned man's head, oddly peaceful.

Cath pulled the car neatly into the empty slot on the left and cut the ignition. The garage door went down.

Rowan grinned as the door between the house and the garage opened and Yoshi, his slim dark form in a white T-shirt and jeans, stood silhouetted. He folded his arms and grinned back through the windshield.

Delgado was not at all prepared for this. She looked genuinely happy and relieved, her eyes suddenly sparkling. He caught a flash of concentrated thought—a communication.

"Welcome home," Rowan murmured, then looked back over her shoulder. The full force of her smile hit him like a baseball bat, drove every shred of good sense from his head. "Glad to be back?"

"Pretty much," he mumbled, opening his door.

Yoshi barely waited before he was at Rowan's door, opening it for her. She accepted his hand, and the slim Japanese man nodded as his eyes flicked over Delgado. Rowan's lips moved slightly. They were communicating again.

Oh, Christ, Del thought. *Please. Not Yoshi.*

It was unfair. Yosh was clinically cool and calm, preternaturally skilled with hardware, a master on the computer decks, and good enough in the practice room to earn grudging approval even from Henderson and Del himself. He was also a nice guy. A friend, if Del could be said to have any friends.

Rowan laughed. She reached up, her slender fingers working, and pulled the ponytail holder free, letting her pale hair cascade around her shoulders.

"I'm on my way," she said, and touched Yoshi's shoulder. No hug, no kiss—that was good. That was very good.

But then again, Del had never tried to be affectionate with her in public, either. He had hung in the background, watching over her, not daring to touch her when anyone else could see for fear of betraying what she meant to him.

That thought wasn't comforting at all.

"Henderson wants us both," she said. "Yoshi, you think you can take care of the gear? At least, until Zeke can manage?"

"What's wrong with Zeke?" Cath stretched, pulling herself out of the driver's seat. "Goddammit, my ass feels numb. I *hurt*. You better have some vodka lying around, Yosh."

As usual, Yosh was unperturbed. "No vodka, but I believe Zeke has beer. And Henderson has been saving a bottle of most excellent whiskey for Del's return. Hello, Del. Took your time, didn't you?"

Del's fingers tightened. It was a good thing the car was between them, because he could see Yoshi's brown hand on Rowan's shoulder, squeezing a little. As if offering support. *Goddamn it, he's my friend. And she doesn't belong to me.*

"I got trussed up, beaten, and shot full of Zed. Not to mention dragged to the high-security part of Sig Zero-Fifteen." He forced himself to shrug. "It took a while before I could ask them nicely to let me play patty-cake with my real friends again."

Cath snorted. "There's our old Del. Come on, I'm bushed. Let's get this crap out of the car, Yosh. Don't want to miss the celebration."

Yoshi murmured something to Rowan, who shook her head, her lips pursing. She slid past Yoshi without further ado.

Also very good. He couldn't help it. Hope was an even better drug than Zed. What if she'd been lonely, or had needed a shoulder to cry on? Besides, he'd made the biggest mistake of his life in the practice room, pushed her too hard. If Sigma hadn't attacked, he might have been able to explain, to repair the damage, to use the subtle psychological pressure he was so famous for in nonlethal interrogation to get her to at least give him another chance.

As it was…it was too late. Or was it?

She looked back over her shoulder. "Del? Are you coming?"

Yoshi's dark, liquid eyes widened. He glanced at Cath. Delgado didn't miss Cath's slight shrug. Loosely translated: *I don't know, so don't ask me.*

"Right behind you," he said, wishing his hands would stop shaking. It took all his concentration to walk in a straight line.

It helped that he could look up and see her. She reached out, using the doorframe for steadiness, and hauled herself wearily up the two steps into the house. Her limp wasn't very noticeable now, but her shoulders were tight as bridge cables. It hurt him, suddenly, to see that small betraying hitch in each step. Her left boot dragged a little each time.

Inside the door was a small utility room with a washer and dryer, both busily running. Cheerful yellow linoleum glared up, and Del *reached*, automatically identifying the people in the house. Familiar presences, all of them—Boomer, Henderson, Zeke, Brew. He heaved a mental sigh of relief. He'd worried about how many of them had gotten away.

Beyond the utility room was a kitchen with pale wood cupboards, also drenched with electric light. Two laptops were on the counter, both closed and silent, the smell of Brewster's beef stew bubbling in a Crock-Pot—set with prissy exactitude on the counter—made his mouth water. There were two packages of soft dinner rolls set on the counter too. It was as different from a Sig installation as day from night. The small things—two pieces of gear left on the counter, the smell of homemade food, and the poster of Jim Belushi tacked to the pantry door—probably Boomer's—brought home the magnitude of what he'd done with walloping force.

I've escaped them. Again. Stole her out from underneath Sigma again. They won't try to capture me again—no, it'll be pure neutralization this time. No decency, no tranquilizers, just a straight-out choice: me or them.

He caught up to her, moving silently, and offered his arm. "Looks like your leg still hurts," he said noncommittally.

Amazingly, Rowan accepted his arm, leaning on it. Tented together like a pair of absurdly unsteady drunks, they walked through the kitchen and into a short hall leading to the living room. That was probably the nerve center. He would have to debrief with Henderson to find out what the critical gaps and safety shorts were, and get a full layout on how bad the damage to the infrastructure was. If he worked hard enough, he might be able to forget the uncertainty gnawing at his chest.

They rounded the corner into dimness and the sense of movement. Del was a hairsbreadth away from pushing Rowan behind him and pulling a knife when the lights flicked on, and the shout of "*Welcome back!*" shook the air.

Del glanced down at Rowan, who was smiling again, a beautiful open smile that made his gut clench and his mouth go dry. Then all four of them—Zeke the Tank, his massive hairy chest only barely covered by a white tank top; Brewster in a red polo shirt, his white teeth gleaming against his ebony skin; Boomer, his muttonchops brushed to bushy perfection; and Henderson, broad-shouldered and looking older but still moving with the same dry precision that bespoke readiness—descended on Rowan and Del, and the babble only increased when Cath whooped and leapt past them to jump into Zeke's arms. Yoshi pressed a cold beer into Del's free hand, and Boomer picked up Rowan, swung her around in a circle, and did it again.

The living room was decorated with a banner that said, *Welcome Home Del!* There was a cooler jammed full of ice and beer and a platter of cocktail weenies, probably Zeke's contribution. Rowan accepted a glass of wine while Cath and Zeke unabashedly liplocked in the corner, Cath's white fingers tangling in Zeke's dark curly hair. The only furniture in the room was two mattresses and a purple-velvet loveseat holding three liquor-store boxes and a pile of kitbags. The fireplace was brick, and the hearth in front of it held a large bouquet of flowers as well as plates of cold cuts, cheese, and crackers.

Jesus Christ, he thought, *how are we supposed to get any work done with this going on?*

But then Rowan looked over her shoulder at him and grinned. It was the same open sunshine smile she'd bestowed on Yoshi.

"I *told* you he was still alive!" she announced, and the statement provoked fresh hilarity. Brew clapped Del on the shoulder, Boomer gave him a gruff hug, and Delgado was surprised to find out that it did, indeed, feel like coming home.

Seventeen

Rowan rubbed at her eyes, yawning. She tried to roll over, dislodging something soft over her, and bumped against something a little less soft, something her leg was thrown over. It felt comforting and cuddly, even though she'd slept in her clothes again. Her left leg wasn't throbbing nearly as much as it had been, and the sense of peace that enfolded her was so novel it shook her out of warm, fuzzy sleep entirely.

Did I sleep next to the wall? The theory was immediately proven as she tried to roll back and found her shoulder hitting something cold and hard that was *definitely* the wall. Wherever she was, she was sandwiched very effectively.

She heard low, soft breathing, and the crackling electricity sliding over her skin felt familiar.

As she did every morning, she kept her eyes closed, counting to ten and imagining Justin was right next to her. Then, reluctantly, she opened them to find that she'd passed out in the living room, on one of the mattresses. Her left leg was thrown over both of Justin's. He lay on his back, apparently deeply asleep.

Rowan blinked, propping herself up on her elbow. The room looked like any room after an enthusiastic party. Cath and Zeke had disappeared—probably to a back bedroom to celebrate in their own way. Henderson slept propped up by the fireplace, his hand curled protectively around a bottle of Scotch. Brew had cleared off the loveseat and was curled up with his back presented to the rest of the world, the polo shirt riding up to expose a slice of his well-muscled ebony back. Yoshi sat by the front window, meditating. She could almost feel the concentration spreading out from him. He had an assault rifle in his lap, his slim fingers resting on the stock and the barrel as the gun balanced on his knees. Boomer was sprawled on the other mattress, breathing heavily and regularly but not quite snoring. She had a vague memory of him refilling her wine glass a few times, then persuading her to try something called "Yeager" with him—something that burned foully on the way down, but only the first few times.

Justin was completely still, his chest rising and falling so shallowly she wondered if he'd drank himself to sleep to avoid Zed withdrawal. The dark patches under his eyes had shrunk a little, but the harsh lines of his cheekbones still stood out. He'd lost more weight than she'd thought, not an ounce of spare flesh on him anymore. The vulnerable notch between his collarbones was exposed since his T-shirt had been pulled down. He had a sheathed knife in his left hand, which was lying on his chest. As she watched, his eyelids fluttered in dreaming sleep.

The yellowing bruise over his left eye was almost gone. He was still as warm as he had ever been. His right arm was squeezed between them, his hand resting on her hip. She could feel his forearm against her bare midriff where her tank top had been pulled up, a patch of feverish skin pressed against hers. The fans of his eyelashes, perfect charcoal, lay against his cheekbones and made him look strangely young.

She let out a soft, wondering sigh, watching as his eyelids stopped fluttering and he sank into non-REM sleep. It was true.

He was here.

He was so deeply asleep she didn't want to wake him. It was rare for anyone suffering withdrawal to get even a little rest. So she stayed as still as she could, ignoring the persistent throbbing in her head and the equally loud insistence from her bladder. Justin's chin was tipped back, and she watched the pulse beat in his throat.

Stop it, she told herself. *You're just making it worse.*

The aching in her chest wouldn't go away. She'd done it—brought him home. So what if he'd changed his mind? She'd still done what she promised.

She'd saved him, like she had been unable to save her father or Hilary.

Well, not precisely. It's more like he saved himself and I just happened to be there. If you want to get technical, that's what really happened.

She told that nasty little voice inside her head to take a hike just as her bladder declared fresh mutiny.

Don't compound an already impossible situation by doing a cocker-spaniel on the mattress, she told herself, and pushed up slowly. It was going to take a bit of work to shimmy free of *this* one, especially since the soft warm thing draped over her was Justin's coat.

Tears pricked at her eyes. She smelled leather and a healthy male, and the indefinable mix of pheromones that shouted

Justin. Her heart began to pound. She had to stop calling him that. From now on it was Delgado, Del if she felt particularly chummy, and she had to stop hoping. She would only embarrass herself, and after the last few months she didn't need any more embarrassment.

Besides, she had another problem, a bigger problem, now that he was out of Sigma's clutches. She had promised herself she would make Sigma pay for her father's death—and for Hilary's. It was high time she made good on that promise.

Rowan made it to the end of the mattress and gave a sigh of relief as she picked her way cautiously out of the living room and to the bathroom. *I hope this house has two bathrooms and a good water heater. I want a decent shower for once.* Traveling with Cath was like having a younger sister you couldn't blackmail.

Rowan found her duffel stowed with the others. Some thoughtful soul—probably Brew—had cleared out the dirty clothes and done a load of laundry. She found a T-shirt and jeans, fresh underwear, and her last pair of clean socks, then carried it and her rig into the bathroom and locked the door. *If anyone else wants in, too bad.*

Her head throbbed a little less once she'd used the toilet, as if some poison had been leached out of her system. Given what she'd done to her liver and kidneys last night, it probably wasn't far from the truth.

Twenty luxurious minutes later, scrubbed and fresh, she stepped out of the bathroom and into the hall, carrying her dirty clothes. The smell of coffee trickled through the air, and she took a deep breath, smiling.

She came around the corner into the kitchen to find Yoshi standing in front of two coffeemakers. That brightened her mood considerably as she neatly stowed her dirty clothes in the duffel and approached the kitchen again. Wordlessly, he handed her a cup of thick black coffee with two sugars, then set a plastic water glass and three ibuprofen on the counter.

Rowan nodded her thanks, downed the ibuprofen, and drank off the water. She was vaguely surprised she didn't have more of a hangover, considering the amount she'd put away.

Yoshi refilled the water glass from the pitcher. He pulled down the hem of his blue linen shirt. "So," he said finally, pouring himself a cup of coffee, with soymilk, no sugar—Rowan shuddered at the thought—and putting the soymilk carton back in the bare white fridge. "Cath said you had some trouble."

Rowan shrugged. "We got out of there with only three-quarters of what I'd hoped. But if it hadn't been for Jus—ah, Del, we wouldn't have gotten out at all."

"Ah." He blew across the top of his coffee to cool it. "Henderson will be pleased."

Yeah, with Justin back you can all go back to normal and I can maybe have some time to plan my grand revenge on a secret government agency. Sounds like a best-seller to me. Wonder if I should start thinking about the movie rights? Rowan Price, martyr to the Psionic Rights movement.

"I hope so," she murmured. *And considering that he didn't want me to go to Vegas in the first place, Henderson should be pretty* damn *pleased.*

Yoshi studied her. His dark eyes were eloquently noncommittal. He was willing to talk if Rowan wanted to, equally willing to let it go if she didn't. Even she couldn't decide.

She far preferred Cath's blithe unconcern. "He's different," she said finally, staring into her coffee. The house was absolutely silent, the feel of dampers crawling over her skin. It felt so *naked* to be under the protective shield. She'd always had trouble with them. Had to be taught how not to blow them down and send out invisible signals that would draw the enemy, but nothing had ever taught her to be comfortable with them.

"You can't have expected him to return unscathed from the darkness," Yoshi pointed out. He leaned back against the kitchen counter, cocking his sleek dark head. The new almost-punk haircut looked good on him. He was barefoot as usual, his sandals left properly placed outside the kitchen, ready for him to step into if necessary. You could always tell when Cath was around by the smell of strawberry incense, cigarettes, and hairspray, and Yoshi when you tripped over shoes on the floor. Rowan wondered if she left her own marks on the houses they stayed in. "The battle marks the warrior, as the warrior marks the battle," he added.

Thank you for that fortune-cookie wisdom. It's ever so helpful.

Rowan sighed and took a sip of coffee. It was strong enough to eat away a silver spoon, very sweet, just the way she'd learned to like it in the past year. "I just…I thought…"

"Thought what?" Yoshi cocked his head, listening. A faintly

surprised expression crossed his face. "I think perhaps we'd best wake everyone," he continued, with no discernible emotion. "I have a rather remarkable feeling of uneasiness."

Rowan closed her eyes, *feeling* around in that nonphysical manner that seemed the most reliable way of scouting out danger. "I don't feel any Sigs," she said.

"Perhaps it isn't them we should be worried about." Yoshi set his coffee cup down with a precise click. "I'll get Cath and Zeke. I think it best if you wake Del and the others."

She knew better than to question him or waste precious time on arguing. Instead, she carried her coffee—*no use wasting a good cuppa joe*—around the corner and into the other hall that led past the front door to the living room.

Where, surprisingly, she saw Justin leaning against the wall, apparently studying the locked front door with great interest. He had his rig buckled on—less graceful than the ones the Society used but still familiar, a piece of Sigma gear. He ran his palm back over his short dark hair, as if he'd forgotten it was shorter now and he was trying to strip it back with his fingers.

Rowan's heart leapt into her mouth. "Good morning," she said quietly. "Yoshi said to wake everyone up. There's coffee, if you want it." Her eyes slid down his shoulder—he wasn't wearing his coat—and to the inner surface of his left elbow, exposed by the short sleeve of his blue T-shirt, the same one he'd been wearing since Vegas.

There, scored into his skin, were track marks. They were ugly, raised and red, and Rowan sucked in a breath. She reached out, her coffee cup almost burning her left hand, and trailed her fingers down his bicep, avoiding touching the nasty hypo-marks. She'd seen enough of them by now on psions caught by Sigma.

The flesh at the hollow of his elbow was bruised as well as scored, the sign of rough handling. Had he been strapped down? There was a bracelet of raw, red flesh around his wrist she hadn't noticed before. From restraints, probably. Cold fingers trailed down her spine, and the skin on her upper arms prickled with gooseflesh.

"My God," she whispered. "What did they do to you?"

He shrugged, an easy fluid movement. "Nothing I couldn't handle." His voice was low, too—early-morning gravel. "Slapped me around a little, got me on some Zed. Seen it before." But his arm was hard and tense under her fingertips. Was he shaking? Or was it some high voltage of rage going through him?

I left him there. Guilt rose acid in her throat.

Rowan flattened her hand against the rough track marks. She had to step closer to him to do so, and she was suddenly aware that she'd spent the entire night sleeping next to him. It hadn't been planned—she barely remembered collapsing on the mattress and listening to others talking, the bursts of laughter, feeling the world whirl under her as the alcohol disorientation released her tension.

"I can help with this," she managed around the lump in her throat. "You must be… God, I'm sorry. I should have done something last night, instead of—"

His fingers closed around her wrist. The contact was just as electric as the heat of his abused skin under her palm. Gently, *very* gently, he pulled her hand away from his arm. She knew how strong he was, guessed he was trying not to hurt her. The touch did something strange, filled her head with heat and robbed her legs of strength.

Keeping my distance is going to be a little harder than I thought, she admitted wryly to herself.

"A little later," he said, his fingers still around her wrist. "When we've found out what Yoshi's nervous about, and when you've had some breakfast. You look a little pale."

I'm not pale, she wanted to say. *My hair's a mess, I haven't worn makeup in what seems like years, and I'm thin and nervous because people with guns keep chasing me. Nothing that fleeing the country won't cure.*

"I'm fine," she said, a little more curtly than she wanted to. "It's been hard, we've all missed you."

"Did you miss me?" He sounded like he wasn't even interested. She had managed to tear her eyes away from the damage done to his arm by the simple expedient of looking at the plain white painted wall.

A brief struggle—she pulled fruitlessly against his hold on her, his fingers clamped just enough to keep her from breaking his grip. Another brief struggle with caution, which she lost just as badly.

"Of course I missed you." Heat rose up to her cheeks. It felt like she was standing over a hot burner. "Justin, I'm so sorry—I mean, Delgado—"

"You can call me what you like." Did he sound, for the

first time, amused? "I like the way you say it. Anyway, you'd better wake them up. I'm going to get clean and find some coffee." His fingers loosened and he slowly let go of her wrist.

I am such a miserable coward, Rowan thought. *I can't even look at him.* "Fine." Her voice wouldn't work above a whisper.

He edged past her, moving a little closer than absolutely necessary, crowding her toward the wall. Coffee slopped against the sides of Rowan's mug, and she finally looked up.

He was staring at her again, with that oddly *present* look making his eyes dark and deep instead of flat.

"I missed you too." His whisper was different from hers, less squeak and more harsh depth. "I didn't even know what I was forgetting, and I missed you."

Rowan's heart banged against her ribs. Her cheeks felt as if she was having one mother of a hot flash. *And I'm only thirty-one, nowhere near menopause. Dammit, Rowan, keep your mind on business!*

But it was very hard to remain businesslike while Justin leaned down a little and inhaled as if smelling her hair, still wet from the shower. *He used to do that a lot. What am I doing? What's* he *doing? I thought he didn't want anything to do with me!*

"Try to stay out of trouble while I'm getting my coffee." He was gone around the corner before she could protest. Rowan blinked. Her knees felt watery. Would the old Justin have done that? Or was it just his sense of humor, sarcastic and difficult at the best of times?

The thought of the track marks made her stomach flip uneasily. *I did that. I may not have held him down and pressed the hypo button, but if it wasn't for me Headquarters would never have been broken and he wouldn't have had to suffer. Maybe he's angry and just trying to work through it on his own.*

In the living room, Henderson still sat with his back propped against the wall. But she thought she heard a smothered chuckle, and she would have bet he was awake. Embarrassment flooded her, and she took a deep breath and a scalding gulp of coffee, promptly burning her mouth.

Get a grip on yourself, Rowan, she told herself firmly.

"All right, I can hear you giggling," she said, hoping her voice didn't quiver. "Get up, General. Yoshi's got one of his feelings again."

Eighteen

Del ran his eyes over the printout. His neck hurt and his bones ached from second-stage Zed withdrawal. He ignored it.

"How much worse is it?" He glanced across the living room. Rowan was occupied with packing kitbags. She took a sip of cold coffee, swirled it in her mouth, and grimaced, downing it as if it contained alcohol. She was so pale her skin appeared almost translucent except for the faint flush that rose to her cheeks whenever her eyes met his.

He wondered what that meant.

He'd actually slept next to her last night, listening to the steady rise and fall of her breath as the party wound down and the others dropped off. When he had finally found himself relaxing despite the aching of withdrawal, he had even dared to turn his head and take a deep lungful of her. He'd tucked his coat around her because she'd looked cold. And this morning she'd been gone when he opened his eyes. That was a nasty shock, but he'd *reached* and found her concentrating on taking a shower. He'd retreated hurriedly back into his own head, glad she hadn't been aware of his quick brush. It made him feel like a voyeur—not so much because he'd done it, but because he wanted to crawl into her mind like a badger into its hole and *stay* there.

The General spared a brief grin. "Actually this *is* the bad news. We've gained a lot in the last month or so—fourteen newbies. We've gone back to the decentralized training. Eleanor's got a bunch of them up in Calgary. She sent word back with Boomer that things are kosher up there. Everyone who was out and away from Headquarters survived largely intact, thank God." Henderson's voice dropped. "If it wasn't for Rowan we wouldn't have made it."

"Ro!" Cath stuck her head in the living room. "Zeke wants to know where you put the—"

"Bathroom, second shelf." She nodded at Yoshi and handed him his full kitbag. "In the blue bottle. Tell him to leave some for the rest of us, and is he taking his meds?"

"You know how he is." Cath rolled her eyes. There was a large, fresh hickey on the side of her neck, and her violet eyes were hooded and sleepy. "Thanks."

"No problem." She flipped the messenger bag she was working on closed, handing it to Yoshi. Del watched, but the Japanese man didn't steal the chance to brush her wrist when he took the bag, didn't lean in toward her like Justin would have done.

That was very good.

"Rowan?" This time it was Brew. "Need anything else?"

"Just another couple clips for Zeke's Walther, if you have any. Oh, and ask Justin what kind of hardware he needs." She hunched her shoulders, shooting Del a guilty look. Her hands kept moving, swift and deft, taking the next canvas messenger bag, stowing the medkit, extra clips, pad of paper, the pen with the digital camera in the shaft, copper wire, Matheson handheld—all the little things no Society op should be without.

"Already did." Brew tipped Delgado a wink and vanished, with Cath, back down the hall. If the danger came closer, into the critical zone, it was Brewster's danger-sense that would warn them to scramble.

Del's throat was dry. His body cried out for Zed. As long as he stayed near her it was tolerable—the red-hot ants didn't jitter so badly over his skin and he didn't feel like he was breathing through wet cloth. The spikes of pain were distracting and intense enough to make him sweat, but still tolerable.

But take Rowan out of the room and suddenly everything got a lot worse. As object lessons went, it was extremely elegant. Something about being around her made the withdrawal easier. If he needed yet another reason to watch over her, that would have done it.

His jacket smelled like her now. It was an unexpected blessing, the faint scent of *woman* attached to the lining of his coat. Not just any woman, either; the only woman Del had ever...

"She's missed you," Henderson said quietly. The table between them was a flimsy portable number, looking barely capable of holding the printouts and maps. The old man's wire-rimmed glasses gave a steely glint to match the white patch at his left temple. That white patch had grown, and Henderson himself looked older. The fine fans at the corners of his eyes hadn't been there before, nor had the slight weary shadows in his eagle eyes. "I had to tie her down so she didn't go running off to 'rescue' you from Sigma."

"Christ." Del's blood ran cold at the thought, and his head

started to pound. He wouldn't have been able to help her. "I *pushed* myself to forget so they couldn't beat it out of me. I don't think they know what she can do."

"I don't even think *she* knows what she can do. I mean it, Del. We had to damn near kneecap her to keep her from raiding any Sig installation she could find on her own."

Del's heart felt like it was cracking and throwing itself against his ribs at the same time. He flipped through a few more printouts, seeing none of them. *So she wanted to come riding in and save me, huh? Well, that's something, at least.* "Glad you kept her from doing that."

"You'd kick my ass if you came back and found out I'd let her go." Henderson's tone changed, became businesslike. "They're sending Carson."

Another chill walked down his back. "Andrews told me." *That's why I got the hell out of there.*

"Andrews. How is the old bastard?"

He would have sent his greetings if he'd known I was on my way to meet you. The man's almost as fascinated with you as he is with Rowan.

"Just like Anton, as fine and sociopathic as ever." Del shifted his weight and looked up, checking on Rowan again. Her head was down, she was packing the last kitbag as Yoshi handed each implement to her. "It's become personal. He'd love to get his hands on her."

"Him and everyone else, huh." Henderson started rolling up maps. "Glad to have you back, Del. Listen, we've picked a new Headquarters. The nest egg Rowan brought back isn't as good as we hoped but it's adequate. I'll need you to start working through security procedures and help Yoshi salvage whatever we can from the old resource net."

Del blinked. Did they just expect him to step in where he'd left off? Didn't they understand he was a danger, that he could be a Sigma mole?

But no, Henderson had trusted him long ago in the dim days of Del's first escape, and never doubted him since. "You should wait until you can trust me," he said, harshly, watching Rowan roll her eyes as Yoshi made a low comment. She laughed, grabbing for the coil of copper wire he held. He tried to move, but her hands were too quick. Her hair had begun to dry. Fine, slightly curling, strands fell into her face. She subtracted the roll of wire from him deftly. They looked very easy with each other.

Very goddamn friendly.

The old man shrugged. "Would you drag Ro in to Sigma, see her shaved and full of Zed?"

"Christ, no." He tried not to sound horrified. "I *pushed* myself to forget so they couldn't use me against her."

"There you go. Help me clean this up. What else can you tell me about Andrews?"

He wants her, badly. It's personal now. He won't stop hunting her down, might even go rogue.

"He's an idiot." He reached down and started shoving the papers into manageable piles.

Henderson made a short, disgusted sound, acknowledging the humor. "Well, goddammit, Del, I knew that."

* * *

"Not a moment too soon," Yoshi murmured, his fingers flicking over the laptop's keyboard. "Four SWAT teams. They must have a high opinion of us."

"I didn't even know they had SWAT teams in Fargo," Brew remarked from the driver's seat. He scanned traffic and changed lanes, the SUV moving smoothly.

Rowan shifted restlessly in the passenger's seat, a movement Del could feel in his own body. "Henderson?"

"Henderson's clear. He and Boomer and the kids got out with two hours to spare," Yoshi said. "They'll meet us in Des Moines. It's all over the television—an anonymous call tipped off the inquisitives at the news stations." Yoshi grinned and glanced over at Del. "Wonder who would do such a thing."

"Can't imagine," he agreed. If there was one thing Sigma hated, it was publicity. They had used the local police force to do their dirty work this time, maybe thinking that deadheads wouldn't trigger Rowan's exquisitely sensitive antennae for danger. They might have been right. It had been Yoshi's nervousness and Brew's insistence that they move on, and Henderson had agreed.

Del's entire body itched, his bones twisting with deep grinding pain as the chemical dependency yanked mercilessly on his nervous system. He was nauseated and shaking, but it wasn't as bad as it *could* have been, not as bad as he remembered from his first detox and certainly not as hellish as when they had recently tried to use withdrawal to break him—as if he could have answered their questions about a woman he had forced himself not to remember. The feeling of being in the same room with Rowan, standing in the path of the lightning bolt of her talent, seemed to make it just bearable.

Only *just*, though.

The miles unrolled under the car wheels. Rowan looked out the window, her profile thoughtful and closed. It was odd to see her without a book in her hands. Odd to be in a vehicle without two bullyboys holding him at gunpoint, odd to hear Brew's humming along with the classical station on the radio as it began to break up at the edge of its range. Odd to move again without the restraints, to know he could suggest a bathroom break or a stop for lunch at any time, odd not to look around and see a handler lurking in the corner. Unfamiliar freedom. When he'd first arrived at Headquarters it had taken him six months just to get used to going to the goddamn bathroom alone again.

Lunch was a mini-mall with a Subway, a teriyaki shack, and a little pizza place. Rowan looked longingly at the Subway before agreeing to go with everyone else for crust and melted cheese. She did insist on a vegetarian pizza, and settled in their back booth with a sigh. He decided to push it a little and slid in next to her. She'd picked the side that would put her back to the wall, good defense strategy.

He finally had a chance to talk to her when Brew went to order the pizza and Yoshi to visit the restroom. "How's the leg?" he asked.

And that was more food for thought. The bullet hole had closed up in an astonishingly short amount of time. She hadn't been able to do that before. Then again, if it made her look as thin and wan as she'd been, he doubted it was a blessing.

"Fine. A little tender, but all right." She rubbed her slim, expressive hands together, and a tendril of ash-blond hair fell into her face. "Boomer insisted on giving me some pain meds, but they don't help. I seem to burn right through them." Her eyes scanned the restaurant, moving in quick arcs, settling on the door. Outside, sunlight simmered down, but clouds were piling up. There would be rain before long, maybe an afternoon storm. "Del?"

His heart sank. She had never called him that before he'd been captured. "What?" The pain in his bones taunted him. He laid his hands flat on the table. If he pressed down on the varnished wood, she wouldn't see how badly they were shaking. He tore his eyes away from her face and checked the restaurant again. The back of his neck was prickling for some reason. He scanned the plate-glass windows with their dusty posters, the staff going about their pizza duties, and smelled cigarettes burning in the smoking section.

"Can I… I mean, your arm. May I help you with the bruises?"

What? "Sure, angel." He felt his eyebrow rise. "Do I have to take my coat off?"

She actually flushed, looking down at the table. "No, that's not necessary. I'll climb in the back seat with you when we hit the road again. But until then…" Her hand moved, and her fingertips met Delgado's wrist.

He was about to turn his hand palm-up so he could take hers, but the sensation—a palpable wash of peace that started at the crown of his head and slid down, coating his skin with liquid heat—nailed him in place. Fire roared through his veins. He felt her slipping through the surface of his mind, but the feeling wasn't the agony of his own talent burning and ripping at him even as it served his purposes. Instead, it was as if every bloodstained moment of his life was washed clean, as if she had taken all the pain from him for a brief moment, both the physical pain and the agony of a battered mind stretched to its limits. When she took her fingers away he had to once again restrain himself from reaching out and grabbing her hand.

She hadn't managed to keep herself completely separate during the touch. The complex wash of emotion from her—relief that he was alive, uncertainty, worry and a powerful crimson-colored guilt—was underlaid with that same strong, clear, pure feeling he hadn't been able to put a name on before. He'd never encountered anything like it. It was *dangerous*. Getting addicted to that feeling would make Zed look like a cakewalk.

But it meant she was still emotionally attached to him. He could use that attachment, to worm his way back into her good graces and see if he could get a little closer. His hands had stopped shaking.

"Rowan—" he began, his voice rusty and hoarse.

Brew slid in on the other side of the booth, carrying a tray with four glasses. "Diet Coke, root beer, plain Coke, and plain Coke. Take your pick."

She picked diet Coke, Del took plain Coke, and by the time

Yoshi had come back the conversation had turned to pizza as the perfect food. Brew was a vocal champion, Rowan a passionate detractor—due to the amount of cholesterol in the melted cheese—and Yoshi weighed in, as usual, with a hymn to the wonders of sashimi. He didn't seem to mind Del sitting next to her.

Del just sat back, sipped his Coke, and watched her grow more animated. He kept an eye on the front of the restaurant and moved a little closer in the booth, almost smiling each time she accidentally elbowed him. To hell with being fair, and to hell with playing nice. He *needed* her. If he had to add the sin of manipulation to his long list of crimes in the service of fighting Sigma, he was more than happy to do so for her safety.

That's the thing, he thought as the pizza arrived. *I've turned into the monster Anton talks about all the time: a rogue freak. I don't care what happens as long as she's safe.*

She elbowed him again and gave him a quick look of apology. Del had to take a deep breath and restrain himself from sliding a proprietary arm over her shoulders.

Nineteen

Rowan sat straight up, her entire body cold and prickling-wet with sweat. She gasped, reaching out to ward off danger, and found her hand caught in slim, strong fingers.

"It's only me," Yoshi said. "Light." And with that warning, he flicked the bedside lamp.

"What's wrong?" She almost choked over the words, and then saw Justin. He was repacking her bag, swift and efficient. Brew was gone. She almost *reached* for him, but that would disturb the portable dampers.

The motel room had two queen-size beds. Justin had elected to sleep on the floor, over her faint protest, and Brew and Yoshi took the other bed. A hideous painting of a lighthouse leered at her from above the television.

"Something's not right." Yoshi was pale under the even caramel of his skin. "Brew had a nightmare and I think we're being followed. Here." He shoved a pile of clothes into her hands. "Del thinks something's up too," he added, apparently thinking that was enough of an explanation.

It was. She knew it was.

Justin zipped the duffel closed. "This is the last one. Get down to the car. If anything jumps, just go. I'll get her out."

Yoshi nodded. "Hurry," he said, and left at a pace too quick to be called walking but not quite an undignified dash, taking Rowan's bag with him. Justin followed him to the door opposite the curtained window, and checked the hall.

The other bed was rumpled. Rowan swung her legs out and shivered. It was chilly in the room, a cold that seemed far more than physical.

"What do you think it is?" *What a stupid question, Rowan. It's Sigma, that's what it always is. Won't this ever stop?*

"Probably Carson and his lapdog." He shut the door quietly, precisely. "Hurry, angel."

The pizza she'd had earlier churned in her stomach as she ran for the bathroom. Yoshi had left her comb, a pair of jeans, a button-down shirt, and her kitbag. She could stuff her tank top and shorts into it on the way down to the car.

The mirror greeted her with a vision of a rumpled, very pale Rowan, her hands visibly shaking as she used the small toilet and changed her clothes, taking a few moments to rinse the taste of fear from her mouth and splash her face with cold water. She decided to keep her tank top on and slide the other shirt over it.

The chill in the room seemed to work its way all the way down to her bones. It wasn't a physical cold, and the extra layer of clothing didn't seem to do much good.

She came out to find the lights off again and Justin by the window, peering out into the parking lot. They were up on the second story. A ground-level room had too many possible avenues of approach. The only trouble was, higher up, the avenues of escape were just as few as the avenues of approach.

The dampers were still running, he would leave them here just in case. "I don't like this," he murmured. "You ready?"

"Ready enough," she managed.

He glanced at her. A thin, tight smile hovered around the corners of his mouth, and her heart began to thump. "Don't worry, angel."

"I'm not worried." Her voice shook. Embarrassment warred with honesty, and a compromise was reached. "You're here." She tried not to sound childish.

His eyes warmed for a brief moment. "That's right. Got your kitbag?"

She nodded. Her throat was dry and her head began to hurt, throbbing in time to her racing heart. "Del…"

"For Christ's sake, angel," he said, peering out into the parking lot again, "it's *Justin*. Now come on."

The hall was quiet, carpeted in brown, and thick with the smell of danger. Rowan clenched her jaw to keep her teeth from chattering, Justin's hand closed around her arm just above her elbow, and she had the sudden feeling that the past was curving in on itself like a snake, doubling like a movie reel. He'd hustled her out of hotel rooms before, in the long dim days of their first escape from Sigma. She had never asked him how he had managed to keep a sedated psion out of the hands of several Sig search teams and bring them both safely to Headquarters, with only two nasty knife wounds and a severe case of exhaustion.

He made a low sound of strained amusement as they reached the end of the hall, under the glowing-green exit sign. "Feels just like old times," he said quietly. "Down the stairs, and we'll take the door to the back parking lot." He pushed the door open.

Rowan stopped dead. The stairwell should have been lit up with fluorescents. Instead, it was a black pit. Danger exhaled from it, and Rowan heard a soft sliding sound. A footstep? Justin yanked her back.

"No other stairs," Justin muttered. "All right."

"No elevator," she said as he stepped back, sweeping the door closed. He gave a quick glance around—nothing he could use to bar the door, which would have been her first thought too. He'd already instinctively put himself between her and the stairwell; she could feel his sudden determination.

"Too dangerous." That was the first rule: *never* use the elevator if you could help it. It was too easy to snip a wire and be caught between floors like a rat in a cage.

She could almost feel his brain clicking through alternatives. He dug in his pocket, fishing the room key out. *Why didn't he leave that in the room?*

"I thought they might have moved in on the stairs," he said, as if reading her mind. He probably was, despite her attempts to keep herself shielded. God knew they had been close enough before for him to hear what she was thinking. At least once they'd started sharing a bed. "Back inside, Ro. Quick."

The naked, fizzing feeling of dampers slid over her skin again as they ducked back into the room. The hall was empty, but for how long? And the stairwell…so dark. She'd never seen that before. Never felt that kind of chill malice before.

"Get the top sheet," he said, pointing, and did a strange thing. He backed up to the end of the short entryway the door gave onto, a gun in his hand. He crouched down and lifted the gun carefully. "It's cotton, nice and strong."

Oh, God, you have got to be kidding. She didn't argue, yanking the bedspread away and tearing the sheet loose. "We could make a movie out of this," she managed in a thready, unsteady voice. Her head began to pound—not with the glassy, needling pain and nausea of Sigma, but a different pain, this one rising and falling like a roller coaster and making her stomach flutter. *What is that? What's going on?*

"Not a very good movie," he replied calmly. "Find something to brace that with, angel. We're taking the short way down."

If he was prepared to risk that, it must be more serious

than even *she* thought. "If they have snipers—"

"This isn't an appropriations or a sweep team. It's Carson and his fucking psychopath. Hurry." He sounded calm, but his mind suddenly knotted inside hers, dark intent and strange exhilaration making a lethal cocktail. His pulse sped up, and hers wasn't far behind. "Seems like every time I get some time alone with you something comes up."

"Curse of living in interesting times, I guess." *I sound calm. Good for me.* She dragged the table to the window, turning it over and slip-knotting the end of the sheet. "Justin—"

He waved at her to be quiet, and Rowan swallowed her words.

Everything slowed down. She finished threading the remainder of the sheet through the slipknot. Her heart hammered, and her palms slipped wetly against the cotton. She had just half-turned to glance out the window at the parking lot when a sharp spike of agony slammed through her head and *twisted.*

I have you now, an old, lipless voice whispered inside her head, pulling, sinking in, and burning. *I have you now. You've run a pretty course, my fine girl, but now it's over. Give in.*

She was vaguely aware of cursing—Justin's voice, a rough sound of effort, a sharp popping roar of gunfire and the sudden whistling sound as a knife clove the air. She was barely aware of her head hitting the floor with stunning force as the old voice burrowed past every defense Henderson and Miss Kate had taught her to painstakingly erect. The dark slicing fishhook *touched*, speared through, and pulled her shrieking out of her own head.

She was struggling, thrashing, mental cords tearing as she fought to stay with herself, to deny him access, to deny him power over her. His laughter, old and unspeakably foul like something rotting from the inside, filled her brain as he chanted the name of the thing he wanted her to do. *Give in. Give in.* The foulness spread, staining every layer of her mind with contagion like a virus, self-replicating. She thought desperately of ocean, clean water, pure rain washing him away, blocking him out, barring his access.

"*Rowan!*" Justin's scream. Rage spilled through her, a rage no more hers than the digging twisting *thing* in her mind. It was *his* anger, and it closed around her like a suit of armor, but oh its black depth frightened her. "*No!*"

He beat at the old voice, smashed it back, and forced a weak cry from her throat. Rowan struggled, thrashing mentally and physically, her wrist hitting the edge of the upturned table with a solid, bruising impact. She felt like a cord stretched between two elephants, Justin pulling from one side, the awful, dry, cracked voice pulling from the other. That rotten fractured voice had smashed through her defenses and sank its greedy claws in, but Justin's black fury pulled her back. He was linked to her far more deeply.

More deeply, even, than she had thought.

Then, as soon as it had come, the voice retreated, leaving behind a sick unsteady feeling and the cold weight of a gun jammed against the temple.

"Let go of her." Justin's voice, low and harsh, as he pulled the hammer back. "*Now,* Carson."

"You kill me, it kills her." The voice quavered, an old man's helpless evil voice. Fury again, burning under her skin, a rage so deep and wide it could consume her.

Rowan screamed, but all that came out was a thready, weak whisper. The voice dug in, tearing, causing damage wherever it could. *Give in. Give in. Give in to me, let me IN—*

A blinding flash. Justin, reaching through her again. It was dangerous for him to split his focus between her and whatever enemy he was facing. She struggled to lift her head, to fight whatever had struck her so hard.

Pain, a flash along her upper arm. She heard his low curse again, and then a meaty *thunk* as if someone had split a watermelon.

Agony rolled through her, a burning as if every synapse had been doused with gasoline and lit. Rowan thrashed blindly, heard a rabbitlike scream. It was *Justin's* pain, the pain he felt whenever he used his gift to break into a mind, the echo of the *push* he used screaming through her own nervous system. It seemed to last forever.

There was a long deathlike pause. Her vision began to return, and she saw the ceiling—oddly skewed because she lay twisted, half on her back with her arm flung out—and something warm and wet was in her eyes. Her lungs burned, and she dragged in a breath. Another. Blinked, vaguely surprised to find herself alive.

Oh, God. God. What the hell was that?

Her head ached fiercely, as if the hangover had only waited for now to make its appearance. The pulsing of some dark intent submerged itself below the layers of her waking mind, and she felt vaguely horrified through the pain and weakness. What was that thing? Where had it come from, and what was it doing in her head?

"When you get back to Sigma," she heard Justin say hoarsely, "if you can still talk, you tell Anton I'll do the same to anyone else he sends after her. Now it's *war*."

A short gurgle. Another one of those wet, horrible sounds, and she heard distant sirens. Someone must have called the cops. Why?

The noise went on. A short, sharp explosion, a gunshot. A thrashing sound. It was a wonder the cops weren't already here. *Oh, God. God, please.*

Footsteps. "Rowan?" Harsh, a croak. "Come on, sweetheart. We've got to go."

His face swam into view above her. Blood dripped down its right side, a shocking scarlet. He bent down, and his mind threaded with hers again, a tentative touch against bruised and scorched mental "skin." Still, she welcomed it. His mind was *clean*, not like the rotted thing that had tried to infect her, to break her to its will.

That wasn't a man. That was a sickness in a human body. How many people did he torture to turn his gift into that? She was suddenly, utterly, glad to have Justin. He'd saved her. Again.

Rowan's mouth worked. She had to drag in another breath as he hauled her upright. "Come on, angel. Walk. We've got to go. Now."

"J-J-J-Justin…" She stammered over the name, relieved when she heard her own voice. The dark thing pulsed, burrowing into her mind, but she couldn't *think*, could not even imagine what it was. "What—"

"Never mind. Come *on*."

"P-P-P-" *Push me,* she thought. He had to help her. There was something buried in her mind, something unholy. It was too hard to talk. Her throat closed up and refused to obey her. She tried again. *You h-have to. Push me…*

"No." He had his arm over her shoulder and dragged her along. Her head dropped forward, her neck unable to hold it up. She saw a slim man dressed in black lying on the floor, half hidden between the two beds. The lamp was knocked over, the television and the mirror smashed too, and blood painted the pale wall in a high arc, gleaming wetly. The television's shell smoked and sparked. Her feet bumped something soft. She bit back a moan. There was a long white stick, like the kind blind people used, snapped in half. "Not gonna push you, sweetheart. Come on, move with me, Ro."

"C-C—" She was about to say *I can't*, when her legs began to work again. She almost tripped, but he lifted her over the moaning body on the floor in the entryway.

It was a pudgy white-haired man, his sweatshirt torn and his khakis dewed with blood, scrabbling weakly on the floor. The owner of the rotted-out voice. A knife hilt protruded from his throat.

A shattered pair of sunglasses crunched under Justin's boot. "That's my girl," he said calmly enough. He winced—she could feel the dragging pain in his chest, his scalp, his arm on fire. What had happened to him while she lay useless on the floor?

"Hurt," she managed. Her wrist throbbed with pain. "You're hurt."

"Doesn't matter." He half-carried her down the hall. The elevator's blank white doors loomed.

Elevator? "I thought you said—" *Help me, please. God help me.* Something blurred and shifted. She could no longer remember why it was so necessary he use his talent on her. It hovered just out of the reach of her battered memory. She gasped in cool air, tried to walk. Failed.

"This is an emergency." The doors folded open, and she managed to help him drag her inside. "You okay? He hit you pretty hard. He's good at cracking empaths."

"H-hurts." That was an understatement. She felt lethargic and pain beat under her skin, a terrible restless pain like nerves twisting, like insects pricking with needlelike feet. It wasn't normal. Something was happening inside her head. The elevator dinged, and he pushed the button for the ground floor. "How b-bad are y-you—"

"Don't worry about me." He hissed in a breath, shifted his weight. The weightlessness of an elevator descending tugged at her stomach.

What if Sigma's out there? She didn't mean for him to hear the thought, but he did, and a flood of reassurance tingled through her tired, battered head. God, even a normal person's open sewer of a mind was better than that blind, rotting touch, squirming like maggots inside her skull. Justin's clear, cold calm dispelled the fog of pain and made it easier to think. The walls between them had been shattered. She had the uncomfortable feeling that a mental door between them had been blown off its hinges and she might not be able to put it back on. And something else taunted her, something about what had just happened dancing just outside her mental reach.

Then I'll get us out. Brew and Yosh can't stay forever. If they're gone we'll have to steal a car. Have to stop and wash up, get the blood off. Chest hurts. Don't think about that. Think he got me with that damn stiletto. Ouch.

Beating under his thoughts was a collage of aches and pains. The feeling of needles all over her skin was his, from the Zed withdrawal.

"Justin." She laid her head against his shoulder, wishing it would stop hurting. Whatever the other man had done, she needed a few minutes to close her eyes and find the wellspring of calm inside herself. She felt filthy, as if the inside of her head had been dipped in slime. Her wrist hurt, a sharp pain under the fuzziness of approaching unconsciousness. "Glad you're h-here."

"Me too, angel." He eased a gun out of the holster, gathered himself to "blur" them. It hurt, but he discarded the pain. Rowan helped as much as she could, but she was exhausted. She doubted she could use *any* of her talent without passing out. "Nowhere else I'd rather be."

The elevator slowed. "Please," Rowan whispered, not sure who or even *what* she was asking.

The doors opened, and Justin went still and cold beside her. But Rowan couldn't worry about it, because her tenuous grasp on consciousness failed and she passed out.

Twenty

It wasn't the lobby. It was a short hall with doors on either side and the double glass doors giving out onto the front parking lot. *Brew and Yoshi should be gone by now. Going to have to steal a car.*

As if the thought had summoned them, he saw the black SUV glide to a stop, street lamp shine sliding wetly off its paint.

I am going to court-martial both of them, he thought irritably, dragging Rowan along. Thankfully, she had passed out. He wasn't sure if he could stand feeling the agonizing pain that beat inside her head. Or the sense of violation. Carson had damn near raped her mind, almost smashing in to take control of her, to break her the way he'd broken plenty of other psions. It was ironic in the extreme that if she hadn't been so goddamn gifted the blind man would have had a harder time with her. He wasn't so effective when it came to precogs or telekinetics, but other telepaths and empaths were critically vulnerable to the Tracker.

Hurt her. He hurt her. Rage rose, and he smothered it. He couldn't afford to get angry and lose his focus.

The back driver's side door opened smoothly. "Let's get the hell out of here," he said, manhandling Rowan into the car. Yoshi leaned over on the passenger side and helped as much as he could, pulling her to safety. Then Del was in beside her, sucking in a deep breath that hurt all the way down.

The stiletto. It hit deep. Hope it didn't scratch a lung. But I'd be having trouble breathing if it did.

Yoshi's dark eyes met his as Brew pressed down on the gas pedal. Pavement began to slip under the car's broad tires. "You look awful." Yoshi offered him a Handi Wipe. "What happened?"

"Carson." Del smoothed it over his face, wiping away blood. The scalp wound itched. "Got to Ro somehow. I put his goddamn psychopath down and hit the blind man with everything I had. Hope it was enough. Goddammit, Brew, can't you go any faster?"

"If you want to be arrested, I can." Brew, used to postcombat jitters, didn't take offense. Yoshi, leaning over the front seat, watched Delgado. Then his dark, eloquent eyes shifted to Rowan, slumped against a pile of hurriedly-stacked gear. Her pale hair had come loose, glowing in the faint light.

It was the darkest part of early morning, the time when old men died. *One old man died tonight, I hope. If he recovers from that* push *he'll...No, he won't. I've killed him. I sank a knife in his throat. He can't have survived that. Please tell me I've killed the two men that nearly killed me the first time I escaped. Have I gotten better or have they gotten worse?*

Hard to get worse than dead. Please let them be dead.

Yoshi continued to study Rowan. Jealousy rose sharp and vicious, and Del took a deep breath.

"She is a very dear friend," Yoshi said suddenly, very clearly. "But no more than a friend."

Oh, Christ. Del leaned over, finding the seat belt and strapping Rowan in. She wasn't physically hurt, but he wanted to check, to run his fingers over her to make *sure.*

"Not like it matters," he mumbled. His cheeks felt hot. Was he fucking blushing? He hoped not. It was too dark to tell, thank God. *You probably deserve her more than me anyway.*

"It matters," Yoshi persisted. "She's very attached to you, Del."

"Leave him alone, mate. He's had a hard night." Brew sounded amused. Almost as if he was suppressing a chuckle, his crisp British accent blurring a little under the weight of laughter.

Don't they realize we're possibly in the middle of a Sig net? Carson and what's-his-face weren't working alone, were they? Then again, Carson usually does work alone. He worked alone the first time he found me. And Ro didn't sense any Sigs. Then again, with Carson there, they might have been under dampers and he could technically keep a small team under wraps, he's talented enough...Dammit, Del, keep your goddamn mind on business. Now's not the time to be debriefing, now's the time to clean yourself up and make sure you can fight again if you have to. Get your team to capacity before unraveling the rest of it.

"Is there a medkit back here?" He swiped at his face again, cleaning off even more blood.

"You bet there is. Look under her elbow."

For some reason, Brew seemed to find this incredibly funny. At least he shook with mostly repressed mirth, though the car didn't waver on the road.

Del worked the medkit out from under Rowan's elbow. She was out cold. Now that he had a chance to breathe, his shoulder wrenched with pain. He probably *had* almost dislocated it. And the knife hadn't helped any. Neither had the shot to the face, and the little Japanese snot had probably cracked a rib. Lucky it wasn't his spleen. His back hurt, too. The shot to his kidneys.

He suddenly realized he hadn't been thinking about Zed withdrawal for the last half-hour. Instead, he'd been concentrating solely on getting Rowan out of a dicey situation. He hadn't bothered to think about his own survival.

Yoshi slid back into his seat and punched Brew lightly on the shoulder. It was a rare gesture of camaraderie. Brew said something too low to be heard over the soughing of tires on the road as he turned onto the main drag. Lights flashed red and blue in the distance. Police lights.

Brew obeyed the speed limit and took the freeway ramp. Del kept watch out the back window, his hand on Rowan's knee, reassuring himself that she was still alive. He caught no breath of pursuit, but he kept checking. Finally, he let out the long breath he seemed to have been holding since realizing the stairwell was trapped.

Rowan made a small sleepy sound. Del glanced down at her, his heart finally beginning to slow down. His lungs didn't hurt quite as much now. She wasn't very hurt, just had a nosebleed and a slight scratch on her scalp as well as a bruised wrist. He spread antiseptic over the cut and wiped the blood away, checked her again. Pulse strong, her breathing even. She was out cold. The best thing for her right now was rest. Her violated psyche needed a little oblivion to distance itself from Carson's filthy touch.

He managed to bandage himself and changed his shirt in the back seat, wincing and hoping his ribs weren't truly cracked.

Then again, hanging around her will heal me up in no time. He swallowed the sick, acid taste of fear. *Just rest, angel. I'll take care of everything.*

"How did they find us?" Brew shook his head. "What should we do? Henderson needs to know about this."

"Goddamn Carson." Del coughed and considered spitting out the window. *How did Carson get so goddamn close?* "Think he triggered the cops on us to flush us out?"

"We were clean. *You* were clean when you came to the house." Yoshi stared straight ahead out the windshield. "I scanned you and every inch of gear you brought in. Maybe they caught some chatter or codestringing. *Damn* it."

Del was about to reply, but a horrible thought froze him. *The Zed. The bag with the Zed. Maybe the last hypo had a tracker, or the bag itself. My God. I could have led Sigma straight to them.*

He didn't know for sure, but it was a damn good guess, and it felt right to his gut. "It doesn't matter," he said harshly. "We got out of there and Rowan's safe. We'll be cautious and go radio-silent for a while."

Brew accepted this with a nod. "Glad you're here, Del. I wouldn't want to take on Carson alone."

If the old man hadn't been so occupied with Rowan, I would have been dead in the water. She was vulnerable to him, but she put up a hell of a good fight. Delgado shivered. Now was not the time to think about what could have happened.

"Glad I was here too," he mumbled, and settled back in the seat, watching Rowan's breathing. "Let's just hope I hurt them bad enough that they can't follow for a day or so."

* * *

Rowan stayed in a soupy, half-conscious daze for a good three days. They reached the new headquarters thirty-six hours after the attack and Del half-carried her into the main house. He had to admit, Henderson had outdone himself this time. The new base for the Society was a former Catholic school and seminary perched outside a pair of cities that glared at each other over a river and a state line. They were close enough to the urban sprawl that the static of so many deadheads would camouflage them, yet far enough away and with considerable grounds attached to the old school to give them some privacy, plenty of escape routes and room for expansion. It was just about perfect, especially since the property was near an old defunct gravel pit. They had already started the excavations that would eventually make an underground complex too, but it would take a good five years or so before they had anything like the extensive transports and other advantages of the last Headquarters. Having the gravel pit next door would provide them with the perfect means to get construction equipment and get rid of the excavation debris. Concrete and crushed rock could be sold and a legitimate business used as a front.

He didn't see much of it for the first day and a half. After dumping Rowan on a bed in the room Henderson had shown him, he'd made sure their bags were in a pile, thrown a sleeping bag down on the floor in front of the door, and collapsed, leaving Brew and Yoshi to make their reports without him. Henderson wisely left him alone, maybe realizing Del was on the fine edge.

He slept deeply, waking only once to stumble to the bathroom as swords of summer sunlight poked through the gap between the navy curtains and lay along the blue-carpeted floor. When he came out, clumsy with weariness, he instinctively crawled into the bed next to Rowan, past caring about guarding the door or giving her space. Fully clothed except for his boots, he pulled the sheet and blankets up, and curled around her. She was on her side, her back to him, and he immediately fell asleep again. It was dangerous to pass out so completely, but he didn't have a choice. There was a limit to even Sigma-trained endurance.

He returned to the land of the living slowly and piecemeal, surfacing with a feeling he hadn't had in a long time—safety and warmth. Rowan's head weighed down his left arm, and he was sweating in the almost-uncomfortable heat from sleeping in his clothes and under blankets.

Rowan stirred.

She yawned and stretched, her head bumping his chin. He moved automatically, easing his aching left arm from under her head. Then he tightened his right arm around her, pulling her back against him. He took a deep breath, waking up completely with the fuzzy feeling of having slept more than twelve hours.

She was awake. For a few moments she rested against him. Del kept his eyes tightly shut, breathing in the smell of her hair and feeling the electricity of her talent against his skin again. She was safe. Here in this room, in his arms, she was *safe*. The relief was indescribable. He kept breathing, waves of something he was almost afraid to call happiness swamping him every few moments. The feel of her tangled hair brushing his skin was almost too sweet to be real.

Finally, she edged away from him and he reluctantly let her go. She pushed herself up, shaking her head, and slid free of the bed, then made her way on unsteady feet to the bathroom. He opened one eye just enough to watch her, and saw she was moving all right. Her long pale hair fell over her shoulders, tangled and beautiful. She shut the bathroom door, and Del stretched, feeling his joints pop and his muscles twinge in various places. He felt better than he had any right to. Even his shoulder didn't hurt any more, and his ribs seemed to be fine. He curled cautiously up to sit on the bed, grateful when Zed withdrawal didn't immediately start pounding inside his head. It still lurked in his bones, a deep half-healed ache, but his skin prickled like a bad sunburn instead of carnivorous ants. He seemed to be…well, if not cured, then at least halfway there.

Sunlight still fell through the same crack in the navy curtains, and the feeling of dampers closed around him. He sensed other minds inside the building, familiar minds going about their business. The room, carpeted in sky-blue, housed a severe missionary style bed and a dresser in matching pale unfinished wood. The closet door was half open, showing a few dangling hangers and nothing else. It was bare and almost soulless except for their suitcases, duffels, and kitbags in a messy heap. His rig lay tangled by his side of the bed, and he pulled the knife out from under his pillow, sliding it back into its sheath.

When Rowan reemerged, she went straight for the pile of luggage on the floor and started digging until she extracted a toothbrush and toothpaste. She gave him a single inquiring glance, her eyes suddenly very green, their depths shadowed.

He tasted morning in his mouth and nodded. She dug out his toothbrush, too, and tossed it to him. He reached up to catch it, and found himself smiling. Actually *smiling*. It hadn't taken him very long to relearn that trick after all.

She smiled back, the expression lighting her eyes. His chest tightened. The feeling that jolted through him was the same deep emotion he'd felt from her before. Was it *her* or something else? He still couldn't figure it out, could not name something so huge it made his throat close and a hot weight prickle behind his eyes.

"Good morning." Her voice was husky. She slowly straightened, pushing her hair back with one hand. His mouth went dry.

"Morning yourself. How do you feel?" *You survived Carson. There aren't a lot of people that can say that. We were damn lucky to get out of that room alive.*

"Sore. Headache. Feel like I got hit with a train." Her smile widened. "But we must be at Headquarters. I knew we'd make it."

He shrugged, deciding that he *did* want to get out of bed. The carpet was warm under his sock feet. He wasn't unsteady, but he did walk gingerly, testing his legs for any sign of weakness. None seemed apparent. "Give me a couple minutes, can you?"

"Sure." She tossed him the toothpaste and bent back down, probably rummaging for a comb. He shut the bathroom door quietly, more out of habit than out of any real need to be silent. *Alive. We're both alive, and she seems almost happy to have me around. First things first, though.*

It was still a luxury to visit the bathroom by himself, especially one tiled in blue and white with a claw footed bathtub. No shower, but that was all right. It was a bathroom, and he was in it by himself. And Rowan was outside the door. The little things about being a free man, he supposed. He still felt grateful.

Ten minutes later they were brushing their teeth together over the gleaming porcelain sink, a strangely domestic chore. It was unexpectedly intimate, especially since the entire time passed in silence and their eyes met in the mirror more than once. She rinsed her mouth out twice, maybe getting rid of a sour taste that wasn't quite physical. Then she carried a comb back to the bed and sat down, sighing. He watched her pull her legs up and sit tailor-fashion, the slim paleness of her ankle catching his eye for a moment. Even her ankles were pretty.

"I feel like I have a hangover." She began to work on the tangles in her hair, pulling with a little more force than Del would have. "My head hurts."

He settled himself next to her. Watched her profile. This familiarity was so sudden and delicate he didn't want to break it.

"I'm sorry," he offered. "I didn't know he would hit you that hard. I thought he'd concentrate on taking me out."

I thought he'd figure me the bigger threat. Why didn't he? Of course, I was busy with his bodyguard.

Did she wince ever so slightly, yanking at her hair? Maybe it was a particularly bad tangle. "It's my fault," she said finally. "All of it."

Say what? He was actually speechless.

She took a deep breath and met his eyes squarely. "If I wasn't such…an anomaly, Sigma wouldn't want me. My father would still be alive, Hilary would still be alive, Headquarters would still be standing and all those people…would still be alive. And Sigma would never have caught you. I'm sorry." Her mouth turned down at the corners, a bitter but beautiful expression that hurt like a knife between his ribs.

Del's hand blurred out and tore the comb out of her fingers. "Stop it. *Stop* it." His voice tore, deep and husky, in his chest. The comb bounced on the carpet, and she flinched. The small, fearful movement physically hurt him.

Great. Christ. Good one, Del. Now she's just as scared of you as everyone else. But the rage boiling in his veins, the utter *injustice* that she would feel responsible for the fucking jackals of Sigma, demanded he *do* something. He wanted to get up and pace, to throw something, to put his fist through the wall, and to find someone to fight.

Startled, Rowan stared at him. Her eyes were luminous, and full of tears. "Justin," she whispered, her lips shaping the name of a dead man.

A dead man she'd resurrected. It had been *Delgado* for as long as he could remember, until she'd showed up.

His hands shook. He reached out carefully, control clamped tight, and touched her cheek, cupped her chin in his hand. He felt calluses scrape against her soft skin.

Be careful. Christ be careful. She deserves someone who can be gentle with her. Give her something, Del. Come on. Use that psychological pressure you're so good at and help her, goddammit!

"Being a psion isn't a crime, Ro." He had to clear his throat before he could force the words out through the fury constricting his windpipe. "You were born with a gift. You used it to *help* people. And Sigma came blazing in with guns as if you were some kind of criminal, because they think of you as a commodity. A *thing*. It's not your fault, Rowan, it's *not*. God*dam*mit, you're the only good thing that's ever happened to me in my entire goddamn life. Don't do this to yourself."

Well, not the most eloquent speech in the world. Why can't I talk to her? He wanted to tell her so much more. Wanted to tell her that she was good, far better than he would ever be. Wanted to tell her that the only thing that had kept him sane in the hell that was Sigma was the memory of the empty room she'd made in him. Space to breathe in, maybe, or just a part of what he felt for her that he couldn't bring himself to forget. He wanted to tell her what it felt like to see her and ache all the way to the bottom of his chest, a sharp pain that was somehow sweet because even if she could never love a damaged ex-Sigma killer, he would still hang around her, breathing in the same air she breathed, and that was enough.

He wanted to say he loved her, but he buried the thought almost as quickly as it rose.

One of her threatening tears spilled out and left a trail of dampness on her cheek. "You might be right," she whispered, her skin moving against his fingers. "But I still feel responsible."

"Don't," he whispered back. "Please." Then he was leaning forward, and he knew he was going to kiss her. He couldn't have stopped it any more than he could have stopped a bullet once the trigger was squeezed.

Their mouths met. She shook with silent weeping as he kissed her slowly, taking his time, his fingers sliding into the tangled silk of her hair. He was ready to push her back onto the bed and try to get through her clothes to find bare skin, so he could get closer and closer to her. But he settled for breathing her in, tasting her, and barely letting her breathe before he kissed her again. Slowly, slowly, the barriers between them melted, his mind sliding into hers, giving comfort, taking solace. When her mouth slid away from his, he kissed her cheek, her forehead, and the corner of her tear-wet eye, tasting salt. He printed another gentle kiss on her cheek before she leaned into him, pushing him over. He ended up lying across the bed with Rowan in his arms, her head on his shoulder and his arms around her. He felt her heartbeat and cherished the small, uneven sigh as she sank even further into him, the borders of their minds blurring together.

"I missed you," she whispered. "God, I missed you."

"Henderson told me he had to tie you down to keep you from running off to rescue me." The grin felt so easy and natural he almost doubted he was smiling. "I'd have killed him."

"I wanted to. I couldn't leave them when they needed me so badly, but I wanted to. I *wanted* to." The black weight of guilt and grief pouring out of her eased slightly as he hugged her and dipped his chin to kiss her hair. "Every day I wondered if they'd killed you, or if they were torturing you, what they were doing to you. I could tell you weren't dead, but I wondered if I was fooling myself, or if…"

Goddamn. If I'd known…there was nothing I could

have done. Nothing she could have done either. "Shhh. It's all right. You did what you should have." He stroked her shoulder, her hair. "Just exactly what you should have."

"I want them to pay," she whispered. "Sigma. I want them to pay for what they've done so that I can get on with my life."

Oh, Christ. But he didn't say anything. She needed a sounding board more than anything right now. The guilt had only intensified her determination, but it was still a raw, aching wound. She'd been putting herself through hell, and she was probably so contained and professional nobody else had noticed. God knew they had enough to worry about with simple survival. It wasn't like when she'd first arrived and her numb misery had seeped all through Headquarters, making life difficult for everyone. Now she was fully trained, and adept at putting on a brave face.

And he'd been far away while she learned how to fool everyone, unable to help her.

Rowan shivered, a small movement he felt in his own body. He was catching far more of her mood and her private thoughts than she knew. The bond between them was deeper than he'd imagined or hoped.

She was contemplating something dangerous. She was *planning* something. Something was coming together inside her pretty head, a constellation turning into a plan.

"I want them to pay," she repeated. "They have to be held accountable. They kill and beat people and ruin lives, and what they're doing is *wrong*. I have to do something about it."

"We are doing something about it," he reminded her. "We're Society operatives. You've caused them a fair bit of damage in the last few months, angel, by keeping the Society up and running. They're like dogs chasing their own tails. Sooner or later they're going to fall. They can't help it."

And they can force their operatives all they want, brainwipe 'em, hook 'em on Zed—but it doesn't stop some of them from wanting to escape. It didn't stop me *from escaping. Twice, now.* His arms tightened around her.

"But why don't we ever go *after* them? At the top? Who's in charge of the whole thing?"

He sighed. *Distract her with something, Del.* "Probably the President. But if you want to know who's in control of the program, it's Anton." The name sent a slight frisson up his back, and he heard the Colonel's rattling voice again. *You've been a very naughty boy, Agent Breaker.* "They call him the Colonel, but I don't think he ever was one. He's got this thing for white linen suits." *And caning. And electroshock.*

She snuggled against his side, and he relaxed. He knew he should be getting her something to eat and then getting down to business, finding out what Henderson needed him to do. But for right now, it was sweet just to lie next to her, feel her against him, and hear the quiet hum of her thoughts under his. He couldn't decipher exactly what she was thinking, but he heard it like soft voices in a neighboring room, a seashell murmur.

"Anton." A sharp flare of complex feeling burst between them. Del smothered a flash of mixed fear and adrenaline, her reaction was tinted orange with…what? Determination? It felt a little off, but she'd just been through the wringer, hadn't she? "Where is he?"

Del shut his eyes. *I would really rather not remember.* "Sig Zero-Fifteen." He shuddered. "The worst Sig installation in the country." The deep nerve center of the rabid octopus that was Standard Integrative Intelligence Growth and Management Agency. Sigma Installation Zero-Fifteen, otherwise known as the Black Hole.

Otherwise known as hell. The place where people died and brain-shattered hulks of Zed addiction and psychic talent were created.

"Where's that?"

"New Mexico." *Don't ask me any more. Please, angel, don't ask me any more. I don't want to think about that place.*

She didn't. Instead, she sighed. "We should get cleaned up and get some breakfast. Henderson will want to see us."

Are you kidding? This is the first time we've been alone, really alone, together in months. And you're not in any condition to start wearing yourself out again. You're still backlashed from facing down Carson. "If there was an emergency, they'd tell us."

"I'm hungry." But she didn't move. Her hand came up and traced his jaw, rasping against the stubble of a few unshaven days. "I'm glad you're here. I thought you were angry at me, that you didn't want to…"

"Good God, no. How the hell did you get that idea?" *Is that what she was thinking? Jesus.*

"I just…You seemed so distant."

"Me?" He could literally feel his jaw dropping. Distant? All he wanted was to get as close to her as possible, for as long as possible.

"Yes, you." For some reason she found that amusing, and her soft laugh suddenly made him extremely aware that he was alone with her, lying on a bed, with no pressing emergency happening, no scramble to survive or get to the next hiding place. It was as near to heaven as he had ever wanted to get.

Well, maybe he could get a *little* nearer. But she was right. They both needed food, and he could feel her headache pounding in his own skull. Now wasn't the time to show her just how happy he was to be next to her.

Though he was very, *very* tempted to see if she still made the same sound when he buried himself in her. He wanted to find out if she still tasted like sunshine, if she would still arch her back and cry out softly when he let his fingers do the walking, and most of all he wanted to find out if it was, like kissing her, better than he remembered. Still, they were both exhausted, and she probably felt like her head was going to fall off from the aftereffects of Carson's psychic attack. He himself was nowhere near fit enough to indulge in any heart-pounding bed games.

But God *damn* it, he was tempted. If his heart gave out he'd die happy, but he hadn't done even a quarter of what he wanted to do with her yet. "Distance is the last thing on my mind, angel."

She sighed, her fingers sliding down to the place in his throat where his pulse beat, leaping out to meet her touch. "We should get breakfast."

"We should. In a few minutes." *Give me just a few more seconds of this. If I can't have you right now, just give me a few more seconds of having you next to me like this.*

"All right." She made no attempt to move, and for that brief precious span of time, Del was content.

Twenty-One

Breakfast was more like lunch, and it was a hurried meal. This new Headquarters was familiar to Rowan, since she had visited it several times while getting everything ready for the grand move in. As soon as they showed up in the half-gutted industrial-size kitchen they were greeted with Tamara pushing bowls of sesame chicken with jasmine rice, chickpeas, and greens at them.

"Eat," the tall redhead said briskly, "then go up and see Henderson. He's in the west wing. There's something heating up."

Justin let out a sound that was halfway between a laugh and a derisive snort. "See? I told you. If it was an emergency, they would have battered the door down."

"Not bloody likely." Tamara pushed a lock of her coppery hair back and grinned. "You two needed a little time alone. Welcome back, Del."

"Thanks." He sounded genuinely surprised, and Rowan had to hide a smile. Being scattered around without the benefit of Headquarters had at least gotten rid of some of the fear with which they regarded Justin. Nobody had realized just how much they depended on him until they were on their own. It was a good thing, as far as Rowan was concerned. The less they treated him like a pariah, the better.

"Good God, who's doing the renovations in here?" Rowan stared at the mess made of the kitchen—exposed studs and a pile of lumber, cans of paint and a drop cloth, stacks of tiles. She shook her hand out. Her wrist felt a little tender, but not bad. "Did Boomer get called away in the middle of everything again?"

"No, it's actually pretty close to being done. It just looks bad. Eleanor brought a bunch of the newbies back from Calgary and six teams came in, so there's no shortage of hands. And Yoshi just accessed and drained the old resource net, so we're actually sitting pretty when it comes to supplies. Good thing, too. I was getting tired of eating oatmeal and beans."

Rowan made a face and took a spoonful of chicken. Tamara was by far the best cook they had. "Is there coffee? Oh, good. So everyone's coming in?"

"Yep." Tamara grinned. "Thanks to you. If you and Cath hadn't pulled out the stops in Vegas we'd still be eating beans and running around the country like headless chickens."

"Well, Justin actually pulled that one off. I had very little to do with it. Got shot again." Guilt pinched sharply under Rowan's breastbone. She managed to pour a couple cups of coffee for herself and Justin. He seemed easier than she'd ever seen him, and Tamara seemed genuinely glad he was back.

"Don't listen to her." Justin took his coffee with a ghost of a lopsided smile, and blew across the top of the cup to cool it. "It was her quick thinking that got us all out."

"That's usually the case." Tamara examined him, as if trying to put her finger on something. "You look different, Delgado."

"Getting beaten up and smashed on Zed will do that to you." His hazel eyes came back to rest on Rowan. "We'd better eat and then go up to Henderson. Where's a quiet corner?"

He does look different. It's not just the lost weight or the shadows under his eyes. She found herself searching his face, looking for the change. It wasn't just that his eyes had lost their screen of indifference. What was it?

Her head gave another pounding burst of pain, and then subsided. It felt like something was buried in the center of her brain, flaring up again to briefly stain the inside of her skull. She stopped and stared at the floor, trying to locate the source of the pain.

"Rowan?" Justin held his bowl in one hand, his coffee cup in the other, and looked quizzical. Tamara was grinning, a wide sparkling smile that spoke of mischief. She turned back to the stove, and Rowan heard a muffled giggle.

What? What just happened? She didn't know, but Tamara obviously thought Rowan was acting like a hormonal teenager. *I was staring at him, wasn't I? No, I was looking at the floor. Why?* "Hm? Oh, somewhere to eat…I'll go straight up to Henderson, and you can eat in the refectory if you—"

"I'll come with you." The slight smile was gone from his face, and the words were clipped. "Lead the way."

Rowan's stomach threatened to cramp. She wanted to go into the long refectory and find a quiet corner to persuade her body to accept some nourishment, but duty called. Henderson needed her. "Fine. Anything you want Henderson to know, Tamara?"

"Just tell Cath she's not getting out of kitchen duty again. I'll sic Del on her." The redhead seemed to find this extremely amusing, and Rowan frowned. She left the kitchen, still trying to think of what was so different about Justin now.

"Penny for your thoughts," he said behind her as she climbed the stairs to the second floor and started wending her way to the west wing.

Great. Now what do I say? What on earth *did* you say when the man you loved came back after being tortured and wasn't…the same? How could *anything* ever be the same again?

"Not worth it," she said lightly, her boot heels clicking as they went down a long hall with windows on one side and thick golden sunlight falling in dusty rectangles on the wooden floor. Her wrist throbbed faintly, and the bruise was yellow-green and fading, looking weeks instead of days old. "You'd probably get change back."

"Still, I'd like to know. Humor me."

She could tell his eyes were on her back. "You *are* different," she said, taking a gulp of coffee immediately after. It scalded her mouth.

"Better or worse?" There it was, that ironic amusement. At least, she was fairly sure it was amusement. She felt it like warm sun against her shoulders.

"Just different."

"Distant?"

Damn the man, he's teasing me. She shot a look back over her shoulder, saw him smiling and stopped short. He almost ran into her, but gracefully avoided collision at the last second. "Kind of," she admitted. *He never used to smile like that. Maybe once or twice. He was just learning to loosen up a little when Headquarters…happened.* "But there's something else. I don't know. I've been trying to figure it out."

"Just relieved to be back, I guess."

"What did they do to you?" *Torture? More electroshock?* The track marks on his arms were healing, of course. Any wound in her proximity tended to heal faster. He wasn't sweating or shaking like a lot of Zed addicts did, though she could feel the prickling running over his skin, a different sensation than the electric crackle she felt when she touched him. It was hard to keep herself so carefully contained, to keep from soaking into the borders of his mind to find out what he was really thinking under that slight smile and behind those hungry eyes that were really just as effective at keeping his feelings hidden as the flat indifference he used to use.

"Nothing I couldn't handle," he said, again. "We'd better get up to Henderson before the food gets cold."

Her head flared with pain again, a brief tearing that was gone almost as soon as it started. Distracted, Rowan blinked, shook her head. "Oh. Right."

Henderson was in the west wing nerve center, leaning over Yoshi, whose slim brown fingers tapped at a keyboard. They'd apparently set up a full system of decks. Code was flashing across a monitor right in front of Yoshi.

"Mark," Yoshi said quietly into the comm-unit he wore. "Move to your right, there's a dead spot in front of you."

Sounds like an operation. Rowan's mouth went dry. She took another hurried gulp of coffee, scalding her tongue again.

Henderson glanced over and nodded. He'd be with them in a moment. Rowan cast a glance around, found a table covered with topo maps, and cleared a space for both of them. She settled down, watching.

"Heavy fire on your nine, watch out, on your nine." Yoshi sounded calm, as always, but Rowan's heart flipped over. Who was out, and where were they? "Cassie, see if you can give him a little cover. Rick, stay down. Cassie's coming in."

Rick and Cassie. Deborah's team. They must be coming in from California. Rowan caught a flare of complex feeling from Yoshi and swallowed dryly. He'd been hanging out a lot with Deborah, teaching her codestringing tricks.

Rowan was about to push her chair back and hover over him, seeking to help, but Justin's hand covered her bruised wrist. "Eat first," he said. "Won't do anyone any good if you collapse. Come on, Ro."

So she sat and listened through the mission gone critical, barely tasting the food as Deborah reported being pinned under heavy fire with Sigs everywhere and half her team wounded. She didn't sound happy, but neither did she sound panicked.

"Just sit tight, Deb," Yoshi murmured. "They're on the way." Then, he said, "Cath, you read me? They're pinned."

Cath's out there? Oh, God. Rowan listened, mechanically eating and marking off the intervals as Yoshi spoke calmly, only his almost-blurring fingers showing the strain he was under. Rowan kept taking deep, even breaths, the tender places inside her head twinging a little as she fought the urge to help. There was nothing she could *do*. Yosh was perfectly calm and Henderson didn't need her. She could help best by staying out of the way. *Cath's out there. Be careful, honey. I hope Zeke's with her. And Brew.*

"Steady, steady... Here they come. Stay *down*. They're coming in fast. There." Yosh sounded relieved. "Get everyone aboard. Don't *worry* about the Sigs, Deb, that's Brew's job. Yessir, I'm working on it." His fingers danced. "Nasty little buggers, aren't they."

He glanced up at Henderson and nodded. The older man straightened, light glinting off his steel-rimmed glasses.

"Thank God." Henderson's mouth shaped the words. He rubbed briefly at the back of his neck and glanced at Rowan and Justin.

Rowan found, much to her surprise, that she'd eaten three-quarters of her food. Her coffee had cooled down, too. She finished it in two long swallows. Welcome caffeine began to make its way through her bloodstream. "Hey," she said as Henderson approached, his boots clicking on the floor. "What can I do?"

"Not a damn thing." Henderson stretched and rolled his shoulders. The long-sleeved shirt he wore clung to him, and his Glock rode in a shoulder holster over it. He wore jeans, but he was barefoot. His dark hair with the white streak was rumpled and ruffled. "They'll be fine. Cath and Brew will bring 'em all in. Yoshi will be glad to see Deb again."

For some reason, Henderson glanced at Justin, who had finished his food and was staring into his coffee cup. "A Sig net in Cincinnati and some heavy fire. They just snatched a new telepath right from under Sigma's nose. How you doing, Del?"

"Better than I've been in a long while," Justin replied. "Hear you've drained the resource net. Any complications?"

"Nope. Goddamn good to have you back. Rowan, I have some printouts I want you to look over, and I wanted to ask you something." Henderson pulled out the third chair at the table and glanced over his shoulder at Yoshi, whose tension had begun to stain the air now that the crisis was over. Yoshi stretched and went back to tapping at his keyboard.

"Sure." *What on earth would you want to ask me? Justin's back.* Rowan smiled at the thought. *He's back, we're at Headquarters, and we're safe. I never thought I'd see that again.* Her head twinged, the bursts of pain getting less frequent. This one wasn't so bad. She sighed in relief. "How are you feeling, General?"

He granted her a tight smile. "Screwed six ways from

Sunday, girl. Glad we didn't lose you."

Give in. Give in. Give in to me, let me IN. Memory rose, a vise clamping around her temples, something working in, burrowing. The pain tore at her. She was still tender inside her head, bruised from the blind man's attack. Rowan shuddered, came back to herself with a jolt. "I'm glad too."

"Was it Carson? What's his status?" He looked at Justin, his steely eyes glinting, and Rowan was suddenly, utterly, relieved that Justin was back. Being Henderson's second was more stress than she needed, mostly because she was always afraid of screwing up and costing someone their life. Thankfully, it hadn't happened yet—unless she counted everyone at the old Headquarters.

And Justin.

"I hope he's dead." Justin leaned back in his chair. He looked better, his eyes bright and his mouth curling up in a familiar half-smile. He moved easily inside his rig, as if glad to have its familiar weight on his shoulders. He hadn't looked right this morning without a couple of guns hanging on him. Rowan supposed it was habit. She touched the butt of her own Glock, a familiar weight under her left arm.

Henderson reached over for a carafe almost buried under the topos and poured them both fresh coffee. "You need sugar, Ro?" She shook her head no, and he turned his attention to Justin. "You *hope* he's dead?"

"I hit him with everything I had and sank a knife in his throat, boss. If he's still breathing it's not for lack of effort on *my* part."

Oh, God, I hope he's dead, too. Rowan wrapped her fingers around the coffee cup. "Should I go and—"

"No, I need you here. What's your estimation of Carson's status?"

Give in. Give in. Give in to me, let me IN. She shuddered again. Why did it have to sound as if he was still whispering in her head, the squirming maggot-voice tender and waxen-white?

"Creepy." Her voice threatened to break. Tears rose behind her eyes. "Filthy. Very, very bad."

Justin made a small sound, his knee bumping hers under the table. Henderson ran his hands back through his hair. She blinked. Why was it so hard to concentrate? She must be more tired than she'd thought. "What?"

"Do you think he survived?" Henderson persisted.

"I wish I'd had time to shoot him once or twice more,"

Justin muttered. His knee bumped hers again. He was trying to comfort her, she realized, and was oddly grateful for it.

"I don't know." She shivered again, her coffee splashing inside the cup. It was hot and strong, and she wanted another jolt, anything to clear her head of the persistent, soft, maggoty voice. Gooseflesh spilled down her back, her hackles rising as if she was in danger. "I hope not. Justin *pushed* him. He also had a knife in his throat. If he survives…"

"He's survived worse, the old bastard." Henderson stared at the table. "Goddamn it."

It was so unlike him Rowan's eyebrows threatened to nest in her hairline. "General?"

"He was my handler." He spread his hands on the table. "Back in the old days of MK Ultra." He shrugged. "He was a bastard even then. Anyway, let's hope he's at least out of commission for a good long while. How far did he get inside your head, Ro?"

Give in. Give in. Give in to me, let me IN.

"Not very far," she whispered, staring at the table and her almost empty bowl. "Far enough to hurt."

"He didn't get anything of value," Justin interrupted. "I made sure of *that*."

"You know how dangerous he is. We have to be sure." The older man glanced at Rowan. "Are you absolutely sure?"

"Absolutely." Justin's certainty felt warm and reassuring, a flood of sunshine in the middle of her head, cleaning away the remaining filth. But something skittered away, burrowing under the surface of her conscious mind, and she found it suddenly difficult to think. One realization swam slowly to the top, as if swimming through molasses.

"You think he can track me if he's still alive," Rowan said, slowly. "I'm putting everyone in danger."

Justin's fingers tightened on her bruised wrist. "Stop it. You're clean. If you weren't, I wouldn't have brought you in. I'd have holed up somewhere with you until you were all right. Trust me, Rowan. Yoshi scanned us both, and we're both clear."

She nodded, biting her lower lip and looking down at the table. *But if it hadn't been for me, none of this would have happened.*

A sudden wave of self-loathing swept over her. She took a deep breath, blinked back tears, and pushed up to her feet. "Excuse me," she said politely. "I'm very tired. I'm going to take the dishes back down and go get some more sleep. Unless you have something you need me to do."

Henderson and Justin exchanged a long look. What it meant she couldn't decipher. Was Henderson asking if she was truly safe? And Justin making that small gesture—a tiny shrug, his face expressionless, eyes dark—was defending her to the General. But how could he be sure she was clean? What if the slime-drenched mindbreaker had inserted some flaw into her, something Sigs could use to track her down like they had last time?

I don't feel clean, she realized. *I feel dirty. I don't think I'm ever going to feel clean again.*

She wished with sudden vengeance that she could take a scrub brush, not to mention bleach and hot water, to the inner corridors of her mind, cleaning out the contamination. It wasn't just the blind man. It was the whole fantastic chain of events, from meeting Justin outside the abandoned house to the fall of Headquarters to this latest debacle. The Society would get along so much better without her.

"Ro?" He touched her hand, his fingertips gentle. "I'll go with you. I could use a little more sleep myself."

Tears threatened to spill out of her eyes. She tore away, shutting her mind to him with a clenching physical effort, stacked the bowls, and took her coffee cup.

"No. Stay with Henderson, he needs you." *Boy, does he ever. And if I'm infected with something that will draw Sigs...*

The sharp upswell of guilt stopped her in her tracks. They hadn't had a moment's peace since she'd joined the Society. Things had rapidly gone downhill. Justin had practically had to twist her arm to get her to snap out of it and start training to be an operative. Although, to be perfectly fair, he hadn't. He'd left it up to her.

"Don't care." Justin's fingers loosely braceleted her wrist. "You okay?"

No, I'm not. I won't be okay for a long, long time. "Fine. Look, catch up with Henderson." *I'm talking about him as if he isn't sitting right here.* "I just need to rest. That was a hard hit, and I think I'm still a little woozy."

"Sounds good. It can wait." Henderson's eyes were on her, kind and utterly ruthless. "Rest, Rowan. I'll need you soon."

Need me? Like you need a hole in the head, maybe. "Sure," she mumbled, twisting her wrist free of Justin's grip. "I'll see you later."

She carried the bowls away and heard Henderson murmur a question. A worried one, to judge by the tone. *I'd be worried too, General. If I'm dangerous to the Society, you should just tell me outright. It'd be a lot easier than all this pussyfooting around.*

Justin apparently decided to let her go. She walked slowly through the new Headquarters back toward the kitchen. When she reached it, Tamara wasn't there, so she put the bowls in the large industrial sink set aside for dirty dishes and leaned against the counter. She held up her hands.

They were shaking. Her fingers trembled, and so did her palms. She watched them distantly, as if they belonged to someone else. The pain vanished as her mind latched onto the single undeniable conclusion, the only course of action she could possibly take.

"Calm down," she told herself. "You know what you have to do."

She might never have another chance. They called Justin *Rowan's shadow* for a reason.

Kitbag, she thought, suddenly glad to have something to focus on. *And I'll need my duffel. And a car. Can I get out without anyone seeing me? I can do that. This is the Society, after all. They trust me.*

Which is exactly why I have to get away from them. I'm the danger. I'm the bad-luck charm, the reason nothing's going right. God, how could I have been so stupid?

Enough. Time to get going, before Justin decided she wasn't better off alone right now. It wasn't like him to leave her alone, but maybe he was having second thoughts about her now. She had, after all, brought him nothing but trouble. She peeled herself away from the counter and set her shoulders, walking quickly out of the kitchen to get her kitbag. She needed a map, too. Fortunately, she could access the Headquarters intranet with her clearance and get any of Henderson's maps that Yoshi had loaded. She was sure one of them would show Sig Zero-Fifteen.

Forty-five minutes later, her duffel and bag safely stowed in the passenger seat, Rowan crossed the state line and pressed the accelerator. She knew where she had to go next.

Twenty-Two

"Is she all right?" Henderson asked, his tone low and worried. "She looks dazed."

"He hit her hard. And you know how dangerous he is to telepaths." Del shrugged, rolling his shoulders back in their sockets. As soon as she left the room, the prickling of Zed withdrawal settled deep in his bones, twisting. The leftover wounds from his run-in with Carson also twinged, a mounting song of discomfort. He set his jaw and ignored the feeling. She needed a little alone time now, time for her violated psyche to put itself back together. He would only make the situation unbearable by nagging at her. The mental walls between them had slammed up, tinted a deep, dark red with pain and guilt, and he'd noted the shaking in her hands. She needed rest and maybe a little good, old-fashioned therapy as soon as they had both recovered a bit. "She'll be okay as soon as she gets some more sleep, I think."

"What if she's not?" The old man's steely eyes met Del's.

"Then I'll take care of it." He didn't bother disguising the possessiveness in his tone. "Take her up to Calgary, maybe, or go start causing trouble in Europe. Get her out of the country, somewhere nice and isolated where she won't worry so much. She's been scared half to death, old man, and withdrawing from everyone as well." He heard his voice rising and took a firmer grip on himself. He didn't need to start shouting at Henderson.

It was just that she had gotten so damn good at hiding what she felt, keeping that brave face pointed outward. It was frustrating, thinking about the pain that lay behind serene façade. It was even more frustrating to think of how other people must have taken it for granted. She was so powerful and outwardly calm it was easy to assume she was all right.

"I know." Henderson took his glasses off and rubbed at his eagle eyes. "I'm sorry, Del. She's so fucking talented it's hard to know how to approach her. She can do things no other psion I've seen can do. And if I try to tell her to back down, to take a break, she just stares at me with those big eyes of hers. It's like she feels personally responsible for every goddamn thing."

"What, like *you* feel responsible for every damn thing?"

The attempt at humor was met with a wan smile. *Let's leave it alone, General. If I think about this much more I'm going to get angry, and I don't want to do that right now.* "What's the situation like here?"

Henderson took the change of subject gracefully. "Good as it can be. We have plenty of liquid assets and are three-quarters done with the infrastructure. Yoshi's been working around the clock with Cath and the new guy, Lewis. Rowan got him out of a dicey situation, and he's been one hell of an asset. Anyway, we've pulled everyone back in to consolidate. The next few weeks are critical, but we've got every fail-safe I can think of—and a few that were Rowan's ideas—in place. We're as safe as we can be. The newbies are flooding in and undergoing intensive training. Most of them have come through wonderfully. The teams are concentrating, shaking free of Sig nets, and coming in one at a time. There are a few out causing trouble, which is good for us. They'll come in once they've finished a shift and we'll send a few more out."

"Nice." It was hard not to sound openly admiring. "You've been busy."

The old man shrugged, his rig creaking slightly. Henderson was the only person Del knew of—other than himself—who carried his knives everywhere. "Well, it's not like cooling my heels in an Italian villa, but it's good enough. Listen, I want you to take a look at these—"

From that point on it was natural. He'd worked with Henderson for so long it was easy to catch the man's train of thought, and Del was suddenly grateful to be back where he belonged. Funny, but before Rowan he'd never considered that he *belonged* with the Society. But wherever she was felt like home, and this felt more like home than ever, poring over maps, coming up with scenarios, crosschecking protocols and procedures. He didn't notice darkness had fallen until he heard a faint sound and looked up from a stack of printouts, seeing Yoshi slumped over his keyboard, asleep.

Henderson, slumped in a captain's chair behind a folding table that served as a desk, rubbed at his eyes. The sound came again, a tentative knock at the door.

Eleanor cleared her throat. She stood framed in the door, a thin beanpole of a woman with messy dark hair. Her rig was supple and well-oiled, she favored Sig Sauers instead of Glocks. Del was relieved to see she'd escaped the ruin of the old

Headquarters too.

"Hey, Del." She seemed unsurprised to see him. "Henderson, is Rowan around? I heard she'd come in, and Bobby has a new trick he wants to show her. He'd love to see her."

Del blinked. He *reached* automatically for Rowan, meeting only the same hard mental walls, curiously thinned and brittle.

"She came in with Del." Henderson rubbed his eyes and yawned again. "She hasn't checked in with you yet? She was pretty hashed."

Delgado pushed himself up. He *touched* the mental walls, probed them delicately. *Ro? Angel, I need to talk to you.*

No answer. Just a strange sensation, as if his chest was suddenly yawningly empty. An empty room.

Adrenaline spiked through his blood and laid copper against his tongue. Stark, uncomprehending fear smashed through him. *Rowan?*

Rowan! He sent the call out along the private path between her mind and his, the deepest level of their shared bodies. The link reverberated with emptiness. Henderson glanced at him. Eleanor had gone suddenly pale under her dark curly hair. Delgado had no idea what was on his face in that moment, but he was sure it wasn't kind or pretty.

"Oh, God," he heard himself say. His eyes burned with something too deep and hot to be tears. It suddenly clicked into place: her seeming distraction, the waves of pain and guilt, the dazed look on her face.

A fucking compulsion. How could I be so goddamn blind?

"What?" Henderson's capable hands curled around the edge of the table, as if he needed to anchor himself. Yoshi stirred, his cheek pressed against the edge of his keyboard. The monitors flashed.

"Delgado?" The sharp bite of command was in the General's old, gruff voice, but Del was past caring. He half-whirled, as if Rowan might be standing behind him, closed his eyes, and fought for control. The old man's chair squeaked as he rose, slowly.

He probably thinks I'm going to go postal. I just might.

Silence ticked by as he wrestled with himself. Finally, he took a deep breath.

"Carson buried a compulsion in her," he said, forcing the

words out through his teeth. "Of course. The fucker knew he couldn't take her from me, so he cracked through the first few layers of her shielding and planted a compulsion. God*dam*mit." *How could I be so stupid? I saw it, all the signs were there.*

"What compulsion?"

"Isn't it obvious?" Del opened his eyes, and Henderson took a step back, sending his chair over to smack on the wooden floor as if he suspected Del was going to come after him. Yoshi groaned, probably catching the tension in the air. "She's heading to parts unknown, and she's going to get picked up by Sigma, pretty as you please. God-*fucking*-dam-mit."

"What's going on?" Yoshi yawned and stretched, dislodging the comm-unit. It made a small tinkling sound as it hit the desk. "Not another crisis. Please." He yawned again. His black hair stood up in wildly-gelled spikes.

"No worries." Del's boot heel ground into the floor as he turned, Eleanor ducked aside from the door, obviously not wanting to be in his way. "I'll bring her in."

"Del—" Henderson began.

Fuck off and die. She's mine. She belongs to me. I'm going to bring her in. "No, Daniel. I'm the best bet. Sigma won't catch me again, and I stand the best chance of catching her. Jump-off's in ten minutes. I'm taking a car and some gear, and I'm going to bring her in if I have to slaughter every fucking Sig in the western hemisphere to do it."

"Del—"

Don't you understand? Have I not made it clear enough? "No." Just one clipped harsh word, but it stopped Henderson in his tracks.

Eleanor put her hand over her mouth, her eyes wide and haunted. *Christ,* he wanted to say, *quit looking like that. I'll get her back. I'll bring her back.*

He was halfway to the door before Henderson spoke again. "How are you going to find her?" The old man sounded weary.

"I trained her," he tossed over his shoulder, gathering speed. "And besides, I've got to find her. She'd find *me*."

She did find me. She brought me back. Goddammit, why didn't I see it? All the signs were there—unconscious for a long time for the compulsion to sink in and replicate to set up a ricochet, the shaking, the guilt, and the uneasiness. She was vulnerable—not enough sleep and worrying herself sick thinking I didn't want her, thinking she's to blame for everything.

"Del? Delgado!" Henderson actually yelled, but Del was already gone. He was running, not bothering to pace himself. She had several hours' worth of jump on him, and it was up to him to narrow that gap and find her before the compulsion Carson had planted brought her into a Sigma net.

Hang on, angel. I'm coming. And when I find you I damn sure won't make the same mistake again. I'm not going to let go of you until you're safe—and until you're exactly sure of how much you mean to me.

* * *

Del grabbed a map, his duffel, and his kitbag; Yoshi showed up right behind him with a roll of cash and an emergency identity.

"Here." The slim Japanese man shoved the documents into Del's hands. "Henderson's climbing the walls. He's got me running chatscans and everything."

"Thanks." Del stuffed it higgledy-piggledy into his kitbag. "Car?"

"Take the black one." Yosh dangled the keys. His dark eyes were wide and anxious. "She hasn't been herself lately. Too wound up. Bad case of combat jitters." Del snatched the keys. Yoshi didn't flinch. "There's something you should know."

"If it's more of your goddamn Sun Tzu, can it. I've got a serious—"

Yoshi grabbed Delgado's arm. "Listen to me, Delgado. *Justin.* Listen to me."

It was so utterly unlike Yoshi that it penetrated the fog of worry and rising anger. Delgado took a deep breath. When he opened his eyes, Yoshi's hand fell away. "I'm listening," he muttered through clenched teeth. "Make it quick."

"She loves you." Yoshi's mouth was a straight line. "Don't hurt her."

That anyone thought he would harm her hit him like a fist to the gut. Christ, she was the only thing he *cared* about. Why would he even *contemplate* hurting her?

"Hurt her? I'm going to bring her *back.*" *No matter what I have to do. Goddammit, I'm an idiot, a stupid, idiotic moron. I should have seen it, should have seen the warning signs. Compulsion is Carson's goddamn motherfucking specialty. I should have seen it.*

"Be gentle." Yoshi looked more worried, his eyebrows drawing together and his mouth turning down.

"Gentle as I can. But if they so much as touch her I'm going to—" His pulse spiked again, he had difficulty bringing it under control. So much to do. So little time.

"Go." Yoshi let go of him. "Think about it. *She loves you.*"

"Fine, thank you." *I don't know if you're right about that, kid. Someone like her isn't going to love someone like me. It's ridiculous.* "Ammo?"

Yoshi handed over five clips, and Del stashed them in his kitbag as Yoshi said, "Call in if you need directions to a cache. Keep in contact. We'll send as many teams as we can—"

"No, you'll just get them killed. Just me." He slung the bag across his body, picked up his duffel and stepped past Yoshi and out into the hall. "Tell Henderson not to worry. I'll bring her back safe and sound."

The other man didn't reply. Del hoped he was praying. He barely saw the rest of Headquarters on his way down to the garage. He was too busy trying to breathe through the massive ball of panic in his chest.

Just stay alive, angel. Just stay alive until I can get to you.

Twenty-Three

Four days later the green slopes of the Santiago City Veteran's Cemetery lay drowsing under mist and the shadows of rain clouds. Dripping trees stood guard over the silence of the dead, fog sliding between slender boles of lamp posts and the thick green-clad lines of cedar and juniper. Rowan, safe in the shadow of a large cedar, scanned the cemetery once again. She'd parked on the east side, in the warren of back streets she knew from growing up, and jumped the fence. Her head was stuffed with pain and the persistent wrapping of cotton-wool. She'd barely slept, impelled by the sudden, irrational, but undeniable desire to see her father's grave, for maybe the first and last time.

I never even got to go to his funeral. Someone else took the flag draped over his coffin. Someone else was here, probably his friends from the VA and the Moose Lodge. Maybe Marta from the bridge club. I think Dad really liked her.

She breathed in the familiar wet air of Saint City—green and damp and smelling of vegetation and the salt breath of the bay, growth exploding from rain-soaked ground and held cupped in air full of humidity. And under that smell of saturated Nature lurked the other smells of cities: car exhaust, humanity, desperation, money, danger.

Tears lodged hard and unforgiving in her throat. Memory turned like a wheel, shattering inside her head. Her father, grinning as he lifted a six-year-old Rowan into his arms. Teaching her how to change the oil filter in Tuna, Mom's old silver Volvo. Celebrating with a bottle of Dom Perignon when Rowan had graduated from college, and celebrating again with a supper at La Tourelle's in the University District when she graduated from nursing school. Dad's hands, veined and old, chopping garlic for chicken noodle soup, and his younger hands bandaging a scrape on Rowan's knee. And his hand solid and firm on Rowan's shoulder, as they watched her mother's coffin lower into the ground. Rowan had sobbed into a handkerchief, numb with grief and wondering guiltily why her talent hadn't warned her of her mother's death, while her father's weeping was done privately. How much had it cost him to be strong for her sake? She had never thought about it until now.

They were so in love, she thought. Her mother had been

laughing and affectionate, a counter to her father's stalwart military rectitude. Dad hadn't been distant or severe, just...well, too martial to engage in spontaneous hugs or celebrations. Despite that, Rowan had never felt a moment's worth of uneasiness about her parents' love for her or for each other. It was the one thing that had saved her sanity in the face of her freakish talents and her inability to control them. The unconditional acceptance of both her mother and father had reassured her at every turn.

Her best friend, Hilary, was buried at Mount Hope. Much as she wanted to visit the grave, Rowan didn't think she could stand seeing Hil's name on a headstone. Although it was anybody's guess when she would have another chance to come back and visit.

Fury rose inside her again, rage and the weird twisting headache that seemed to burrow into her head, impelling her through the increasing haze of exhaustion. She decided it looked safe enough and slipped out from the shelter of the cedar, brushing bark off her hands. Each step was a struggle. Even the slight hill up to the section housing her father's simple white marker seemed to steal the breath from her lungs and the strength from her legs. She was gasping by the time she fought her way up the slight rise, glad nobody was among the headstones to hear her.

Justin had given her the photos and the map of her father's gravesite, trying in his own way to help her deal with the shattering grief. The thought of Justin tore at her head. For some reason the headache got worse when she thought of him. No amount of pain medication or quiet meditation would make the headache go away. It was as if her head was a large glass pumpkin balanced on her wobbling neck. It invaded her sleep, this harsh sucking pain, until she could barely think straight.

She checked the markers. No. No. No.

Oh, God. God help me. There it was.

Major Henry Price, US Marine Corps. His rank, his date of birth and death. The carved letters were rough under her fingers as she knelt, tracing her father's name.

"Oh, Dad," she whispered. "I miss you. God, how I miss you."

He'd liked Justin, liked him almost immediately. Of course, Justin had chased off that Sig in the parking lot. At the time, neither she nor her father had any idea that a government agency would be trying to kidnap or kill her. Now Rowan wondered how much of Dad's liking Justin had been a small *push*, nothing harmful, just enough to insert this seemingly innocent stranger into their lives.

Her head gave another sharp twist of pain. It hurt to think of Justin. But what else could she think of? What else—and *who* else—did she have left?

Nobody, that's who. Sigma had robbed her of everything.

"I'm going to make them pay." Her voice shook as her fingertips brushed the P, the R, and the I in *Price*. Dad believed in honor and truthfulness. It would have hurt him to think that the government and country he'd fought for was responsible for the things Rowan had seen Sigma do. Broken bodies, battered minds, psions screaming as they suffered through Zed withdrawal—a whole parade of horror unreeling through her memory. If she hadn't *seen* it with her own eyes, been shot at, lived with the suffocating fear, she might not have believed it. Probably wouldn't have believed it. It defied belief.

"Anton." That was the name of her enemy. Colonel Anton.

But if you want to know who's in charge of the program, it's Anton...Sig Zero-Fifteen...the worst Sig installation in the country.

Where's that?

New Mexico.

Henderson had cautioned her never to go near White Sands in New Mexico, or near Mount Shasta in California. "Big Sig installations, like Langley. Just isn't worth the risk," he'd said, and his face had been so grim she hadn't asked more. She should have asked more, maybe she could have done something sooner, maybe stopped this endless parade of pain and death.

The sight of her father's headstone blurred as tears slid down her cheeks, welling up hot and acid from the deepest part of her grief. *Oh, Daddy. I'm going to do what I can. I'm so sorry.*

It occurred to her that this was her fault too, this bare white stone with the bloodless carving on it—nothing to tell how her father was one of the greatest cooks alive, how he could turn anything into a feast, how he loved books on hauntings, the unexplained, psychic phenomena, all sorts of woo-woo, and how just the sound of his voice could make a little girl feel safe and special. There was nothing here but this chunk of rock, carved with birth, death, name, and rank. No color, no *life*, her father's comfortable old age in the house he'd paid for with the daughter he loved all cut short by the goddamn fucking Sigs. Because his daughter was, to put it kindly, a freak.

Rowan straightened. She scanned the cemetery again. No sign of any activity except herself, the fog, and the silent trees keeping watch over the brave dead.

"I love you, Daddy," she whispered, and wished she had time to visit her mother's grave. It suddenly didn't seem right that they were buried in separate cemeteries, her mother on Mount Hope with Grandma Parker, and Dad here. They should be together.

Yet another thing Sigma would pay for.

Rowan ghosted through the cemetery, found a handy spot and muscled herself over the high stone wall. If there were video cameras or the like, let them see her. She hadn't been here before because it was too dangerous, the one place Sigma could be sure of kidnapping her. It was anticlimactic to show up and have nothing happen. Of course, Sigma couldn't be watching *all* the time, and they probably were busy with the teams Henderson had sent out to cause havoc all over the US in order to cover the withdrawal to Headquarters.

She found the car—the faithful blue Subaru, this time with Missouri plates instead of Georgia—undisturbed and got in, resting her aching head against the steering wheel for a moment. *Justin.*

Thinking of him hurt, but it paradoxically made the pain easier to bear. She was used to missing him, true, but the brief period of being near him again drove home just how *much* she missed him. It would have been just as true to call her Delgado's shadow. She had never felt very comfortable away from him for very long. He was the only stability in her fragmented world.

Her fault, again, that he'd been taken and tortured, suffered God-knew-what that he didn't want to talk about, not even to her. Self-loathing crawled over Rowan's skin like the soft maggot fingers that had squirmed inside her brain.

When she surfaced, staring at the world outside the car, the fog had thickened. She twisted the key in the ignition and was rewarded with a softly-purring engine. She switched on the headlights and spent a few minutes driving aimlessly down the hills. When she found herself on the very north end of Smyrna Avenue, she knew miserably what she was about to do, and couldn't stop herself. It was like a train wreck or an automobile accident. She simply could not look away. She drove down Smyrna, stopping at stop signs and creeping through uncontrolled intersections, passing the laurel hedge that blocked the sight of the dilapidated old Taylor house. She didn't want to look. Gooseflesh stood out hard and knobbed on her arms. A right on Ninth Street, two blocks… and she brought the car to a halt, her heart rising in her throat.

The neat, well-kept two-story house they had worked so hard on was now a shambles. Rowan made a small, hurt sound in the back of her throat as she stared at the broken windows, and the lawn rank with weeds. Nobody had bought the house. Had it stood abandoned since that night? Yellow crime scene tape fluttered on the porch where Rowan had sat so many summer evenings, where her mother had almost fallen off while watering the roses—and oh, the roses themselves were dead or dying, brown rot all over their lovely leaves and stems. Dead leaves clustered under the old oak trees, and a fallen branch lay buried in weeds and leaves. The door was broken down, barred only by the yellow crime scene tape. She wondered if anyone had cleaned out the fridge, if her books were still upstairs swelling with moisture from the damp coming in through the front door and broken windows. And if there were still stains on the kitchen floor. Big, dark, bloody stains.

There were no cars behind her, but Rowan started violently as if hearing the blast of a horn. She sat upright, wiped at her eyes with the back of her hand. More tears spilled down her cheeks.

Got to get going. She checked over her shoulder for nonexistent traffic and pulled out, hoping she wasn't weaving. Her vision ran and blurred with both pain and tears. She navigated with ease through familiar streets, each new change—the Martin's house was repainted, and yards were redone, businesses had gone up and others had faded—slamming into her stomach like a badly taken punch. Each time she lost a little more air.

Oh, Justin, she thought, ignoring the spike of pain his name sent through her. *I need you. I'm sorry.*

Then she hit the freeway heading south. She would cut east past the state line and start wending her way into the land of desert, rattlesnakes, Four Corners, and White Sands. She just had to get close enough to Sig Zero-Fifteen and get herself arrested or caught, and Sigma would take care of the rest.

And then, Rowan could get her revenge.

* * *

Four days later she woke in the middle of the night, her breath coming short and harsh in her chest, the soft maggot-writhing voice whispering inside her head. Sweat cooled on her skin as Rowan sat up, gasping, reaching blindly for a light, any light. The lamp on the two-drawer nightstand next to the bed toppled alarmingly before she could catch it and find the button to turn it on. When it finally clicked, the hotel room resolved itself into horrid pink and beige around her.

She let out a coughing breath as her head twisted with pain. *Justin?* Instinctively, she had reached for him again on waking. Why did thinking about him hurt her head so much? What was wrong with her?

Rowan found herself clutching the phone, her fingers poised above the keypad. She laid the phone back in its cradle, hoping she hadn't dialed. Who would she call? There was nobody *to* call. If she called in, Henderson would have a fit and probably officially throw her out of the Society. And Justin…What did he think? Did he think she had betrayed them?

Never. I never would.

But if they started to torture her or injected her with Zed, how long would she be able to hold out? She had no illusions about her capacity to deal with torture. Justin might be able to endure the unspeakable, but Rowan knew very well *she* couldn't. Though she had, since joining the Society, done some amazing things when forced to. If they tortured her before she could get her revenge, she would just have to see how strong she truly was.

Rowan lifted her hands and examined them in the warm, forgiving light of the bedside lamp. They shook, her fingers almost blurring. "Look at that," she said. "I'm so brave. What am I *doing*?"

Revenge, the persistent little voice whispered in her head. *Revenge. Revenge.*

She settled cross-legged into the creaking mattress, pain cresting inside her fragile, aching head again. *Something's wrong. Something's very, very wrong. I'm not thinking clearly.*

Just then, the sensitive fringes of her mind registered a *touch*. It was light and fleeting, simply a brush against the very outer borders of her awareness, as if someone had stepped into a room and hastily stepped back.

All uncertainty faded. Rowan reached under her pillow for the knife. She wasn't close enough to be sure she would be taken to Zero-Fifteen. There was another installation just thirty miles from here they would probably drag her to. She wasn't even under dampers, was she? She couldn't remember turning any dampers on, and the funny, naked feeling she always had under dampers was gone.

The knife blade gleamed in the bright electric light. She jammed her feet quickly into her boots and slid out of bed, her jeans rasping against the bleached sheets, then ghosted on silent feet to one side of the door, knife held low and reversed along her forearm. She was sleeping in her clothes, only taking her shoes off and sometimes not even that. She might have to move quickly and couldn't afford the time it would take to get dressed if she was attacked. Adrenaline washed the pain from her head and narrowed her concentration.

Now she could hear someone fiddling with the doorknob. Air-conditioning washed chill over her skin, and the unit in the window made a racket that would cover any noise she made. Rowan slowly sank down, crouching, wishing she hadn't turned on the light. A dark room for eyes adapted to the light outside in the hall would have given her an advantage.

The cheap deadbolt was eased open. Someone was very good with a set of lock picks, not everyone could tickle a deadbolt. The chain on the door was almost useless, held only by one flimsy screw. She had left it open. Why? That was a violation of procedure. Even a flimsy chain was better than no chain at all.

Now the doorknob began to turn, a millimeter at a time.

Whoever this is, they're going to get a big fucking surprise.

If it was a Sig, she intended to do some damage before letting them catch her. If it was anyone else…

The doorknob turned. The adrenaline freeze poured over Rowan's vision, everything standing out sharp and clear—the nap of the cheap bedspread, the horrid beige carpet, the print of a fruit-basket over the useless television, the individual scratches left on the painted wall from other people banging their luggage carelessly around. Rowan's pulse slowed. She was still and quiet as an adder under a rock, buttoned down tightly, not daring to scan outside the door in case the attacker was a psion.

The door released. The attacker waited a moment before opening it an inch at a time. Chill industrial-filtered air swept across Rowan's body as she slashed, her legs turning into coiled springs, driving a shoulder into the attacker's hard-muscled midriff and spilling them both to the cheap harsh carpet out in the hall. She struggled wildly, her right wrist caught in a bruising grip and locked, twisted mercilessly until the knife dropped. Then he grabbed her other wrist and rolled, effectively trapping her. A sharp twisting psychic attack smashed into her already bruised and vulnerable head.

She shunted the force of the attack aside, not even bothering to turn it back on him. Rowan found her mouth near his shoulder, so she did the only thing she could, training suddenly shoving aside fear. She *bit* him as hard as she could, thrashing wildly.

He let out a short barking cry. She brought her knee up swiftly and rolled free as his arm loosened, scooping up the knife as she made it to her feet. She threw a kick, catching the man squarely in the face, and catching a glimpse of blond hair as he collapsed backward. Then Rowan was on him again, the knife sinking into flesh with a solid sound.

Memory cascaded inside her head. She seemed to remember a blond man clutching her arm as Justin, bloody and battered, raised his hands slowly, one full of a knife blade that glittered through the drugged haze of sedation.

The man swore in a vicious whisper and Rowan stabbed again, the knife sinking in just as Justin had taught her, the shock of blade meeting bone jarring up to her shoulder. *Twist it, break the suction of muscle on the blade, good girl. Just like that.*

The man gurgled on the floor under her. Rowan got one foot on the floor, her knee in his midriff. She let out a short, sharp breath. The man was in Sigma gear. They'd found her, all right.

A small *psshht!* sound jerked her halfway around, but not before a spear of ice buried itself in her shoulder. *Ow! What the hell—*

Comprehension burst inside her head just as the compulsion broke, shattered by its consummation, and Rowan's entire body turned to lead. The drug was quick, the tranquilizer dart loaded with something icy and prickling that flooded her. For one agonized moment before her head hit the floor she understood that she had been trapped like an idiot, and she was very, very grateful Justin was safe back at Headquarters.

Sigma had her now.

Twenty-Four

Del watched from the screen of thick bushes at the side of the parking lot as the Sigs carried down two limp forms. One was Rowan, her pale sheaf of ash-blond hair rising on the faint, chill night breeze. Two Sigs carried her to the black van and bundled her in.

Del's hands turned to ice.

The second person they carried was a man with familiar blond hair. *Andrews. I'd bet anything that's him.* A hard, satisfied agony burst in Del's chest, and his arms and legs turned to ice. He drew back into the shadows, but they weren't scanning for him. They had what they'd come for. If he'd been a little quicker he might have saved her, but now it was too late. She wouldn't be served by him getting himself caught too.

Oh, Rowan.

The limp male body *was* Andrews, the bastard recognizable even in death. They bundled his body into the second black van, and more of them carried her duffel and kitbag. It was the off season and the parking lot was empty of everything except a smattering of cars. Not many people came down south in spring or summer when the heat got unbearable. By tomorrow her hotel room would be empty and wiped, no trace left of the woman who had stayed there.

He had narrowly escaped the Sigs himself in Saint City while following her. She had taken suicidal chances by operating without dampers and doing everything but getting arrested and shouting, *"Here I am, boys!"* It was a wonder she hadn't been picked up until now.

Too late, too late, I'm too fucking late. Where are they taking her?

She'd accessed an old map from the intranet at Headquarters. He could have told her it was out of date. There was an old Sig installation near here, but it had been closed for a good five years. That made the closest installation Zero-Fifteen.

The belly of the beast itself.

Are you crazy, Delgado? You just escaped from there. There's no way you can go back in. Christ, they'll eat her alive and there'll be nothing left but a husk. They'll break her. Anton will break her. Don't do it. Please don't do what you're contemplating. It's insanity. You won't make it out alive.

He reached out blindly, his hand closing over a juniper branch. He squeezed, hearing the crackle of dry wood under his fingers, strangely removed. *Besides, she doesn't love you. She couldn't. She's not that type. She's good, and you're not. What the hell are you thinking?*

The vans roused themselves, purring like beasts. The one carrying Rowan made a short, sharp half-circle in the parking lot, its headlights splashing wetly against other cars. Del ducked instinctively, even though his cover was good and he was sure they couldn't see or sense him. The invisible man, Justin Delgado.

The receding fire of Zed withdrawal burned under his skin. He felt cold. His legs had turned to solid blocks of ice.

If they caught him, he was done for. He was *finished.* There was no way he could penetrate Zero-Fifteen and get her out. None.

I'll just have to be careful then, won't I? I escaped once.

But *escaping* was not the same as penetrating a high-security installation without backup and bringing out a potentially broken psion. It just wasn't.

He fumbled for his cell phone. Then he shut his eyes and breathed in the smell of dust and junipers. Here he was crouching in the bushes, looking for a snakebite or worse, dithering. None of it mattered. The only thing that mattered was that van, carrying Rowan away to a fate she probably couldn't imagine but Del could picture all too well.

The vision of the empty room, Rowan's room, rose again. Drenched in sunlight, he could almost feel his pupils contract against the force of that light. The scarves thrown across the bedstead glowed in rich blues and greens. The plants grew green and lush, healthy, and the bookshelves were jammed full. The French door to the small balcony was open a little, wind stirring the curtains as they hung. He took a deep breath, smelling Rowan's skin.

I missed you. Her voice, soft and vulnerable, the feel of her hair under his fingers, and the weight of her head on his shoulder.

It didn't fucking matter if it was impossible to get her out of there. Nothing mattered except finding her and freeing her.

He opened his eyes, faintly surprised to find himself still crouched in the bushes. The second black van idled with its side door open. They were coordinating in there. It was against procedure to have the side door open, but being in there with a dead body probably meant they wanted a little ventilation. It was a picture-perfect opportunity. He slid the cell back into his pocket and eased out of the shadows, sliding the knives free of their sheaths.

Hold on, angel, he thought. *I'm coming to get you.*

There was really no other choice.

* * *

The *push* left him in a scalding wave of fire, slamming over the top of the driver's mental defenses. There were three in the van: driver, handler, and Zed-wiped psion. Blood dripped down Delgado's face. He ignored it in the cresting agony of his talent as he rammed through walls and false trails, breaking the driver's mind and taking what he needed. His hands shook as he held the garrote, a simple thin piece of wire with wooden handles. No other Society op carried this. It was his own little secret. He yanked back, keeping the pressure on and hearing the crackles as the small, deep bones in the throat snapped. The driver was like Andrews, a complacent psion, a military man used to unquestioning obedience.

Del kept the pressure on, and the man's hands flailed wildly. One hit the window with a hollow sound.

I am not a very nice man, he thought, with a kind of dark hilarity. The *push* rang inside his head. Behind him, the Zed-wiped psion moaned.

The driver's mind broke in a shower of psychic sparks. Del coughed, his injured shoulder throbbing. He'd made sure Andrews was dead by sinking another knife into the man's throat and wrenching back and forth. Andrews's body laid half-in, half-out of the van, his head dangling out toward the pavement. *Have to pull him in and get that door closed.*

His fingers ached as he released the garrote. *Rowan.* She wouldn't like this at all. No, she would be horrified. *Suppose it's a good thing she can't see, right?*

He pulled Andrews back in and closed the side door. Then he settled back against the side of the van, his head resting against a small console. This van, like any other Sigma workhorse vehicle, was stuffed with electronic equipment, screens glowing green, strings of code flashing across two monitors. The small space available for humans was taken up with bodies. In the very back, the psion moaned again. He was handcuffed to a console to keep him out of the way. Del scrubbed at his face with his hands. He needed a plan. *Deep, even breaths*, he reminded himself, as if he was talking to a trainee. *If you can't breathe, you can't think.*

Breathe, Delgado. Just keep breathing.

It took a while to get the limp body out of the driver's seat. Thank God, the van was still in "park." The last thing he needed was to be in an uncontrolled vehicle with three dead bodies and a moaning, handcuffed idiot. Del slid into the seat and spent a few seconds looking at the steering wheel, trying to remember how to drive. *Goddammit. Stop it. You're not in shock. Rowan needs you. Get your ass in there.*

"Section 511, report in," a voice crackled from the radio on the dash. He almost jumped. The smell of death was thick and rank in the close confines. He thought briefly, longingly, of opening the window. "Section 511, report. Zero clear?"

He reached for the radio, the information he'd wrenched from the driver's mind sliding fresh and bloody into place. "511 reporting," he said into the handset, in what he hoped was a normal voice. "511 is zero clear. Proceeding as planned, over."

"Ten-four. Over and out." Apparently satisfied, the voice retreated.

Del closed his eyes. *I need a plan.*

Trouble was, he didn't have one. He buckled the seat belt, slipped the van into gear, and coughed rackingly. First he had to get rid of the bodies.

Then he was going to call Henderson.

Twenty-Five

Darkness. Soft, forgiving darkness. Burn of a needle in her arm.

"It's not Zed," the voice said. Male, slightly whistling, familiar. "Calm down. It's not Zed. It's just a little cocktail to keep you calm while we discuss things."

Rowan's eyelids fluttered. Light slowly, slowly flooded into her aching head. The drugs took effect quickly, wrapping her in a warm blanket. She could not move, but she was upright somehow.

Justin. Where's Justin?

Her head pounded dully. Her eyelids were heavy, so heavy, and she was strapped against something hard. Her head lolled to the side. "Whaaaa…" It was a long, slurred word. Her mouth wouldn't obey her.

"Just be calm," the familiar voice said, and uttered a high whistling giggle of glee. "Nice and calm. I've waited a very long time for this. Shame we couldn't have done it earlier, before the testing was complete."

I know that voice. I know *that voice. Where am I?*

But she knew. Sigma had her.

With that revelation came a flood of memory and the strength to lift her head, even through the blurring disorientation of the drugs.

What greeted her was obviously a lab—long bare counters, different apparatus set at intervals, and two monitors at the far end blinking with screens of data. She was strapped to a chair, leather restraints around her wrists and ankles, as well as her knees, elbows, torso, and throat. The effect was almost total immobility, though she could wriggle a little and loll drunkenly from one side to another. Wires dropped from her forehead, probably attached to electrodes. She could see an IV pole, some kind of drip. Sedation? Maybe.

The lighting was clear and low, obviously turned down, and she blinked as a familiar face swam into view. Moist, dark eyes behind horn-rimmed glasses, thin cheeks and sawlike cheekbones, liver-spotted hands trembling as he raised one and shoved his glasses higher on his nose. He wore a rumpled white lab coat, and recognition slammed into her.

"Jilssen," she breathed. The traitor who had shut down the security grids and let Sigma into the old Headquarters was standing right in front of her. Justin had mentioned seeing him again and confirmed that he was the one responsible for the carnage. It was small consolation that Rowan's instincts had been right about the good doctor all along. If only she'd known what her instinctive response to him had *meant*, she might have been able to avert the massacre. But even Justin hadn't been able to find anything at the old Headquarters. Jilssen had covered his tracks too well.

"Hello, Rowan!" He beamed at her, as if she was a prized specimen. His yellowed, strong, crooked teeth almost glowed. "It's *so* good to see you again, without any interference."

"Traitor." Her mouth wouldn't work quite right, and her head seemed too heavy for her neck to hold up. She sagged against the restraints. "*Traitor.*"

He shook his head, his smile dimming a little. "You'll soon see things in a different light, my dear. There's important work for you to do. You'll be serving your country, and that's very important. You should feel proud."

She could see a rack of test tubes, and wires leading off to something. The air smelled like chemicals and burned insulation. There was another faint pervasive stench—human pain and desperation. Wherever this place was, several people had suffered here. Suffered terribly. "What…What are…"

"When the Colonel gets here, we'll begin. You see, Rowan, Sigma is just the first step. We've been trying to create something very important, a physical bulwark, as it were. Several years ago…" He muttered something, scooped up a clipboard and checked it. "He's late. Dammit, it's not like him to be late."

The Colonel. Adrenaline flooded her, fighting the sedation. It became a little easier to think. *Anton? Maybe. Where have they taken me? How long have I been out? If the Colonel's here, I can…*

The dream of revenge faded, replaced by a cold feeling in the pit of her stomach. *Stupid, stupid, stupid!* The blind man had buried something in her head, something deep and foul, pushing her through the maze until Sigma could scoop her up. He'd distracted both Justin and her with pain and slipped the fishhook in, neat as you please. Rowan hadn't recognized or felt it because she'd been too busy worrying. Useless, frantic worry. She should have listened to Justin. She should have…

Well, too late for that now. Her head was clearing rapidly. Her freakish talents did that, burned up pain medication and tranquilizers much faster than normal. She tested the straps, taking care not to make any sudden moves.

They were tight and hard. She couldn't get free even if she tried. Now was a fine time to wish she was telekinetic like Cath.

What's going on? Come on, Ro, keep him talking. She let her head drop to the side, as if she was still drugged. "Whaaat?" she moaned, deliberately trying to make her voice loud and drunk.

Jilssen's watery eyes moved over her, a touch almost as filthy as the maggot-squirming blind man's. "You see," he said pedantically, "all along, we've been trying to *create*. We need reliable means of reproduction. There's only so much a coerced psion will or can do. Agent Breaker proved that, at least. We can't offer the type of benefits the private sector can, and we lost a great deal of talent to the private sector before we started pursuing our policy of necessary persuasion."

I wish he'd stop pontificating and use a noun, give me something to work with. She took a deep breath and tried to still herself. If this Anton was due along any minute, she might not have much time to figure a way out of the restraints.

The idea came like a gift, a haphazard plan depending on instinct, as usual. *Oh.*

It was risky, but she had to try. She didn't know what the drug he'd injected her with would do to her ability to concentrate, but it was worth a shot.

It took more effort than she thought possible to still herself, to reach for that space of quiet calm where most of her talent lived. She listened to Jilssen's babble with half an ear while she let her breathing lengthen. Her pupils dilated as she found the space of alpha waves and pressed, sliding home. Immediately the room seemed a little brighter and the situation a little more hopeful.

"That's why we try to get them young, raise them right. Unfortunately, there's something amiss. They are always highly resistant."

Of course they are. You're a bunch of repressive fascists. The thought braced her. It sounded steady and amused, with an edge of ironic anger, just like Hilary. She *reached* delicately, searching for the fringes of his mind through the blur of the drug. It was hard, slippery, exhausting work. Rowan felt sweat trickle down the channel of her spine, smelled the chemical reek of exhaustion and her body metabolizing the drug, pushing it out through her skin.

Jilssen leaned against the counter, watching a monitor turned away from her. "Heart rate steady, respiration normal," he murmured. "EEG normal. Very good. *Very* good. You like the alpha waves, don't you, Miss Price? Empaths always do. Anyway, we discovered we had to *create*. It was a farfetched scheme, but one I felt was viable. And of course, it was shelved until we came across the perfect psion, one who can alter cell metabolism and body functions almost at will. A psion capable of producing the focused bioenergetic fields necessary to alter genetic material and…" Jilssen paused, shaking his head. Rowan breathed deeply, firmed her concentration, and tried again. The borders of his mind were so slippery, and the touch filled her with disgust she *had* to push aside to make this work.

He continued, evidently liking the sound of his own voice. "There's a time factor, of course. Your body isn't capable of producing more than one at a time. But once we have three or four good stocks to breed from, we can begin to approach the problem of stem cells. There's been some promising advancement—"

Contact.

The sewer of a normal mind flooded her. Jilssen didn't have any psionic talent, which made his ability to hide his intentions from the Society all the more remarkable. There was the shadow of another mind behind his, a psion whose mental footprint filled Rowan with a frantic loathing and made her wonder if she'd ever feel clean again.

Ah. So that's why he was so nervous when some of the kids in Kate's class practiced their talents on him. He was afraid they would find out.

The mental walls holding his secrets were strong and thick, oozing slime. She didn't even try to breach them. She didn't want any of Jilssen's secrets. She would settle for getting out of his reach.

She *pushed* again, very gently. Very delicately. Jilssen, still babbling, moved toward her, his liver-spotted hands trembling. He placed one hand on the restraint on her left wrist and began to unbuckle it slowly, unaware of what his hands were doing under her mental grip.

"—and of course, we have to pick the stock very carefully. We have samples to be cross-checked, and you can be artificially inseminated. With your penchant for healing, it won't take long, and I wonder if the gestation period will be shortened because of your accelerated healing? It's a question I've often posed to myself. Anton thinks you'll gestate normally. We have a rather large wager."

Another psion built defenses for him, defenses so good we couldn't tell what he was planning. Who?

Loathing bloomed under her skin as her attention drifted across Jilssen's words. They wanted to breed her.

He unbuckled the restraint at her left elbow and then moved to her right wrist. Rowan's head pounded with the effort of keeping him under control, pushing him so gently, so carefully. A soft beeping began, a red light flashing down at the end of the lab. He didn't notice, and Rowan hoped he wouldn't. She strengthened her hold on him carefully, one fine thread at a time, every lesson Henderson and Miss Kate had taught her standing her in good stead.

The old Rowan would have never been able to shut out the waves of disgust and terror threatening to swamp her. She trembled with both effort and repressed anger, her will turning to steel. The *push* tipped delicately, subtle mental control so insidious she was almost horrified at herself.

Her right hand was free. He moved slowly, so damn slowly. She gathered herself as his hand came to rest on the restraint over her right elbow.

"Of course, we had hoped to have you and Agent Breaker at the same time," he breathed. His halitosis was rank and foul, and she saw with frenzied revulsion that his free left hand was playing with the button on his khakis, reaching down to cup his genitals. No wonder this man had always repulsed her. "A specimen with his talent and yours would make a very fine soldier. *Very* fine, once we breed out that regrettable streak of independence."

Something in Rowan snapped. Pure unadulterated rage boiled out. *Haven't you fucking done enough? Breed me, breed Justin, like animals? Would you watch while we copulated or just inseminate me at a distance?*

Jilssen's eyes cleared. He stared at her from behind his horn-rimmed glasses, his gaze suddenly confused. Horror and comprehension wandered across his face as he looked down at the unbuckled restraints.

Too late. Rowan struck.

Fear. Agony. Guilt. The fury of her retaliation, the absolute incandescent rage she had never dreamed herself capable of. She battered at him with the full force of her horror and loathing, her thirst for revenge. For each traumatized, broken psion she had nursed back to health, each grief she had swallowed, each horror she had witnessed. She poured it all into his brain, striking like a snake, severing vital connections, smashing and burning everything she could reach.

He fell as if shot, straight down, his head clipping the arm of the chair by her hand with murderous force. Something sparked wildly in the lab, the monitor closest to her emitted a shower of fireworks and popping noises. She reached up, her hands clumsy, and unbuckled her throat, her torso. Had to get her legs free. *Oh, God.*

Jilssen lay still on the floor, crumpled in his soiled lab coat. She blinked back tears. Her head pounded fiercely, the dull red smolder of rage like the aftermath of a forest fire through ash and trails of smoke, a wrecked mind, a wasteland. She smelled blood and feces—death had not come gently for Jilssen. She'd seen enough death by now to know about the sphincter's loosening with its advent. He lay twisted on his side, a bloody gash in his temple where it had hit the arm of the metal chair, his arm curled awkwardly under his body. If she hadn't known better she would have sworn he was sleeping. Except there was no glow of thought, not even the banked messy fire of a normal mind at rest.

I think I'm going to throw up. Please, God, don't let me throw up.

She managed to get her legs free, her fingers shaking, then ripped the electrodes off her forehead and tossed them. She tore the IV out of her arm. Immediately, she felt better. Not by much, but better.

Her duffel and kitbag were nowhere in sight. No weapons. The red light flashing at the other end of the lab taunted her. She was in her sock feet, jeans, and a tank top. She dragged her fingers back through her tangled hair, trying to think. Why were the lights turned down in here? What had Jilssen planned on doing to her before Anton came? She shuffled away from the chair and the slumped human body, needing to get away. Her skin crawled.

A shiver bolted up her spine. *Where am I? The installation I was nearest to was thirty miles away. Or did they take me to Zero-Fifteen? What do I do now?*

She crouched behind a lab counter, her breathing coming hard and fast as she tried to *think*. Anton, this Colonel, was due any minute. He was late for a meeting with Jilssen, maybe to gloat over her capture. She cast around wildly for a weapon, any weapon.

Could she do it again? She'd killed Jilssen with her mind. The very thought made her sick to her stomach. Sick, but also…Well, there was an unholy glee to the thought. A cleansing, murderous satisfaction. A step toward revenge, no matter how small.

Good God, I'm no better than they are. The thought flashed through her mind and was immediately discarded. She could almost hear Justin's voice. *Move and think, operative. You've got to move* and *think. One without the other is useless. Get going.*

She searched for a weapon and found none. Even the clipboard had only a flimsy plastic pen, not likely to stand up to any real abuse. The red light and soft beeping continued. She glanced at the two monitors and discarded them as useless. Her fingers curled around a heavy, empty glass beaker. Didn't Jilssen at least have a gun here? *What I wouldn't give for my kitbag. And boots. I'm in my frigging socks.*

The thought was welcome and rational. She let out a sigh of relief just as a soft chime rattled against her ears. She threw herself down, taking cover behind a long, low counter as there was a whoosh—the sound of a door opening. *Voice activated? Or maybe some kind of key? They had those sorts of doors at Headquarters, too.*

The thought of the carnage at the old Headquarters filled her with fresh fury. It was as if all the anger she'd ever pushed away or repressed in her life was now welling up, demanding an exit. Demanding to be *used.*

And God, the idea of using that fuel scared and exhilarated her in equal proportion.

"Jilssen?" A hard, old voice, smooth as silk over a steel table, slightly rasping. "Henrik?"

She shuddered, crouching behind the counter. She heard a tapping—a cane, a footstep, a cane.

Oh, my God. The image of the blind man's cane tapping, sweeping the floor, rose. *No. Not again. Not again!*

She absolutely could not endure another rape of her mind.

Rowan came up into an easy crouch, her head still well below the top of the counter. Her breathing evened out and she closed her eyes, seeking the stillness inside herself. She felt the static of another psion approaching.

Her breathing calmed, her pupils dilated, her hands stilled

a little. She now knew what a trapped animal felt like when the hunter approaches the snare. She clutched the glass beaker so tightly her fingers ached. It was the only weapon she had.

That and her mind. The freakish talent they wanted to breed her for.

Silence. The tapping footsteps stopped. Could he see the wreck of the chair and Jilssen's body? If he could…

"Why don't you come out, Miss Price?" The voice tugged gently at her, whispered comfort. "I don't blame you. Jilssen was a pervert. Why don't you come out and talk to me? I can make everything right."

Breed me like an animal, hunt me like an animal, and now you want to make everything right? There is no way this could ever be right, you son of a bitch, whoever you are. The borders of her mind were clear and strong, bolstered by the anger that even now filled her blood with a siren song of vengeance.

One more tapping step. She could almost hear the creaking of the cane. Then she heard another sound—the definite click of a hammer pulled back.

Come out so you can shoot me? How stupid do you think I am? On the other hand, here she was, captured by Sigma through her own stupidity. Her own weakness. Nevermind that it had been a compulsion. She should have been strong enough to resist it.

"Come out, Miss Price. We can discuss this like civilized beings. I know you are at heart a very calm, rational person." He sounded so *sure* of himself, so certain she could come creeping out like a stray dog to a food dish.

Oh, I'm calm and rational all right. But not now. You've pushed me too goddamn far. And all this time I thought it was Justin who was the dangerous one.

"Your psych profile indicates a high degree of compassion and empathy, probably a by-product of your rather unique gifts. We can offer you a chance to serve your country and be a legal citizen, as well as help others, Miss Price. Daniel Henderson and his ragtag little group can't offer you that." The voice pulled, tugged, sang, cajoled, enticed. It was easy to see what this man's psionic talent was. Rowan shut her eyes, leaning her forehead against the slick, cold plastic of a cabinet door. "They are, after all, only criminals. Offenders with warrants and prices on their heads."

Cath. Brew. Zeke. Henderson. Yoshi. She thought of them

desperately—of Cath's fierce loyalty and irrepressible optimism, of Zeke's phlegmatic good sense and plain, unadorned love for Cath, of Brewster's quiet efficiency, and Yoshi's calm, practical endurance. And Henderson, who worried about them all, and for whom perfection wasn't good enough when the life of an operative was on the line. She thought of them in the dark tunnel beneath the wreck of the old Headquarters, thought of Brew pressing a bandage over her bleeding gunshot wound and hustling her to safety, of Cath driving with the windows down and her cigarette fuming, of Eleanor and her clutch of newbies, of Boomer's crusty exterior covering a heart softer than Rowan's own. And the children—little Bobby, little Elena, a whole collage of young-old faces. The kids Eleanor and Tamara had taken up north to get them away from Sigma, each one marked with a difference like Rowan's. Each one at risk of being bred like an animal or mindwiped by Zed.

"Come out, Miss Price." Another tapping step with the cane.

Last of all, she thought of Justin, of his eyes now awake and alive and hungry. *Nothing I couldn't handle. They just slapped me around and strung me out on Zed.* He'd said it so casually, as if he wasn't broken and bleeding inside, as if he wasn't afraid of opening himself up even for a moment because of the danger of someone hurting him again. That was what was so different about him this time, she realized. He held himself so tightly closed even she couldn't get in.

She opened her eyes wide, the world snapping into place, and took a deep, soft breath. Just as the man with the cane rounded the corner, pointing the 9mm at her, she rose to her feet smoothly and flung the glass beaker, striking at his mind as hard as she could at the same time.

The bullet zinged wide, his aim thrown off by the beaker flying at his head. Rowan followed, smacking into him hard enough to knock her own breath out, driving him back. *Move in, get going, do it faster, faster, precise, put your weight behind it, sweetheart! Move!* Her sock feet slid on the slick linoleum as she flung herself forward. He flinched, the beaker shattering somewhere behind him, and then he went down.

With his thin old wrist in her hand, she squeezed and twisted as his leg buckled, her knee sinking into his leg as they landed with a jolt. She tore at the gun, wrenching it free, and then she backhanded him and his wire-rimmed glasses flew off. He wore a white linen suit, and dead dark eyes glared at her from under a white buzz-cut. He fought her, but she got a knee in his ribs and the breath slammed out of him with a groaning huff. The gun reversed in her hand, and she suddenly remembered Brewster training her to use a firearm in the dim, long-ago time when she'd first joined the Society.

Squeeze, don't pull, love. His English accent made every word crisp. *Squeeze nice and easy, and don't flinch. Good show.*

Oh, God, her brain was imploding, memories colliding with each other, smashing and burning.

She had him on his belly, gun jammed against his temple, knee firmly in his back, his left arm twisted savagely behind him. "Who the fuck are you?" she whispered, through a throat gone raw and dead.

"Anton," he choked. "Richard Anton." He heaved and struggled. She dug her knee in and pushed forward, smacking his head into the linoleum. "Head of...Operations…*fuck...*"

"Colonel Anton." Her voice sounded strange even to herself. Strange, flat, uninflected. Just like Justin's.

Kill him, Rowan. Do it. Kill him.

Her finger tightened on the trigger. *Eight pounds of pull on the trigger*, Justin's voice said, from his own long-ago training of her. *When you get to about six and a half, you better mean business. Don't go that far unless you're ready to kill, Ro.*

The man below her was a psion. He struggled, his talent caught in her own sure grip, and she saw, suddenly, the twisted thing that lived in his flesh. He had also used his talent to hurt people, to torture them. Sigma was made in his image, and he was proud of his access to the corridors of power, proud as well of the extralegal status he enjoyed. Kidnapping and torturing psions was only the first step.

She also tasted the same mind that had built the defenses inside Jilssen's head, and sent him to the Society like a poisonous gift. If Jilssen was the traitor who had made the rape of Headquarters possible, here was the hand behind the traitor, the finger on each trigger that had killed and on each hypo of Zed.

Kill him, Rowan. He won't stop. He won't ever *stop.*

She choked on bile and rising rage, a fury so intense the world shaded with red in front of her staring eyes. Her finger tightened, tightened.

"Get it over with," he snarled. "There's a whole complex

of armed guards and psions on alert out there. You'll never get out. They'll catch you and pair you with a handler anyway, it's inevitable. Go ahead, Price. Pull the trigger."

Daddy. Her father's face, the chilling little gurgle as he died on the kitchen floor, in her arms, choking on his own blood. Shot by Sigs.

She gathered herself and *reached.*

The man under her bucked and screamed as she poured her rage into him, a twisting, barbed flood of agony and grief. She tore at the root of his talent, clawed at it, and yanked it up by the roots, burning it, cauterizing the open, festering sore of his psionic ability. He screamed again, the sound of a rabbit in a trap, and Rowan let him go, rising up on her knees. Her hand flashed down, the butt of the pistol becoming a club. There was a solid *chunk* and he lapsed into merciful unconsciousness.

"I'm better than you," she rasped. "I'm one of Henderson's Brigade, you sack of shit."

She sagged over his slumping, unconscious body, her breath coming harsh and loud. Then she pushed herself up to her feet. Sock feet, no kitbag, and a whole installation to get through.

But at least she now had a gun.

She rifled his pockets, coming up with a wallet, seventy-three dollars in cash, a white plastic card with a magnetic strip—*door card,* she thought, *just like in a Vegas hotel, let's hope they don't use retinal scans in here*—and another clip of ammo for the gun. It was a good thing she had pockets in her jeans.

Her head throbbed with acid pain, and white-hot needles were bursting into her skull. She wiped at the wetness on her face—tears on her cheeks, and a hot thread of blood coming from her nose.

I'm a mess, she thought, and it was such a practical, despairing, everyday thought that she laughed until she cried, hunched over the unconscious, bleeding Colonel.

In the middle of her laughter, she got up and headed for the door. She was going to see if the magnetic card in her hand would open it.

If not, she would figure out something else .

Twenty-Six

I cannot believe I am doing this. Del nodded, the gun pointed up, and Henderson slid around the corner and covered. The sage-brushed chill of a desert night touched Del's cheeks. They were just about to penetrate the second ring of buildings on the east side. Sigma Zero-Fifteen was being infiltrated successfully. So far.

The team had fortunately been right behind him, following the same signs to Rowan he had and monitoring him through the tracker Yosh had secreted in his kitbag. They were a little less than half an hour away when Del dialed in. After a short, crisp scolding from the old man, Del had gotten rid of the bodies and made the rendezvous, picking up the team in the Sig van and hitting the road. The information gleaned from the driver's broken mind told him that 511 was a cleanup team sent to wipe down the hotel room and head back to Zero-Fifteen in six to eight hours. It was a long drive that wasn't made any shorter by Del's inability to think of anything but Rowan. The mindwiped psion had been turned over to Eleanor, who would take him back to Headquarters and get him started on rehab. If there was anything salvageable in his broken, Zed-stained mind, they would try their damndest to save it.

Rowan could do it, if she gets out of here. Christ. Please be safe, angel. Please still be alive.

Everything had gone smooth as silk, the transponder on the Sig van getting them into the underground garage. Yoshi accessing the Sig intranet from the console in the van. Brew staying behind to help support Yosh and keep a weather eye on the parking lot. The complex was several concrete cubes and hangers tucked into the side of a mountain, a collage of underground labs and facilities burrowed into the rock that were virtually impenetrable. The back of Del's neck prickled. It felt like a trap.

Cath followed them, Zeke lumbering silently in her wake. Boomer, carrying the plastic explosive, would peel away from them to visit the core, if they could infiltrate that deep. Blowing the power and security grid might give them enough time to get the hell out of here. For a seat-of-the-pants plan to infiltrate the most secure Sig installation in the country, it wasn't half bad.

If they could pull it off.

Adrenaline lay copper against his tongue. They might even get in and out of here unseen.

Yeah. And next pigs will fly. Stay focused, Del.

"Stop," Yoshi's voice suddenly breathed in his ear through a comm-link held in with spirit gum. Everyone froze. "There's a sweep heading your way. Stay where you are."

Del heard them pass—footsteps and the snuffling of a tracker-psion. Zeke exhaled a slow, soft breath. His imperviousness to psionic attack also generated a useful bit of psychic "static." It was that static footprint that allowed them to move without detection. Once Zeke went with the other half of the team to take out the grids, it was up to Del and Henderson not to trip any psychic alarms.

"Safe," Yoshi said. "Boomer, Cath, Zeke, your turn coming up. Move to your right at the next intersection, hug the left wall. Del, Henderson, straight ahead."

They moved out in waves, the team functioning precisely, like a well-oiled machine. *If we pull this off...Christ, if we pull this off I might just start believing in miracles instead of percentages.*

Cath, Zeke and Boomer peeled off and vanished at the next intersection. Del's gaze met Henderson's. The old man nodded, his mouth pulled tight in a straight line. It hadn't even occurred to him to disbelieve Del's report. If Del had been Sigma they would have been trussed in a trap by now. It was an odd feeling, realizing how much Henderson implicitly trusted him. He never thought he'd be so grateful for such an unspoken assumption.

I owe him big. I owe him, and I'm not even nervous about owing him.

They slid into the building Yoshi had marked, a massive concrete pile in four stories, ugly as sin but secure enough, Del supposed, inside the outer defenses. It took him forty-five seconds to get the maglock on the door to chuck open, and then they were swallowed by the building's maw. If Yoshi was right, Rowan was in here somewhere. Del just hoped she wasn't on an IV of Zed. He was fairly sure it wouldn't work on her, but with something like that you could never be sure enough. There were other procedures to break a psion, especially a female one. Rape, drugs, sleep deprivation, torture. Now there was an idea. Her capacity to heal would make her an ideal candidate for torture.

Stop thinking like that. Concentrate. Just be safe, Ro. Please, angel, just be safe.

"Stairs at your nine, Del. Zeke, tighten it up."

Delgado blinked and eased around another corner. Clear. Of course, all the mindwiped psions that weren't on chatscan, codestringing, or intra-security patrols with handlers would be locked securely in their cages, and the handlers would be catching some rest. Mission Control was on the other side of the complex, and that was where any activity was likely to be. Over here were the labs and training rooms, deserted at night except for the patrols Del and Henderson were eluding. If anyone in Control found their comm channel, things would get real ugly really quickly.

"Standby, Zeke. I'm initiating the code for the doors. Del, you're going to go down to the end of the hall, turn right, four doors on your left. That's the best pinpoint I have on her according to the listing here." Yoshi's voice crackled. He sounded just as calm as ever. You couldn't tell he was navigating two teams at once through an unfamiliar complex on a console that might trip him up at any moment, working with an enemy computer system and stringing code by the seat of his pants.

Del nodded, forgetting Yosh couldn't see him except through the security cameras. Brew was probably doing the security trip-loops, jacked into the cameras and running safe footage through them to keep any other onlookers blind. Henderson covered another ghostly hallway, made sure it was deserted, and moved to the next cover position. It was agonizingly slow. All Del wanted to do was charge in, guns blazing, and drag her out.

As if the thought had summoned it, there was a sudden clattering racket around the corner at the end of the hall. The pops and zings of gunfire echoed suddenly against linoleum and metal doors. Del's heart started to hammer.

"Oh, shit." Yoshi sighed. "Guys, Rowan's making a break for it and just ran across some armed guards. Brew, take over with Zeke and Cath, on my mark, mark. Del, Henderson, get the fuck *down*, she's heading your way."

"Get down," Del mouthed, but Henderson was already in a crouch, his own comm-unit glinting in the dimness. Del found himself crouching too. There was no cover in the hall. They had to fall back.

"Ro's making a break for it." He felt compelled to say it, as if speaking made it more real. *That means she's ambulatory, and thinking.*

"Cheeky girl," Henderson mouthed, and pulled the hammer back on his automatic. "Shit."

Del agreed wholeheartedly. They dropped back to the defensible intersection, Henderson behind a bank of stacked chairs, and Del crouched and melding with the shadows. Running feet, more gunfire, and a high agonized scream of pain. The empty hall, smelling of industrial floor-wax and human pain, echoed and rang eerily in the dark.

"Just hang tight, guys," Yoshi murmured. "She's not hit, not hit, not doing half bad. She just took out two guards, nice shot. Here she comes. Get ready. She's got four more guards after her."

Shouts echoed, and another scream, high and girlish.

God, I hope that's not her.

Then the cacophony tumbled nearer. "Guys? They're setting the detonators now. Get ready to move like a motherfuck." Yoshi's voice dropped to a murmur, the only audible sign of strain.

"Lovely," Del murmured.

"Always a pleasure," Henderson murmured back. He raised his gun, and Del's own automatic came up in a weirdly synchronized movement.

"Oh, wonderful." Yoshi sounded disgusted, and Del's pulse kicked up a notch. "The whole complex is starting to wake up. Can we move it along, please?"

And then, skidding around the corner, Rowan appeared. She dropped down, taking advantage of cover and aiming back around the corner, her pale hair glowing in the dim light. He heard her breathing come fast and light. She squeezed off two shots, reached into her pocket as she ejected the empty clip, and reloaded with blurring-fast fingers.

He couldn't have stopped himself if he'd tried. The connection blazed to life between them, his head suddenly thudding with pain and her fear singing between his veins. She hadn't been slammed with Zed or shaved yet. How had she gotten loose? He didn't fucking care. All he cared about was that she was *alive*, and he almost rocketed to his feet and ran for her. *Rowan! Dammit, move back here. We've come to get you out.*

She glanced around wildly, not seeing them. "*Rowan!*" He had to shout over the sound of running feet and the howling, which had taken on a weird animalistic quality that raised the fine hairs on his nape. She backed up, covering the intersection in front of her, her ribs flaring with deep, rough breaths. Moving too slowly. They would be on her soon. They were right behind her.

Her mind flooded his with pain and urgency. *One clip left. Pick your shots, headshots if you can. Remember, most gunfights end with a lot of noise and nobody getting hurt. Pick your shots. Take your time,* her voice whispered in the middle of his brain. He could feel her head hurting, her feet bruised from slapping the floor, and the exhaustion weighing her down. She wasn't going to last much longer before making a fatal mistake.

He moved forward, sliding along the side of the hall. "What are you—" Henderson began, shocked at his breaking cover. It was the first time Del had ever heard the old man sound surprised in the middle of a job.

Rowan didn't whirl, but she stiffened and began backing up more quickly, a fast light shuffle.

"Come *on!*" Justin shouted. "Trust me, Rowan. Let's just get the fuck *out* of here!"

That did it. She whirled and ran for them, her hair a pale banner and her sock feet hitting so hard he winced sympathetically. Then they had no time, because the trackers piled around the corner.

Human, but scrabbling on hands and feet like monkeys, the bald psions drooled and gibbered. Thin as scarecrows, their bodies moved in ways human joints weren't supposed to move. They howled as soon as they saw her, and streaked forward on thickly callused bare feet, their palms slapping the flooring.

Revulsion cramped Del's stomach. Training took over. He picked a target and squeezed the trigger. There were three of them, Henderson picked off another. The third was rapidly drawing nearer, Del shot and missed.

Goddammit.

"*Down*!" he yelled, and Rowan threw herself down, rolling with sweet natural grace as he and Henderson peppered the lone tracker with lead. She gained her feet again in a skidding rush, not bothering to look behind her, and he realized just how beautiful it was to see her running again. He'd missed seeing her go all-out. She looked like a cheetah, as if it was no big deal to be moving over the ground so easily.

She almost ran into him, barely slowed, Henderson whirled and took point to lead her out. Del checked the hall, turned on his heel and fell in behind to cover. The crackle of her talent washed over his skin, a lightning storm about to happen. Bullets pocked the wall as they slid around the corner, the guards shooting wildly and uncomfortably close.

As they scrambled down the stairs, he wished he could stop and give her some shoes. When they hit the gravel outside she was going to get hurt.

Yoshi's voice suddenly crackled to life in his ear. "Keep moving. You're clear for now, so go. Go, go, go. The timer's set, counting down, twenty seconds. Eighteen. Fifteen. Watch your flank, Del. There's heavy fire coming your way, Henderson take the left turn. Move, guys. Move." A pause sizzling through the comm-unit, Yosh letting them work and keeping his mouth shut when he had nothing to offer. Then, "Five. Four. Three. Two. One. We have liftoff."

A massive faraway boom shook the air as Henderson kicked the door open, and then they were outside, cutting across a graveled drive, Del's boots crunching, and more bullets popping and digging into the dirt. Darkness, movement, and confusion reigned supreme and conspired to make every shot miss. Fire began in the bottom of Del's lungs. He'd abused not only himself tonight but before, with no time to heal between Carson's bodyguard and this little shindig. But Rowan's pale head in front of him made it worthwhile.

Henderson jerked and skidded, as if he'd been hit. Rowan, right behind him, caught his arm and hauled him upright. And yes, it was official. She had perhaps gone crazy, because she was laughing as she hauled the old man along, her eyes wide and wild and her waxen cheeks slick and shiny with tears Del could feel against his own face.

Then, wonder of wonders, he heard tires on the gravel. A black van, headlights dark and dead, speeding toward them and throwing up chunks of crushed stone. "It's us, guys. We're coming to get you, so continue on present course. Zeke got clipped and Boomer's furious, but otherwise we're at a hundred percent."

Henderson didn't bother correcting him about the hundred percent. Neither did Del. He needed his breath for running. A skidding, smoking half-turn and the side of the van was open, Brew leaning out. Rowan all but boosted Henderson in and Del was right behind her, crowding her, his hands on her waist. He fairly threw her into the van and hopped in, grabbing the quick-release catch. Cath floored it. Boomer already had his comm-unit off and was ripping open packs of gauze. Del slammed the door, the noise of bullets suddenly distant. The blackness pressed like a wet bandage against his eyes despite the faint glow of monitors. The plastic explosive had worked better than even Yoshi had suggested. All the lights in the complex were out.

"Goddammit! Mother*fuck!*" Cath was swearing, a low steady monotony of obscenities so familiar Del could have mouthed them with her. He ignored them, sliding his guns back into the holsters. The air was suddenly close and rank.

"Rowan? *Ro?" I sound like I'm fifteen again.*

"How bad is he?" Rowan's voice broke. She sobbed openly. Brew was already sliding into the passenger seat while Yoshi braced himself in the tiny chair, his fingers dancing over the keyboard while he strung code. They weren't out of the woods yet.

"Bad news, Cath!" Yoshi yelled. "Front door's closed!"

Cath's only answer was an unrepeatable term that raised even Del's eyebrows and the sudden jolt of acceleration as she smashed the gas pedal to the floor. Del lost his balance and fell, managing to land on something soft and familiar. *If I'm going to die, I'm going to die kissing her*. He found her cheek against his in the darkness. The van careened over a bump, and Rowan let out a short cry of pain he smothered with his mouth.

"You're bleeding pretty badly," Boomer muttered. "Dammit, old man, say something."

"You sound like an old woman." Henderson's voice, tight with pain. Del wondered where he'd been hurt and found he didn't care. "Quit it."

"You're stepping on me." This from Zeke, uncomfortably wedged in the back of the van.

Del didn't care who was stepping on Zeke. He slid his fingers into Rowan's hair and kissed her again, savagely, teeth pressing into her lips. She gasped into his mouth, and he tasted the chemical sourness of some drug. Fear smashed into him. Zed? Or something else? There was a slick wetness on her cheeks, and she shuddered so hard it was almost convulsions. Her hip was braced against the door and a small wounded sound rose in her throat.

"I'll be all right. Just my leg. I'll need a fucking cane." Henderson said, his hand white in the dimness as he reached up to steady himself against the edge of Yoshi's console.

"Watch the guns, watch the guns!" Brewster's voice hit a pitch Del had never heard before.

"Get ready!" Cath shouted. "Or this is gonna be one *fuckuva* short trip!"

"Oh, cra—" Whatever Henderson intended to say was lost in the impact as Cath barreled through the fence. Bullets chewed along the side of the armor plating on the van, but with the grid down and the backup power disabled, the entire brooding anthill of Zero-Fifteen was critically disabled. By the time the Sigs got their wits about them, the Society ops would be lost in the urban wilds of Taos, scattering to rendezvous back at Headquarters. The van would be abandoned, the bodies of Section 511 would be found at the bottom of a dry gulch, and the Society would have pulled off another hat trick.

Jesus Christ. He kissed Rowan's cheek, her ear, the slippery tangle of her hair. Then communication, as he flooded the link to her mind with his crazed relief at finding her again.

Don't ever do that to me again. Don't you EVER do that to me again. Goddammit, woman, I thought I'd lost you. I thought I'd lost *you. You could have been killed. You could have been—*

"How we doing, Yosh?" Henderson heaved himself up, his voice brittle with pain. Boomer made an exasperated sound and braced him, trying to keep compression on the wound high on the old man's right thigh.

"No pursuit, General. There's some kind of snarl in the chain of command, and nothing's getting done. Better than we'd hoped." Yoshi sounded cautiously optimistic. "Cath?"

"We didn't lose any tires, so I'm happy. Zeke? Zeke, baby, talk to me."

"I think I sprained my ankle, and Boomer stepped on me," Zeke answered morosely. "Great drivin', Cathy."

"Amen to that." Boomer made a short, snorting sound. "How's that for payback? *Yeah!*" It was the closest to unadulterated joy Del had ever heard from the man.

"Anton," Rowan whispered, and Del's skin went cool and

rough with terror and gooseflesh. “He… *Jilssen…*”

“Later,” Del promised, taking a little pity and struggling not to crush her. She probably couldn’t breathe with him lying on top of her. A spike of frustrated heat went through him, an animal reaction to the adrenaline surge.

Every time I get some time alone with you, something else happens. I swear to God I’m going to lock you in a room and spend some time getting to know you again in the best way, angel.

It was the sudden rubber-band snap of released tension, postcombat jitters. “You were under a compulsion, Ro. I didn’t spot it. My fucking fault. I’m sorry. I’m so goddamn sorry—”

“They’re not even scrambling helicopters,” Yoshi said, wonderingly. “Wow. What the hell?”

“Anton,” Rowan choked again. “I killed Jilssen. He’s dead. I killed him.”

Christ. His knee felt bruised, but he wedged it against the floor and dragged her up to a sitting position. He propped her back against the locked door and started feeling for any damage, mostly to reassure himself she was still alive.

“Road’s clear,” Brewster said from the front. “This is fantastic.”

“Let’s not get cocky. Yoshi, find out what the hell’s happened. Rowan, what about Anton?” The bite of command in Henderson’s voice made her stiffen. Del almost opened his mouth to take the old man down a peg for barking at her, but Henderson was right. They needed to know.

Rowan gulped in air. He touched her collarbone, her arms. Then he felt her knee, her ankle, and spread his hand against her belly. Her tank top had ridden up. He felt warm, soft skin and almost groaned.

“Jilssen.” She choked on the word. Delgado realized she was crying, taking in great sobbing breaths and shuddering. “He wanted to *breed* me. *They* wanted to breed me. I killed him. I killed him and then Anton came in—”

“Christ.” Del caught her shoulders and stopped himself from shaking her by a sheer effort of will. “Did he hurt you? *Did he?*” His stomach boiled at the thought.

“Let her talk, Delgado.” Henderson moved irritably so Boomer could tighten the tourniquet around his wounded leg.

“H-he had a gun.” She held it up, fingers locked on either side of the trigger guard. “T-tried t-t-to use his t-talent on me.

I burned him, I burned him out. I wanted to kill him. God, I *wanted* to kill him."

You're not the only one, angel. I want to kill him too.

"Burned him?" Henderson sucked in a breath as Boomer yanked on the tourniquet, tightening it.

"Sit the fuck down, General. You're bleeding on me."

"Bite it, soldier. Burned him, Rowan?" Henderson cocked his head.

Dammit, leave her alone. She's just been through the wringer. But he shut up. Henderson needed this information, needed it desperately, or he wouldn't be pushing her.

"He's not a psion anymore." Her breath hitched in. "I burned his talent out. Then I p-pistol whipped him. Maybe I killed him. I don't know. I didn't stick around to find out."

Silence rang through the car. Then Cath whistled out through her teeth. "Good fucking deal," she summed up. "Hope you did kill him. Brew, how we doing?"

"No pursuit that I can see. Yosh?"

"None here, either. Their tails are still tied in a knot back there. Hope you used enough C4."

"Of course I did," Boomer replied irritably. "I used enough to knock out the whole fucking grid. All the lights were fucking out."

"Rowan." Del shut out the sound of the others. Acceleration pulled against his body as Cath took a curve. He cupped Rowan's face in his hands. "You all right?" His voice almost broke under the sheer inadequacy of the question. "Goddammit, talk to me. *Talk to me.*"

"I'm not all right." A sob cracked under her words. "I killed him. I used my talent to kill him."

She bent forward, curving into his arms. She cried against him as if her heart was breaking, and he closed his eyes, stroking her tangled hair and tasting bitterness. She should never have had to do that, face that, alone. He should have gotten to her before the Sigs did.

The full horror of what she'd experienced soaked into him. His arms tightened around her, and he held her as tightly as he could. Fortunately, Henderson didn't ask any more questions, just submitted to Boomer's ministrations and started organizing the finer points of their escape.

Twenty-Seven

Rowan fell into a thin, restless doze, barely paying attention when the van stopped and everyone leapt out. Justin took care of everything, ushering her out of the van and into the clean chill of a desert dawn. Wind touched her hair and mouthed her cheek. Her head throbbed, and she knew someone was hurt—probably more than one someone—but she couldn't bring herself to care or offer help.

The empty Sig van, wiped free of fingerprints and cleared of all Society gear, went over the side of the road, down a long sheer fall into a ravine. The crunches, crashes and tinkling broken glass were very loud in the predawn hush. On the other side of the road, parked far over on the shoulder against the mountainside, were three cars, waiting patiently to spirit the Society team into the distance.

"I'll take care of it," Justin said. "I won't let her out of my sight."

"Good." Henderson sounded tired. "I'd hate to have to do this again."

She winced. It was all her fault, the suffering, the death. Her fault. She was a plague. She tainted everything she touched. All because of her freakish talents.

If I could burn out Anton's talent, maybe I could burn out my own.

But if she did, she would be helpless. Once Sigma regrouped, they would be after her. Who knew who would be in control now that she'd destroyed Anton? Or if she hadn't killed him, would he still be in charge?

Maybe it would be best for everyone if I disappeared. Just...disappeared.

Her head was heavy. She leaned against Justin, feeling his exhaustion close around her. Exhaustion and grim determination. His arm was around her, solid and warm, accepting her weight.

Someone grasped her shoulder firmly. "Rowan?"

She raised her eyelids with an effort and stared at Henderson. "General." Her voice wouldn't work quite properly. "I'm sorry." Two words, pale and utterly unable to carry the full burden of her guilt. "If I hadn't—"

His steely eyes were softer than she had ever seen them, and his mouth pulled tight, as if he tasted something bitter. He squeezed her shoulder. "We didn't spot the compulsion, Rowan. It's my fault, not yours. I should have known Carson would pull something like that. Listen, Del's going to take you north until everything calms down. Stay with him, all right?" His tone was gentle, gentler than his usual briskness by far. "Don't torture yourself. Do you know why we came to get you?"

She shook her head numbly. Two fat tears brimmed up and spilled hotly down her cheeks.

"We never leave one of our own behind, Ro. You're one of us." He leaned in, and she saw the glint off his wire-rimmed glasses in the pale gray of false dawn. There was a stain of orange light on the horizon, some desert city. Which one? She didn't know. Justin would know. "You hear me? You've proved yourself time and time again. *You're one of us*. Understood?"

She gathered herself. "It's my fault," she said dully. "My fault."

Henderson squeezed her shoulder again, his fingers turning to iron. "Sigma isn't your goddamn fault. They started before you were born, little girl. The only thing you're guilty of is being a good person, and that's no crime." He let go of her. "Stay with Del. Listen to him."

She nodded. Henderson limped away, leaning on a silent Boomer.

Cath stepped in and kissed her cheek. The smell of Juicy Fruit, cordite, and strawberry incense clung to the younger girl. "Be safe," she whispered, with no trace of impatience. "I'm glad we got you out. *Don't* do anything stupid, okay?"

Yoshi merely bowed slightly, his almond-shaped eyes glittering. Brew and Zeke had already walked away, Cath following them to the second car. Yoshi drifted after Boomer and Henderson. Before he was out of sight, though, his mind brushed Rowan's briefly, a warm friendly touch, as if they were in the middle of an operation again.

You are my very dear friend, Yoshi said. *Be gentle with yourself for a while, Rowan.*

Gentle? Her breath hitched in an unsteady laugh. She didn't feel like being gentle. All she wanted to do was find somewhere dark to curl up and pass out.

She was left with Justin, standing on the side of the wide paved road. He pulled her back from the edge of the ravine as two car engines roused and their headlights cut a wide swath through the gray. No traffic, but he looked both ways before guiding her across the street and to a cream-colored Volvo.

He unlocked the passenger door with a sigh. "We'll stop to get some sleep as soon as we cross the state line. Afraid you'll have to wait a little while for a change of clothes. Cath packed some for you and you can change when we stop for breakfast, is that okay? I've got a kitbag for you, so at least you won't be helpless. We can get coffee in Taos and—"

Her shoulders shook. She couldn't seem to stop crying.

"Hey." Now he sounded alarmed. "Christ, Ro. Please. We've got to get out of here, sweetheart. You're safe now. I promise you're safe." He stuffed the keys back in his pocket and stroked her hair, hugged her, kissed her forehead and might have tried to kiss her mouth if she hadn't buried her face against his chest, smelling the clean healthy scent of a male who had just undergone a hard workout. She wasn't sure if he was wounded, couldn't bear to look up. He also smelled like night wind, of cordite like Catherine—of course, there had been a lot of gunfire—and like the only safety she had now. "Shhh, angel. It's all right. I'm here."

Of course you're here. How can you forgive me? I left you there in that horrible place. With Jilssen, and with that...that filth. Anton. Shudders racked her. She didn't resist when he opened the car door and pushed her down inside to sit, buckling her seat belt. The smell of a new car filled her acid-tasting mouth. *Of course, they drained the old resource net, plenty of funding. Newer cars, nice and clean. We can use them for a while before they get hot.*

He dropped in on the driver's side with a sigh, settling his kitbag on the console between them. He was pale, his mouth a hard line and his eyes glittering darkly. He slid the key into the ignition and twisted it. The car started. His hands curled around the wheel, and she saw through the tears that blurred her vision that his knuckles were white.

"I am never going to forgive myself," he said, harshly. "I'm taking you north. Eleanor's cleared out the house in Calgary, but we'll stay somewhere different. Sigma will never find you, Ro, not in a hundred years. I'll make *sure* they don't. If you still want to come back and run operations for the Society we can do that too. But I am never, *ever,* letting you out of my sight again. You decide to go on an operation, I'm going with you. You decide to go civilian and disappear, I'm going with you. And if you decide to get out of this car and throw yourself over that cliff, guess who's going to be right behind you."

Her entire body hurt. She closed her eyes, her head moaning and rippling with pain. "I killed him." Her voice was dry as a bleached skeleton. "My mother always said I should use my talent for good."

"It *was* good." Though there was no traffic, he checked over his shoulder as he pulled out. His leather jacket made a slight creaking sound as he shifted his weight, and he passed his hand back over his hair again as if forgetting it was cut short. He looked, as usual, impossibly calm and precise. "You got rid of a fucking plague upon the earth, angel. Believe me, I know how you feel. I can't touch anyone's mind without killing them or driving them fucking mad. Anton trained me by hooking me on Zed. I couldn't get my hit until I broke some poor bastard's mind to some appropriate degree. More often than not, they were used for target practice afterward." The car moved smoothly over the road, tires whispering. "I hope you killed Anton too. I just wish I would have been there to do it so you didn't have to. I am *never* going to forgive myself, Rowan."

"Forgive *yourself?*" She couldn't stop the bitter little laugh that boiled out past her lips. "I left you there, Justin! And I… I…"

I betrayed the Society, she realized. *I could have been tortured into betraying Headquarters. Especially if I was strapped into that chair and Anton touched me. I don't think I could have stood it if he'd gone to work on me.*

Her hands shook as she lifted them blindly, and her right hand smacked against the window.

Justin reached over and caught her left hand, gently. The touch sent another wash of crackling soothing energy over her skin, sinking in. "Calm down, Ro. It isn't as if you had any goddamn choice. Now just get some rest. We got you out of the heaviest Sig installation in the country, and you may have killed their head of Operations right after I took out that blind bastard. They're in for a major bureaucratic shakeup. Only good thing about the goddamn government is that they need paperwork to go to the bathroom."

You don't understand. It soothed her to speak to him without words. Regular speech didn't have the tones, the shades of meaning, nuance blending into nuance. She wanted to slide into his mind and stay there, secure in his certainty. His mental house was *clean*, not like the diseased pit of Jilssen's brain or the squirming, twisted parasite that was Anton. And also, the fishhook maggot-squirm that was the blind man twisting in her head. She was never going to feel clean again.

"Revenge. I wanted revenge." Her voice broke again. "I still do. I thought I was better than that."

"You are. Just rest, angel." He sounded so goddamn sure. He slid his fingers through hers, holding her hand as he drove. "Take it easy for a little while. Breathe."

She stared out the windshield while dawn came up. Despite herself, her terrified grasp on consciousness began to fade. The wheels of the car made a low soothing sound against the pavement, and she began to believe that she might almost be alive. And safe. Not that it mattered.

Her breathing hitched on a last broken little sob, and she passed out gratefully, sliding into darkness.

* * *

The first night they stopped she thrashed into full terrified consciousness in the darkness, a sleeping weight on the mattress right next to her in the dark. For one vertiginous moment she thought she was strapped back in the chair, Jilssen tightening the restraints as he leered and cupped his crotch. Anton leaned on his cane in the background, the lab stretching and distorting like a funhouse mirror behind him. A scream tore at her throat, and when Justin lunged into wakefulness and grabbed her wrists she struggled, thinking he was someone else. But his hands were gentle, and he held her while she sobbed, the borders of her mind clean and intact. Even so, he *reached* through the link to her, calming her, his steadiness reassuring and the last fading burn of Zed withdrawal skittering over his skin with insect feet that she felt against her own flesh. He reached to the bedside table and flipped the cheap green-glass lamp on before he pulled her into his lap and rocked her while she shuddered and sobbed.

She finally quieted, his fingers stroking her back through her tank top. She sighed and began to relax a little, though the shivers coming through her in waves didn't stop. The naked feeling of dampers soaked through her skin, familiar, helping to dispel the nightmare.

"Better?" he asked finally, his mouth against her temple. He didn't sound sleepy at all.

No, I'm not. This isn't going to get better. How can *it get better?* "Better," she whispered, and took in a deep hitching breath. "My God. I could have given away Headquarters. If they'd tortured me—"

"You wouldn't have. You're stronger than you think." The headboard, bolted to the wall, creaked as he leaned back against it. If he was uncomfortable with her in his lap, he gave no sign. As a matter of fact, when she tried to wriggle away he tightened his hold on her, and an almost-contest ensued, her trying to squirm free and Justin almost negligently keeping her still. They were both breathing hard by the time she stopped, and she leaned her head against his shoulder, cuddled against his chest. His heartbeat thudded under her ear.

"It's not ever going to stop," she whispered. "What are we going to do? When we get old, or if…" *Stop it, Rowan. Just stop it.*

"Old age and treachery will always win out over youth and inexperience," he quoted solemnly. He actually sounded amused.

"That's not what I meant." Her head hurt, but the tearing, ripping pain of a compulsion buried below the surface of her conscious mind had ceased. He touched her shoulder and lifted a slippery strand of pale hair. "I can't do this." It was a soft, despairing moan.

The volcanic anger had extinguished itself, leaving only a howling emptiness. The rage that had possessed her in Zero-Fifteen was gone, replaced by ashes and smoke drifting through her mental landscape—burning, wrecked pieces of trauma.

"Give yourself a little time," he said into her hair. "Don't worry so much. Even if it is a losing goddamn fight, at least we're on the right side of it. That's worth something, don't you think? Look." He shifted a little, as if his legs had started to go to sleep, but his arms turned to iron when she tried to slide away. "One day, sometime, somewhere, they're going to lose. They can't keep it up forever."

She let out a choked half-sob. "You know what Jilssen said? He wanted to breed us. He said if he could breed out the stubbornness, it would make a good soldier."

Her lips moved against the bare skin of his shoulder, and she felt him take in a soft, deep breath. She shifted her weight a little, feeling a familiar insistent hardness pressing against the outside of her hip, and a wild panicked laugh rose behind her teeth. *Well, at least I know he's still interested.* Guilt slammed through her again. How could she even *think* about sex at a time like this?

"He's probably right." He paused. "Of course, I can't see any child of yours lacking for stubbornness." He stroked her hair, untangling it with infinite gentleness.

The laugh jolted its way free. "I'm sorry," she whispered.

"Don't be," he whispered back. "Take your time, angel. I'm not going anywhere."

"I want to forget." She somehow, somewhere, found the courage to lift her head from his shoulder, felt the heavy weight of her hair slide against her back. She was going to have to cut it, dye it somehow. It was too distinctive, even for a psion practiced at blending in. Thinking of expending the energy to redirect attention away from her hair made her feel even more tired. "I wish I could forget everything."

"Everything." His face was closed, but his eyes were dark and finally alive again. He watched her face, his lips gone soft and somehow amused, the arches of his cheekbones perfect in their severity, one eyebrow slightly lifted in unconscious imitation of Henderson.

I wonder if he knows how much he copies the old man? she thought, and tried to hide a smile. It felt odd to smile, odd but also a relief.

"Everything except you. I missed you."

That made the faint shadow of amusement leave his expression. His face turned solemn. "I missed you too." He let go of her, sliding his hands down her arms, callused palms gentle against her skin. "And here we are."

"Alone. Nobody chasing us."

"Yet." Now he reached up and skated his fingertips over her cheekbone. The touch was so gentle it made the tears rise again. The fading echo of Anton's voice—*Go ahead, Price. Pull the trigger*—finally receded into the place nightmares went when faced by daylight. He tensed slowly, muscle by muscle, as she memorized his face over and over again. "Don't ever do that to me again. You hear me?"

Relief made her slump backward a little. It was the closest to a statement of need she'd ever heard from him. "I love you too."

"Christ." Was he actually *sweating*? He was trying to stay still as she moved in his lap again, deliberately teasing him. It had been a long, long time for both of them. "Rowan…"

"Turn the light out," she told him, and he reached out slowly as she found the hem of her tank top with trembling fingers and pulled it off over her head. His hand never found the lamp, because he traced the lowest curve of her ribs with shaking fingers. Their mouths met, and from there it was easy. He pulled her down into the tangled covers, his mouth on her throat and breasts until she made a soft pleading sound, his fingers hooking in the waistband of her panties. She had to lift her hips to get them off, for once not worrying about getting dressed if there was an emergency, only wanting to get the confining material out from between them. He tossed them over the side of the bed, and she kissed along his jaw as he struggled with his boxers, muttering a curse she laughed at before he finally kicked the offending material away and slid his knee between hers. She felt the sensations spilling through his nerves as acutely as if they were her own; the rougher silk of his skin against hers was exquisite torture magnified by the link between them.

*Rowan. Christ, Rowan...*The words faded under the onslaught of pleasure echoing inside her head, cleaning away the fear and pain and hatred. The edges of his hipbones dug into the soft flesh of her inner thighs, he shoved the pillow away from under her head and wound his fingers in her hair.

He didn't want to hurt her, struggled to retain his control, but she pulled his head up to hers and kissed him, tasted the faint fading echo of toothpaste and the spice of him. She arched her back and rocked her hips up, pleading, her fingers tangling in his hair and his mouth exploring hers. Still, he tried to hold back, fear and caution warring with need. He was being so damn careful she almost exploded with frustration before he gave up, bracing himself on his elbows and easing himself slowly, so slowly, into her. She closed her eyes, linking her ankles at the small of his back, and sighed as he moved, settling in, the hard length of him pulsing as she shifted, a small sound of satisfaction caught deep in her throat.

Finally, the moment of *connection*. Her mind sank into his like water. He shuddered in her arms, on the fine edge of losing control, one thought beating through the red haze of pleasure his mind had become.

Home. I'm home.

So am I, she thought before all words were lost in sensation. He moved and she rose to meet him, relief and arousal and sheer heat blurring the borders between them. No longer two separate beings, she felt her own hand sliding down his back, tasted her own mouth through his. Two short, hard thrusts settled into a longer one. Faint stubble on his chin rasped against her cheek, and she kissed under his jaw, catching the hollow of this throat where the pulse beat and fastening on, wanting to leave a mark on him. She felt the sharp point of almost-pain in her own throat, and when he moved again, thrusting into her, she felt her fingers driving into his shoulders, hard ridges of muscle tensing in his back, sweat stinging someone's eyes, hers or his? She no longer knew.

Rhythm caught her. Her body knew what to do, and it shifted instinctively to catch the feedback of pleasure from his. He whispered something broken in her ear as Rowan gasped, tilting her head back, curiously calm in the middle of her body's frenzied need to prove that yes, she was still alive.

More, she thought, the word becoming his, the need becoming shared. *More, for God's sake, don't slow down—*

Speeding up, he was no longer so careful, plunging into her as if he was a drowning man. A cry caught in her throat, and he took her mouth and swallowed it. His voice, echoing hers, was lost in the connection between their hungry tongues. Volcanic heat spilled through her, tightening every muscle and nerve. She let it happen, wanting the release.

Then came the brief moment when their psyches overlapped, white-hot silence exploding through both of them. He stiffened in her arms, a low, hoarse sound of agonizing pleasure spilling from his throat as her release tore through his nervous system and his crisis slammed through her in concentric rings of scarlet spurring flame. And if he used his talent gently, very gently, a featherlight brush of pressure against the surface of her mind to help her forget some of the horror and shock and guilt, it was no less an act of love. One she welcomed even as she forgot for a brief moment why it was necessary.

He never did get around to turning the lamp off that night, and when Rowan finally fell asleep there were no more nightmares.

Twenty-Eight

Six months later

Delgado set the gun against the man's temple. "How many with you?" He sounded bored even to himself, but his pulse slammed inside his wrists and throat even as he shoved his knee more firmly into the man's back. Outside rain swept restlessly down. The winter storms had started. Soon the whole city would freeze, making Montreal looking like a gigantic sugar cake from above. Light would glimmer on the snow, but if they'd been found, neither he nor Rowan would see this city in another twenty-four hours.

Just when I was starting to like it here. Just when Ro was starting to relax.

Rowan, the book bag dangling from her slim fingers, closed the door quietly. They'd taken this small, light-filled apartment not for economy's sake, but because a house wasn't safe. He'd been feeling a little antsy for a while now, and Rowan had started to look pale and drawn again, no matter how many bookstores or lectures they visited. Her nightmares had gotten progressively worse, too. He hadn't had a good night's sleep in two months.

Of course, the fact that he liked to calm her down the old-fashioned way probably had something to do with that. Oh, well. Anything for the cause.

He pulled the hammer back, knowing the click would resonate through the man's skull. Tall, dark-haired, reasonably fit and experienced, the intruder still had no chance against him. Sigma had simply trained Del too well.

Besides, the agent on the floor, whoever he was, was a normal. He couldn't sneak up on two psions.

Here in the entryway, a small table lay on its side, the day's mail scattered over the floor from the quick, vicious fight. The man gasped, probably winded from the shot to the solar plexus. Justin wondered how their visitor had gotten in. Probably the kitchen window.

He better not have knocked over the African violet, Del thought. *Rowan loves that plant.*

"Unarmed! I'm unarmed!" The man almost squealed with fear. A quick, thorough search proved this to be true, and five minutes later their new visitor was trussed with duct tape to a solid kitchen chair. Dark hair, leather bomber jacket, jeans, and a pair of good boots—he looked like miserably out of place here. Nobody in Montreal wore a bomber jacket, for Christ's sake. Not at this season.

Del saw with relief that the African violet was still on the windowsill, but the window had been jimmied. The kitchen lay under a gloom of gray light, the blue dishtowels set just so, the breakfast dishes drip-drying in the rack. Rowan hugged herself near the door, staring at the man with wide luminous eyes under a short, chic cap of sleek dark hair. She was still fragile and jumpy. If this sonuvabitch had set her back Del was going to have to see if he could get a little creative.

Del tossed her the man's wallet. She caught it with a sweet, natural grace and flipped it open. "Barry Holgrave, NSA. Looks real." She tossed her head slightly, still not used to short hair. *I look completely different*, she'd said mournfully, staring into the mirror.

That's the point, he'd replied, and kissed her. A good memory, one he liked. "What's the NSA doing here?" He looked down at the man, aching to wrap his fingers in the intruder's hair and pistol-whip him a little. "You've got thirty seconds to convince me I shouldn't kill you."

Barry was old enough to have been in the spy game awhile. His eyes widened, fine fans of wrinkles spreading out from the corners. His haircut was too butch. He was making a shoddy job of undercover. His Adam's apple bounced as he swallowed, wincing when Del tightened his hold on his hair.

Rowan's hand dropped, weighted with the wallet. "It's about Sigma," she said softly, and shook her head, her hair swinging to touch her cheeks. The green wool sweater she wore made her skin seem even paler, and the blue scarf loose around her pretty throat heightened the contrast. Water still clung to her hair and shoulders, little jewels of rain. She had largely lost the circles under her eyes and the nervous small tremble in her expressive hands. Sometimes she even laughed. "Loosen up on him a little, sweetie."

You make a great good cop, you know, he told her privately, and watched the gleam of amusement touch her eyes, but not her solemn, beautiful mouth. She'd put on a little weight, but not nearly enough. "I think we should kill him." He used the soft pleasant tone he knew was the most terrifying.

Mmh. And you make a good bad cop. The amusement in her tone was tight and thin, a veneer over adrenaline and the sudden plunging of her heart.

Easy, sweetheart. We didn't mark anyone on the street outside. We've got plenty of room to jump if we have to. He felt her take a deep breath and reach for reassurance, answered her silently with all the comfort he could.

"They've shut it down." Holgrave almost choked in his eagerness to talk. "Sigma's shut down. There were closed Congressional hearings, and Anton's at a maximum security prison for the criminally insane. He's totally fucking nuts. All sorts of shit about what he was doing with the agency started to come out and everyone clamped down, from the top down to the lower echelons. It was a goddamn mess, still not sorted out." He took a deep, racking breath. "In the living room there's a briefcase. It's got documents. Proof."

"What does this have to do with us?" Del eased up a little on the man's hair.

Rowan tilted her head. *No activity outside, nothing I can feel. Want me to go check?*

Her heart was pounding; he could feel it in his own chest. *No, I want you to stay right where I can see you, angel. Not letting you out of my sight, remember?*

Oh yeah. This time she did smile. He had to swallow dryly, though his attention didn't waver. Damn, the woman was dangerous to his self-control.

"Rehabilitated," Holgrave swallowed so hard his throat actually clicked. "You're rehabilitated, your identities wiped clean. We want you to work for us, legitimately. No Zed, no electroshock, no torture."

"And if we don't want to?" Del felt his entire body go cold. It had to be a trick. *Had* to be.

"Then you're free. As long as you don't make waves or work for a foreign power, you're free as birds. That's the deal. It's all in the briefcase."

Barry's eyes were as round as plates. He wasn't trying to struggle, but he did crane his neck to look at Rowan, pleading. *He thinks she might stop me if I get crazy and decide to kill him.*

"It's true," Barry said suddenly, shifting in the chair. Del hadn't been gentle in taping him down.

Del uncocked the hammer. "Ro?"

He's telling the truth, and I don't think he's been tampered with. A faint line was etched between her eyebrows.

"What's the catch?" *And don't lie to me,* he thought privately, keeping it from her with an effort. He paced back to Rowan at the door, took the wallet, and glanced through it. If it was a fake, it was better than any other fake he'd seen. *Lie to me and not even your own mother will recognize you.*

"Some of the Sigma infrastructure is still operating, lots of the operatives were taken by the private sector. We want you to hunt down whoever bought them. We're recruiting Daniel Henderson, too. We want you to work with us."

I doubt Henderson would give these guys the time of day, Del thought, not bothering to shield the thought from her. He dropped the wallet on the floor, dispelling the urge to strip the cash from it. They weren't hard-up yet. And if they ever were, a few nights in the underside of any city, a few drug dealers relieved of their bankrolls, and they could move on to the next town. Rowan didn't like it…but she wasn't the naïve idealist she used to be either. *Get what you want, angel. We're leaving.*

Her shoulders slumped. *I'm so tired of this.* "So now everything's supposed to be all right?" she asked, softly. "Now that you need us, that is. Where were you when Sigma was killing innocent people and turning others into animals?"

Holgrave didn't even have the grace to look ashamed. He simply blinked at her as if she was speaking a foreign language. "I wasn't a part of it, ma'am. I didn't know."

I'll deal with this, Del reminded her. *Go on, sweetheart.* He crossed the black-and-white squares of the kitchen linoleum, eyed the man, and heard Rowan padding away behind him. She would get the bags they'd packed for emergencies, but probably not the briefcase. The risk was just too high. She moved very quietly, and he reminded himself she was armed and well-trained—as well-trained as he could make her in such a short time. Besides, her mind was linked to his. If she ran across *anything* he would know.

"We'll see if what you're saying is true," he said finally, tearing off another strip of duct tape. Holgrave's eyes widened. "We'll even call the cops to come rescue you from your little throne there. You can tell them whatever you want, but you take this message back to whoever you run for, dog. If I even sense another one of you behind us there won't be any warning.

Clear?"

"What are you going to—"

Del smoothed the duct tape over the man's mouth. "You can breathe?"

Holgrave nodded frantically. Sweat beaded on his forehead, and the rank smell of fear was suddenly overwhelming. Fear, and a sweet chemical scent he recognized. Idiot deadhead, thinking he could sneak up on them. Just as idiotic to wear Aramis on a job like this.

"Now, do you fucking understand what I told you? Don't send anyone else unless you intend to lose 'em. Clear?" Delgado smiled into the man's face, a hard delighted smile that didn't reach his eyes. "'Cause I want it clear as *crystal*."

More frantic nodding. Delgado nodded back reflectively, studying the man. Holman obviously thought he was contemplating murder, because the agent shook his head, sweat rolling down his face. The pale gray light from the window fell over the entire kitchen, the dishes Rowan had bought, and a copy of *Leaves of Grass* lying open on the table where she had been reading before leaving the apartment this morning.

Justin? Let's go. She sounded sad.

He took the time to pick up the African violet from the windowsill. It might not survive the trip, but he wanted Rowan to have it. And if anyone could keep it alive, she could. When he got to the entry hall, stepping around the knocked-over table, he saw the two duffels. Rowan ducked through the strap of her kitbag and settled it on her hip, then pulled on her gloves. Set near the door was a neat leather briefcase with gold clasps.

Dammit, Rowan, there could be something in there. There was no heat to the words, since she wouldn't have picked it up without scanning it.

She shrugged. *Curiosity, my besetting sin. Come on, let's go. It's a shame. I really liked this place.*

Del privately agreed. He, too, was getting a little tired of running. *Oh, well, at least we won't hear the neighbors anymore. I'd rather have you safe, angel.*

* * *

That night, hours away in a motel room with a chill wind moaning at the window, the briefcase sat between them on a cheap rickety table. Rowan tucked her legs underneath her, unwinding the scarf from her neck with a sigh. "We could call in," she said, the line between her eyebrows deepening. "Or string some code. They would be glad to hear from us."

Del nodded. He finished the last of the scans, putting the small handheld instrument away in his kitbag. It was the second scan, standard procedure, but not likely to come up with anything. "Well, it's not going to explode and kill us, and there's no tracker in it," he said. "You want to do the honors?"

She looked down at the table, her hair falling softly over her face. It was a sweet piercing feeling, knowing he could look at her as much as he wanted, seeing the curve of her cheek and the shape of her flawless mouth. "If we open that, it's as good as admitting we want to go back."

I wondered when you were going to realize that, sweetheart. You've been itching to do something useful for a while now. Don't think I haven't noticed. It felt strange not to automatically share the thought with her.

She gave him a wry smile. "I can feel you thinking, even if I can't hear the content." She stretched, yawning, and gave the bed a longing glance. "What do you want, Justin? Do you want to go back?"

He considered the question for a long time. The pink-and-brown curtains over the window stirred a little. The weather-stripping in here wasn't up to code, but they both needed the rest. Besides, this place was in a perfect part of a small town, easy for them to escape without notice, and that was worth a little chill. And if it was cold he might wake up to her cuddling into his warmth, and that was always pleasant.

"Sex fiend." She shifted uneasily in the chair, and he sighed.

"Well, that's the goose calling the gander, isn't it?" He gave her a smile that felt natural and treasured the quick grin she flashed. "You really want to know what I want?" He folded his arms, feeling the familiar safety of dampers crackling in the air.

She rolled her eyes, and then sobered. She glanced around the motel room, then at the African violet sitting safely on the small bed stand under a pink ceramic lamp shaped like an elephant. The plant didn't seem any worse for wear. "Of course."

"I want you happy. You want to go back, we're still not required to do anything other than hang around Headquarters and train a few psions. Or just do the paperwork. I'm sure the old man has a mountain of it."

Her eyes were dark, almost troubled. "You miss him, don't

you?"

The idea of missing anyone was strange. Unfortunately, she was right. "Yeah, I guess I do. Don't tell him, though."

"Silent as the grave." She put her legs down, leaned forward in the chair, and stared at the briefcase as if she had X-ray vision. He watched the thoughts moving behind her eyes, the faint blush on her cheeks from the cold, and the mussed silk of her hair.

"All right," she said finally, wrapping up whatever internal conversation she'd been having. "I suppose…" But she didn't finish the sentence.

"It's up to you, Ro. We can toss it off the next bridge without even opening it." *Fat chance, sweetheart. I can see it in your eyes. You're thinking about going back, aren't you?*

If it *was* true, it was good news. If it wasn't, Henderson probably needed them. If it was a trap, Henderson would need them even more.

She reached out decisively, and the locks clicked open. Taking a deep breath, her gaze met his.

"We can call in tomorrow morning," he said. "There's a train station in the next town. Risky, but quick."

She nodded, her hair swinging forward. The butt of a gun dug into Del's side as he stretched muscles gone a little stiff from so long in the car.

"If this is true…"

"If it's true, Rowan, you brought down Sigma. Congratulations. Now open the damn briefcase. The suspense is killing me."

"I love you too," she said, opening the briefcase with one swift, decisive movement and stared at the inside.

I don't think I'll ever be able to tell you how much I adore you, angel. If this is true and we go back, I'll keep you safe. "Well?" he finally asked.

She nodded. "We're going back. Henderson's going to need us." Her chin lifted decisively, and he thought she could probably stop his heart if she ever looked at him the way she was examining whatever was in the briefcase. She reached down and pulled out a sheaf of papers, flipping through them and collating them swiftly with a single glance. She set aside two videotapes, flipped through more papers. Her eyebrows rose.

He waited.

When she spoke again, it was in a clear, firm voice that made his heart triphammer inside his ribs. "Transcripts from closed Congressional hearings, admittance papers for Anton, workups on jobs they suspect were done by Zed-wiped psions taken by the private sector…" Her gaze swung up, met his. She looked dazed. "If Sigma's destroyed there's no reason to stay away."

"I guess not." He settled himself in the chair, watching her closely.

"I want to go home," she finished. Her eyes glittered with unshed tears, and high hectic color stood out in her cheeks. She was so goddamn beautiful it actually *hurt* to look at her, all the way through his chest and lower, too.

Justin Delgado gathered himself. "Great. We'll catch the train in the morning. Give me a look at what's in there, angel. I love you too."

Printed in the United States
63436LVS00002B/82-105

9 781933 417806